FAKING IT WITH #41

PIPER RAYNE

Cover Design: Okay Creations

1st Line Editor: Joy Editing

2nd Line Editor: My Brother's Editor

Proofreader: My Brother's Editor

About Faking it with #41

Fake.

Being the heir to Jacobs Enterprises, I've been around fake people my entire life. I promised myself a long time ago that I wouldn't change for anyone. Which is the only reason I'm a professional hockey player who lives on the beach and does as he pleases without answering to anyone —except my father.

And now, my daughter.

Being a single dad wasn't in the plan but after a one-night stand who took off after the baby was born, this is my reality.

My dad's been harping on me to quit hockey and join the company for years and now that I'm a father, he's only intensified his efforts. Until he makes me a deal I can't refuse.

Insert Lena Boyd, the Jacobs' family PR rep. She's beautiful and intelligent and not at all the woman for me— ask anyone.

My dad needs us to act happily engaged and sell the idea that we're in love. If we're successful I won't have to join the family legacy—ever. Of course, I agree.

That's when things get complicated. I thought I had her all figured out until I found out there was more underneath her judgmental sneers and eye rolls. It feels like everything is coming together for the future I really want—with Lena—until my past ruins everything.

Faking It with #41

CHAPTER 1

"Let Lena in, Ford."

Ford

As the starting right wing for the Florida Fury, I'm used to hearing a woman scream in my bedroom in the middle of the night, but the wailing from the nursery down the hall that startles me out of a dead sleep… not so much.

My life has done a one-eighty in the last four months since my daughter was born.

I run a hand through my hair, walking into her nursery wearing a pair of sweatpants. There's only a crib in the middle of the room, so it's easy to find her even without the blaring siren of her scream. What can I say? My daughter has a good set of lungs.

I scoop her up, seeing her bright blue eyes matching mine, staring back at me. Please tell me she doesn't have that mischievous rebel living inside her like I do. My mom says the blue eyes made it difficult for people to be hard on me. That I've gotten away with too much in my life. And she's right.

I'd say she was smiling if I hadn't read that it's most likely gas. I've binge-read book after book on raising a baby over the past six months, though it's not done me much good. I still feel out of my depth.

I change her diaper and nuzzle her into my chest

before I take her downstairs to warm a bottle. Once it's ready, I sit in the big lounge chair in the corner of my family room, seeing the letter her mother left me earlier today laying on the end table.

I'm really sorry, Ford. I can't do this. I'm not meant to be a mother. You're so good to her. Love her extra for me.

The anger swells inside me all over again. How does a mother leave her baby? Especially in my incapable hands. I'm fairly sure Britney thinks I'll be a good father because I have money. Not only from playing in the league, but because I'm a trust fund baby. I wanted to raise Annabelle without the help of a nanny since my arrangement with Britney was that I'd have Annabelle on my off days during the season. Now I'm a full-time dad, so I'm not sure I have much of a choice but to enlist someone else's help.

I had nannies growing up and it wasn't all bad. They could rarely keep me in line and we went through a full dozen of them before Mrs. Gardner arrived. She was a classic British nanny and wasn't scared of my rebellious antics at all. She retired once my youngest sister got into high school, but I'm wondering if she'd be available somehow. Then I remember how harsh her punishments were and the fact that I don't want to look to the nanny for answers of how my daughter's day was.

"I guess it's just you and me."

A small sound comes out of her.

"I hope you like *Yellowstone*. You'll see some horses, and don't worry, I'll cover your eyes at the bad parts."

I click on my DVR, pressing Play on the last episode I was bingeing. Maybe this is a bad decision, but as the music starts, her eyes slowly close.

"You just wanted to be with Daddy, huh? Well, that's

one thing I'm used to when it comes to the female population. But you're a better date than any of them." I chuckle to myself and watch the show.

Feeling her weight in my arms reminds me how big of a responsibility this is and how I've never been a very responsible guy. After placing her in the bassinet next to me, I gently sway it back and forth until my own eyelids grow heavy. Since she has a crib in her room, I keep the bassinet on the main floor for when I need to set her down.

I come awake to the sound of my phone vibrating on the kitchen counter across the room—or more accurately, the sound wakes Annabelle. Daylight streams into the room and I can't believe the clock says it's ten in the morning.

I stand up with Annabelle and grab my phone off the counter. My sister Imogen's name flashes on the screen.

"What's up, little sis?" I answer, putting the call on speakerphone.

"I should ask you that."

Annabelle makes some kind of gurgling sound in my arms, so I adjust her.

"Is that my niece?" Imogen asks.

"No, it's my date from last night. She's looking for a tit to suck on."

"Language, jeez, Ford." Imogen blows out a judgmental breath.

"She's four months old."

"Do you want her first word to be tit?"

I chuckle. "It would make for a funny story."

Another breath sounds through the phone as though she thinks I'm going to be the worst dad ever. Nothing I don't already know.

"Well, I just wanted to give you a heads-up. We're leaving the airport."

I glance around at the dirty bottles stacked by the sink, the dirty diapers overfilling the garbage, and the basketful of washed clothes I've yet to fold that I set on the island two days ago and haven't moved since.

"Who is we?" But I already know who she means. And he's only coming here because word must've already reached New York that I'm a single dad now.

"Rumor is you've been left with a baby on the porch." Imogen confirms my worst suspicion. "Dad says he doesn't want you doing anything stupid. So I'm tagging along to play peacekeeper."

"You gotta stop him. I don't want him here. I can handle this myself."

She sighs, familiar with the wall between my father and myself. One we've built brick by brick over the years. It's the same old story—he wants me to run the family business and I want no part of it. He'll try to use Annabelle as leverage to get me to leave my professional hockey career and take my rightful place as he sees it. He's going to put a hard sell on me, I just know it. And with how exhausted I am, I might not have the usual fight in me.

"I don't think I can stop him. In fact, I gotta go. See you in a bit." She hangs up the phone.

My doorbell rings. I groan, hoping it's my housekeeper who is somehow telepathic and knows I need her magic cleaning powers.

I open the door. Sadly, my wish wasn't granted.

My mom barges in first, swiping Annabelle out of my arms like a professional thief.

"Nice to see you, Mom."

But she ignores me because she's already cooing at her first grandchild.

My dad's busy on the phone, so I'm rewarded with a stern glare as he follows my mom in.

Next is my youngest sister, Morgan, who graduates from high school this year. She at least pauses and kisses me on the cheek. "What's up, Daddy-o?" She laughs and continues into my beach house. "You don't mind if I swim and lie out?"

"Have at it," I say, looking at Imogen. "What kind of heads-up was that?"

She laughs. "Sorry, I didn't realize we were so close already." Her laughter continues as she walks past me into the house.

I move to shut the door, but another voice alerts me to someone else before the woman in question emerges from around the corner. Our eyes meet and I swear it's like we're two cowboys in a standoff in a western movie. It's no secret the two of us dislike one another. Always have—except for that brief kiss on New Year's Eve, but that was ten months ago.

"Lena Boyd," I say, distaste clear in my tone.

"How much shit can you step in?" She shakes her head and tries to slide past me, but I step to the side, blocking her from entering my house.

"You're not welcome here."

She loses her footing for a minute and falters back. I don't bother to grab her arm. It must be her casual day today. Jeans, a T-shirt, sandals, and an open sweater. Not very professional. Although with the way her tits are snuggly fit into that shirt, I'm not complaining.

"Don't be a bigger ass than you already are." She steps forward.

I block her again. "Why are you here?"

"Because I have to spin this story somehow so you come out looking like the doting father and not some rich prick who chased off his baby mama." She crosses her arms, clearly not in the mood for my shitty, sleep-deprived attitude.

"Let Lena in, Ford," my mom says from behind me. "And you cannot raise my grandbaby in this filth."

Lena shoots me a look because she knows I never disobey my mother. I step aside and she walks past me as though she's the fucking president or some shit.

I slam the door and rest my forehead on it. Then I grab every ounce of patience and courage for what is surely going to be a shitty day.

CHAPTER 2

"The baby's not here, you can swear."

Lena

My shoulder brushes Ford's arm as I walk into his beach house that's not nearly as big as he can afford. As if he purposely picked a home that didn't showcase his enormous wealth. But what the house lacks in size, it makes up for in location. He's on a private inlet in the Gulf, along with a bunch of other wealthy people who live here.

Mrs. Jacobs sits in a chair, staring at her granddaughter as though she could hang the moon, while Mr. Jacobs lingers on the back patio, continuing his phone call. Morgan has already changed in the bathroom and walks out in a bikini that shows off way too much skin. Imogen is starting a pot of coffee and says she already placed an order with Grub Hub for muffins and donuts and they're on the way over as though we're planning a conference or something.

I sit on the couch.

Mrs. Jacobs holds up the baby to me. "Isn't she beautiful?"

She has Ford's eyes. That stunning blue of the lightest part of the ocean. The same ones that suckered me into kissing him on New Year's Eve. Not that it meant anything.

The only reason he did it was because I came to Florida to force him back to New York to meet with his dad after his stupid stunt of fighting some guy in a bar. But sometimes late at night, I swear I still feel his lips on mine.

"She's gorgeous." I'm not lying. Annabelle will be a knockout someday. Given the genetics of her dad and Britney, how could she not be? It's not like Ford to dip below model status for his hookups, and Britney was no exception.

We sit in silence for a second while Morgan comes over and bends down to kiss Annabelle's forehead.

"Jesus, Morg, I can see your ass. Don't you have anything else to wear?" Ford covers his eyes.

She turns around and juts out her hip. The bikini isn't crazy revealing, but the ties on either side that could easily be undone is what would worry me. "If I was someone other than your sister, you'd be drooling."

"Mom!" he screeches, looking incredulous. "Are you going to let her go out like that?"

"She's only going out on your patio." Mrs. Jacobs puts her face an inch away from Annabelle's, not paying full attention to her children's bickering.

"Give her a break. She's right. If she wasn't your sister, you'd probably have hit on her." Imogen comes in with a cup of coffee and sits next to me on the couch.

"Ew!" Ford exaggerates with a full-body shiver. "Don't say shit like that."

"The baby," Mrs. Jacobs warns.

"She's four months old," all three of the Jacobs siblings say in unison.

"If I'm not careful, your first word will be a bad one," Mrs. Jacobs coos, tapping her finger on Annabelle's nose.

"That would make it clear she's Ford's then." Morgan laughs and walks outside, half her ass cheeks hanging out.

Ford shakes his head and turns his attention back to us. "Why are you all here?"

I lean back on the couch. Has he really not figured it out yet?

"Do you watch any television, listen to the radio, or look at social media?" Imogen asks, then sips her coffee.

He sits on the ottoman by his mom, staring at Annabelle. "Look around, Imogen, does it look like I have time for that?"

"It is disgusting in here." The doorbell rings and she gets up. "Food is here."

She disappears down the hall and Ford sets his gaze on me. I hate that it unnerves me, makes me self-conscious that he'll say something and I won't be quick enough with a comeback. That's essentially our communication style. And with his mom in the room, he knows he has me because I would never dream of giving him a hard time with her present. The amount of money the Jacobs family pays me is irreplaceable.

"So the story is out? The press knows Britney left?" he asks.

I nod.

"Fuck!"

"Language," Mrs. Jacobs scolds.

"At the moment, she's the one being raked over the coals. The public has a lot of sympathy for you. We need to keep it that way." I speak the truth.

His forehead scrunches. "Seriously?"

Imogen returns with the food in hand and shakes her head at her brother. "You're the hot hockey player and now a single dad. You thought you had a lot of women before? Just wait until they see you with Annabelle." Imogen places the donuts and muffins on the counter, snagging herself two donuts.

I have no idea how she keeps her figure, other than she has a personal trainer five days a week.

"And that's exactly why I'm here," Mr. Jacobs' deep voice says. I guess his phone call is over. "Imogen, call someone to clean this place."

"I'm busy," she mumbles over her donut.

"I have a cleaning lady," Ford says.

Mr. Jacobs briefly looks at Annabelle without much interest and sits in the chair opposite Mrs. Jacobs. He's dressed in navy slacks and a lime green polo shirt. His usual golf attire for when he goes to the country club. For a moment, I wonder if he'll make it a point to golf while he's down here. No one said how long we'd be in Florida.

"Then call her. Why isn't she here now?" Mr. Jacobs says.

"Because I'm a single man. She only comes twice a week."

His dad eyes him. "You're no longer single."

Ford looks around, giving his sister and mom a look that suggests Mr. Jacobs is stupid. It's clear that grates on Mr. Jacobs' nerves. I've never seen anyone get under Mr. Jacobs' skin as well as Ford does.

"You're not the only one here. A baby is messy. She can't live in her own shit," Mr. Jacobs barks.

"We really need to watch our mouths around the baby." Mrs. Jacobs moves Annabelle onto an activity mat on the floor. She's trying to get the baby to interact with some of the items dangling down, but Annabelle keeps sucking on her pacifier and staring at herself in the little mirror. I guess the apple doesn't fall far from the tree.

"She's a baby, Gabi," Mr. Jacobs says to his wife.

"Well, I warned you around Ford when he was a baby and look at him now."

Mr. Jacobs nods, lips pressed together. "Noted."

"What the fu—heck?" Ford raises both arms and looks at his parents in disbelief. "I know I might not live up to your standards, but a lot of people think I'm pretty awesome. And a damn good hockey player."

Mrs. Jacobs sits up on her ankles and pats her son's knee. "You are."

"You'd be a better CEO if you got your head out of your ass," Mr. Jacobs grumbles.

The smile that almost hit Ford's face falters before it ever shines.

Here we go. Round one thousand twenty-seven between Ford and his father on why he's not working for Jacobs Enterprises.

"I think it's terribly sexist that I'm not asked to take over the company. This isn't the nineteenth century, Dad." Imogen starts her second donut.

Ford rolls his eyes and looks over at her. "You're getting a graduate degree in art history."

She opens her mouth for a rebuttal but Mr. Jacobs cuts her off. "You're already there part time, Imogen, and do nothing but complain about it. You want to take over the company? Fine, quit graduate school and start full time next week and I'll teach you everything I know."

Her eyes widen and she stares at him for a beat.

"That's what I thought." Mr. Jacobs lifts his ankle to rest on his knee. He zeros in all his attention on Ford. "Having a baby is a lot of responsibility."

These are the moments I want to leave the room.

"That wouldn't change whether I work for you or play hockey. The responsibility of Annabelle is the same." There's a bite in Ford's tone now. One he reserves only for his father.

"The difference is you wouldn't travel for days at a time. You wouldn't have the temptations you have when you're a professional athlete. God forbid something like this happens again. You could have five illegitimate kids before you leave the league."

Ford walks into the open kitchen and pours a cup of coffee. I've only been with the Jacobs family for a couple years, and during that time, I've witnessed Ford's persistence to stay in hockey dwindle. A year ago, that comment would have set Ford off, and screaming and yelling would have commenced. Either he's learned to control his emotions better—doubtful—or he's losing the will to fight his father.

"I'm not gonna let it happen again," Ford mumbles, walking past his father with a cup of coffee in his hands. "It was a mistake. You've made your fair share of them, I'm sure."

His father's jaw tics. "We're not talking about me. It's the smart decision to come work for me."

"Why? So I can be gone all day and night like you were? At least with hockey, I have an entire off-season to dedicate all my time to her. Not to mention my days off."

Mr. Jacobs rolls his eyes while Mrs. Jacobs scoops up Annabelle. "She doesn't need to hear her grandfather and father fighting."

Imogen crosses her legs and pulls out her phone, always more than willing to witness the two of them go at one another.

"I'll just go with Mrs. Jacobs," I say, excusing myself and standing.

"Sit down, Lena. We need to discuss the PR narrative on this situation." Mr. Jacobs then turns his attention back to his son. "I've had to explain too many of your mistakes over the years. Now I have to explain that you're a single dad because the woman you knocked up isn't ready to be a mother."

Ford laughs dramatically. "Who the hell cares about what people think?"

Mr. Jacobs stands and points at himself. "I care, Ford. Perception is everything in business, and how people see you matters. I can't have everyone snickering behind my back because I can't control my own son, let alone a multi-million dollar company."

"I haven't embezzled money. I'm not an addict. I'm a fucking hockey player who likes pussy. That's all." Ford throws his arms out at his side. "So what?"

I cringe.

"It's not just the women. It's the fights. It's the…" Mr. Jacobs blows out a long deep breath. "I don't expect you to understand." He stands and looks outside at where Mrs. Jacobs is holding Annabelle. "One day you will. One day she's going to break your heart."

"She won't because I don't give a shit what she wants to do as long as she's happy."

Mr. Jacobs laughs. "There you go, Lena. Tell the press that Ford Jacobs is a reformed man, a single father who has his shit together. I'll wait until the story unfolds that you're out late at night while a nanny raises your kids."

"Nannies raised me."

Imogen smiles at her phone. I don't know what she's chosen to do now that she's about to graduate from college, but I do know that the girl loves gossip.

Mr. Jacobs steps forward and my breath lodges in my throat. "You act like you wanted for something growing up. I never sent you away to boarding schools, and yes, we had nannies, but only because to live the life we did, your mother and I had obligations. Obligations you'd like to forget you have."

Ford shakes his head. "I'm over this conversation. I knew you'd try to get me home again, but I've told you a million times and I'll tell you again, I'm a hockey player, not a businessman."

"It's not only about you anymore." Mr. Jacobs points through the floor-to-ceiling windows to where Mrs. Jacobs is holding Annabelle. "You're responsible for another human being now too."

"I'm not an idiot. I know that." He places his hands on his hips.

Mr. Jacobs is silent for a long time, but his eyes are focused on Ford. He finally raises his finger. "Mark my words, you're going to fuck this up."

"Is that what the problem is, Dad, you think you fucked up with me?"

"You have no idea what I think," he says, stuffing his hands in his pockets and walking toward the door that will lead to where Mrs. Jacobs is. "Lena, spin this in a positive light. Say Ford is excited to have more time with his daughter and up for the responsibilities of being full-time dad. Then get some pictures to show them bonding and give an exclusive to someone."

I hate when he dictates the plan of attack to me instead of asking my opinion. He hired me for my expertise, but that's what happens with powerful men. They trust no one but themselves.

"Now I have to let some schmuck take pictures of my daughter for a damn magazine? This is bullshit." Ford walks to the other side of the room and up the stairs.

"Man, that was a doozy," Imogen says once it's just the two of us in the room. "How are you going to pull this off?"

I blow out a breath and steal her fourth donut, taking a big bite. "I have no fudging clue."

"The baby's not here, you can swear." Imogen laughs, sipping her coffee.

I exhale on a sigh. Nothing about any of this will be easy. I have a feeling I'll be biting back curse words for months to come.

CHAPTER 3

"Whatever gets this over the fastest."

Ford

"See, you can't take pictures of her in a onesie," Saige says to Paisley after they change Annabelle's outfit and put on some kind of bow thing that wraps around her head.

Saige and Paisley act as if my daughter is their personal practice baby before they marry and have kids with my teammates, Aiden and Maksim. Speaking of, those two are sitting on my couch, laughing at some stupid prank show on the television. We've got a game tonight and shouldn't be sitting on our asses. We should be getting our heads in the game.

"When is Lena coming with the photographer?" Saige asks, playing peekaboo with Annabelle, who doesn't seem that into the game.

"I have no fucking clue. Soon, I guess." I strip off my fourth shirt to put on another one I picked up from the cleaners.

"Can you please stop stripping in front of my girl?" Aiden says.

"Why? You afraid she'll come over to my side?" I waggle my eyebrows.

"You have the baby she wants, so…" Aiden laughs.

Saige shakes her head. "I should clarify, I want a baby

with you, not Ford. I love this little one, but she still has half his genes." She makes a silly face at Annabelle as if that's going to spur a laugh out of her.

"Hey, that's offensive." I button up my shirt.

Paisley eyes me. "You look too professional. Not like a single dad with a baby."

I groan. "Want me to get the shirt she spit up on earlier?"

Paisley shrugs. "I'm just saying." She goes over and snuggles up to Maksim.

"Relax, he's just testy because Lena's coming," Maksim says.

Just the name makes the hair on the back of my neck stand up. Lena Boyd. The woman drives me insane. Constantly at my father's beck and call. Doing whatever he wants her to do. Have some self-respect.

"Come on, I know you're hot for her," Saige says, still googly-eyed over Annabelle.

"You're kidding, right? The woman wears pants all the time and blouses that cover every inch of her body. Heels? Forget it. She's constantly in flats. And the woman is stuck up my dad's ass to top it all off."

No one says anything. I unbutton my shirt and grab my brown V-neck sweater without putting a shirt on underneath, then I push up the sleeves.

"This good enough?" I direct my question to Paisley.

"Much better. These pictures are going to make women's ovaries explode," she says.

"Kotik," Maksim grinds out his Russian nickname for her.

She blushes. "I didn't say mine. My ovaries only explode for you."

They bring their heads together in an Eskimo kiss that makes bile rise up my throat.

I can't believe my two best buddies have fallen in love. We're in the prime of our lives, hockey gods making bank, and they decide to put on a set of handcuffs. Not to say I don't like Saige and Paisley, they're awesome, but they've taken my boys away from me.

"I'm only doing this shoot to appease my dad," I grumble.

"I thought you hated your dad?" Saige asked.

I don't hate my dad. We don't see eye to eye on almost everything, but my dad is still a decent guy. He just doesn't understand me, and the more he tries to control me, the harder I push in the opposite direction. It's been our relationship for as long as I can remember.

"I have to do some things so he stays off my ass. As long as I'm playing hockey, it's just the way it is." I shrug.

"What's your long-term goal? Like after you retire from hockey, will you work in the family business?" Paisley asks, her psychologist's brain never staying in the therapy room.

"All I know is that I want to retire as a hockey player. While I'm still good and am still wanted, but as old as I can be."

"Amen." Aiden and Maksim raise their water bottles.

"And then?" Paisley pushes.

"And then I'll retire with my money from the endorsements, league play, and my trust fund. I'll have no reason to work."

She tilts her head. "But won't you get bored?"

This is the first time I've really thought much about what will happen after I retire. I always felt like retirement was the finish line for me, but I'll be lucky if I make it to forty still playing in the league. That's young.

I quickly do the math, realizing Annabelle will be twelve if I make it that long. If she's anything like me, she won't want to be hanging with her dad all the time. I guess

I'll still be young enough to live my life the way I was before she was born, but to my surprise, a tinge of loneliness hits me right in the heart. I rub the spot, not understanding why it's there.

"Being a single rich guy who lives on the beach and does whatever I want every day? Sounds terrible."

"Are you saying you never want to get married?" Saige asks.

"You girls are barking up the wrong tree," Aiden says before downing the rest of his water. "This man right here is the only one I can see never falling into monogamy."

"That true?" Saige asks, clearly wanting to hear it from my mouth.

I shrug. "Haven't ever thought much about it. All I know is right now, my hands are full."

The doorbell rings. Thank God for the interruption, even if it is Lena.

"I'll get it." Paisley jumps off Maksim and heads to the door.

Lena's familiar voice echoes down the hall from the door and my back straightens. I ready myself to do something I don't want to.

"I love your pants," Paisley says.

Sure enough, when the two emerge, Lena Boyd is buttoned up as tight as her ass. She's wearing long pinstripe pants and a puffy blouse that hides the curves I know she has because I felt them on New Year's Eve when she was in my arms and her lips were on mine. That night, she wore a pair of leggings that showed off what these pants hide.

"Oh, thank you. They're more comfortable on the plane. And fall has set in back home."

One thing I miss about New York City is Central Park in the fall. But I'm sure I'll be beckoned back to

Manhattan by my dad before all the leaves have fallen from the trees.

"I take it we have you two to thank for this adorable outfit." Lena goes over to Annabelle, smiling at her. "She's beautiful."

"Isn't she?" Saige beams as though Annabelle is her daughter, holding her up in what I've been told by the ladies is "blush pink." The lace dress looks adorable on Annabelle, but she has shoes on that have no purpose since she can't walk. "He was going to put her in a onesie. A Fury one at that."

All the women turn to glare at me.

Aiden and Maksim laugh, sharing a look of better me than them.

"That could be cute too," Lena says.

Cue record scratch. Did Lena Boyd just agree to something I want? Hell must've frozen over.

"Maybe we could take some at the game tonight? Do a few poses before you go on the ice." Lena presses her finger into Annabelle's stomach as though she expects her to laugh. I want to tell her to stop because I want the first laugh out of my baby girl, but I don't.

Aiden raises his eyebrows. "Ford's kind of serious before a game."

"Of course, we can scrap it." Lena waves off the idea, never making eye contact with me. I'm unsure why she's being so agreeable with me at the moment. "Your dad just wants enough to convince everyone you're happily settling into the role of single father."

The room quiets and my face heats.

"Oh, sorry, I didn't mean to suggest—"

"I am happy." My fists tighten at my sides.

"Of course you are. I meant more that the surprise of it all hasn't shaken you."

She really can do a good spin job.

The doorbell rings again. I hope this is her crew because I want to get this photo session over with.

"I'll get everyone in and organized." She walks down the hallway as though she owns the place. Under other circumstances, I might show her around my place, but I'm already annoyed.

I hear her polite conversation with the people my family hired and/or the people she coerced to write up this story. The next thing I know, in walks a photographer, a videographer, a makeup person, and a smiling man whose eyes bulge out when he sees Maksim and Aiden are here too.

"This is Gavin," Lena says. "He was my teacher's assistant at school and does freelance work for a bunch of magazines, including *Sports Illustrated,* so I called in a favor."

All I hear is blah blah blah except for when my mind circles around to the fact that he was a TA and these two clearly have some kind of rapport. Maybe Lena isn't as wholesome as I thought.

I put out my hand. "Pleasure."

His grip is firm, so I squeeze a little harder to win the battle. What am I winning? I have no fucking clue, but my dad taught me from a young age to be the strongest, most powerful person in the room. Since I opted for a career in hockey, there are times I switch that up to be the most charismatic person in the room and I do just fine.

"You're probably familiar with Maksim and Aiden. This is Saige and Paisley." I point toward each person as I name them.

Gavin goes around the room, shaking hands with everyone.

"Let's get this photo shoot going since Annabelle's

dressed and ready to go. There's a good chance she could spit up on her outfit at any moment," I say.

The makeup woman plops down what sounds like a fifty-pound bag and pulls out stuff. She brushes something on my cheeks and puts a small amount of eyeliner on my eyes. I try to be a good sport about it, but I'm anxious to get this over with.

Gavin and Lena have decided that we should shoot in the family room and out on the patio with the ocean behind us.

I pick up Annabelle, who was chillin' in Saige's arms. She relaxes into mine like I hoped she would since it's been just her and me for the past week or so. I've lost all track of time. But the fact that Annabelle seems to recognize me makes my chest warm with a strange sensation I'm not familiar with.

Maksim, Aiden, and the girls all rush to leave, wishing us good luck, and I tell them I'll see them at the game tonight.

I sit on the couch with my daughter in my arms. The photographer snaps a few pictures, having me change positions a few times. Then we're off to the patio by the pool.

"You know what women love?" Gavin says to Lena. "Those things you wear that carry the baby on your chest."

"Yeah, well, I don't have one." I lean Annabelle on my lap, her back on my chest, and her pudgy little fingers grip my index fingers.

"That's a shame. They're a chick magnet," Gavin says.

I don't bother asking how he knows. He probably wouldn't answer me even if I did. He's only really granted Lena any attention since we started and that's bothering me. I wish I had an explanation.

"What about him reading her a story? Maybe we can do some shots in her nursery," Gavin suggests.

Lena touches his arm and shakes her head.

"Why not?" I ask, forehead wrinkling.

"Since this is new, Ford hasn't had the time to decorate the room," she tells Gavin.

He tilts his head, then turns to give me his attention. "You knew for months that the baby was coming. I understand you didn't know about the mother leaving her, but—"

"Let's just leave it at this. I can get her a book." Lena glances at me as if I might have a book at the ready that I read to her every night.

She's four months old, it's not like she'd comprehend a storybook.

Lena must see my puzzled expression. "There will be more opportunities for those kind of pictures in the future. Let's just capture these and get this article out."

Gavin nods as if there's an underlying agreement between them.

"This is the last pose I'm doing." I say it in a tone that I'm sure no one will challenge.

Lena's phone rings and she holds up her finger, stepping back into the house.

"How about you on the floor and her under her jungle gym thing?" Gavin points inside.

"Whatever gets this over the fastest," I mumble.

They move the lighting back inside, and as I walk into my house, Gavin stops me with a hand on my arm. "Lena's a great girl. She worked hard to get here. I'd listen to what she has to say if I were you."

I narrow my eyes and my jaw tics. "She works for my father, not me. I have a game to get to."

He huffs as though I'm an asshole. Whatever. Lena gave him an oyster nestled with a pearl with this Jacobs' family heir exclusive and he didn't even have to fish.

CHAPTER 4

"I didn't peg you for a spy."

Lena

I should put in my notice with Mr. Jacobs right now because the thoughts going through my head about his son are far from professional.

Ford is model hot in a clean-cut, wealthy way. Men like him aren't usually my type. And although he's a pompous ass, seeing him with his daughter makes me want to jump him. Makes me wish the one kiss we shared had gone further.

He seems to have adopted the role of father as masterfully as he skates. The house isn't as messy as it was the day his family ambushed him, which I'm guessing means he's getting into a rhythm. There are prepared bottles in the fridge, neatly folded baby clothes in a laundry basket by the stairs, and Annabelle looks happy. Neither of them have bags under their eyes.

"That about it?" Ford asks, standing from the floor. He pulls Annabelle out from under the activity mat as she's getting cranky. "This dress is cute and all, but Annabelle's like me and wants to dress for comfort."

Gavin glances at me. Ford has no idea how hard it was for me to get Gavin to push aside his plans for this shoot, and I shamelessly used the fact that Gavin hit on me all through school to make it happen. I never did anything about it back then, but I did promise him dinner tonight as friends to thank him.

"Sure. We'll move on to the interview. Do you have someone to watch her?" he asks.

Ford's eyebrows raise. "Do you see someone else?"

Gavin nods. "Yeah, okay. So you don't use nannies?"

"Only when I have to. For out-of-town games. Otherwise, she has a babysitter when I'm playing in town." He flips up his wrist, an expensive watch adorning it. "She'll be here in two hours when I leave for the game."

Gavin groans. He's not going to want to do an interview with a cranky baby interrupting the whole time.

I raise my hand as though I'm in school. "I'll take her."

"It's fine. I'll feed her and lay her down, but you owe my babysitter some extra cash because she won't go down for her nap this afternoon now."

It's heart melting how much he already knows his little girl, but then I remember that although Britney left a week ago, Ford's had Annabelle for half the time anyway. During the time when his dad wasn't up his ass and I didn't have to come down here to straighten him out on New Year's Eve, Ford Jacobs has become a father. Responsible for a little girl. Amazing, really.

"I can do it," I say.

He carries Annabelle toward the stairs. "I wouldn't want to put you out." Then he's gone.

Anger bubbles up inside me that he's being a dick about this. I turn to Gavin and the crew. "I'll be back."

Walking up the stairs, I find myself tiptoeing because I've never ventured up here before. It feels private. Just as I stick to Mr. Jacobs' office, the kitchen, and the family room at the Jacobs' penthouse, I've done the same here. One time Imogen asked me to go to her room, but when I saw Mr. Jacobs in the hall in a pair of pajama pants and no shirt, I decided never to venture outside of the main rooms of the house again.

I hear Ford's voice before I reach Annabelle's room. "You look beautiful in the dress, sweetie, but I bet it's itchy. When you're older, don't let people dress you."

I peek in the room behind the door to stay hidden, addicted to seeing this big strong man be so gentle with his daughter.

"I'll never allow anyone to change you." He's cooing.

Annabelle lets out a little noise that could be a laugh.

I lean forward to get a better look.

"Are you laughing at Daddy?" He puts his face on her belly and vibrates his lips against her skin. She makes the same sound and he lifts his head. "You are laughing. That's not gas, right?"

The amazement in his tone has my hand landing on my stomach because I'm pretty sure my ovaries did a three-sixty. Who would have ever thought he had it in him to be this man? Certainly not me.

He does it three more times and Annabelle laughs every time.

Picking her up, he circles her around in his arms, his smile as wide and as bright as when he's on the rink after a win. I'm so enthralled that I don't realize until it's too late that he's stopped and is staring at me.

"I didn't peg you for a spy." He lowers Annabelle to the changing table again.

I slowly step into the room. "Sorry."

"At least this was something good for you to tattle back to my dad."

"Is that what you really think I do? Tattle?"

"You're my father's fetcher. So yes, I do think you tattle because that's partly what he's paying you for." He changes Annabelle's diaper without a problem and puts her in a cute onesie that says "Daddy's Girl" with pink lettering and small flowers.

"Your family is my business. I was hired to make you look good."

"You were hired to make sure to spin any fuckups." He picks her up and holds her.

"Yes, but—"

He spins to face me. "I've always been curious. Why?"

His anger spurs me to step back. "Why what?"

"Why would you take this job? You can't have much of a life. Always having to be on call to fly down here to stop me from having any fun. My dad doesn't even talk to you with a modicum of respect."

I say nothing about the way his father talks to me. He talks to me like a paid employee, and I've been talked to in a lot worse ways, so it doesn't get to me. At least Mr. Jacobs doesn't talk down to me, which is more than I can say for how he talks to his son.

"It's none of your business, but if you must know, I went to school for this."

"Sure, but why not work at some big firm? You seem like the nerdy type. Surely you had good grades." He takes the headband off Annabelle, and I swear I hear her release a sound like a sigh of relief. It reminds me of when I take off a tight dress and my Spanx after a long night out.

"I hate to break it to you, but jobs aren't just lined up waiting for you when you graduate college unless you know…" I don't finish because I'm growing madder by the minute and I'm going to say something I shouldn't.

"What?"

I shake my head. "Nothing. Let's just get this interview over with."

He widens his legs and his blue eyes focus on me.

"Come on. Give it to me, Boyd. I'm sure it's nothing I haven't heard before."

"I don't have a rich daddy to set me up in his golf buddy's business," I say. I saw it so many times where I'd be one of the top two candidates for a position, and it would go to the person with connections. No one knew my dad except for maybe the shelter managers.

He laughs smugly and it makes me want to smack his face. "I didn't use shit. My dad doesn't know anyone in the National Hockey League. I earned my spot myself."

"I wasn't suggesting—"

"Sure, you were. And if I had to work for any company, we both know it would be Jacobs Enterprises." He stops right next to me, leaning down so he can speak directly into my ear.

My breath hitches from the scent of his expensive cologne.

"Money isn't everything," he whispers.

I turn toward him. Our faces are millimeters apart, so close that Annabelle's hand touches my cheek, but he doesn't back away. "Says the trust fund boy."

He huffs and straightens up, moving Annabelle's hand from my cheek. "That's all you see me as, huh?"

"And all you see me as is some pathetic woman who does your dad's bidding and has to nag you to live your life on the straight and narrow."

He doesn't move. The longer he stands there with his gaze on me, the more I want to fidget. But I'm not going to show him how much he intimidates me. I straighten my back instead and force myself to not do so much as even blink.

"At least we have that straight." He holds out Annabelle for me. "Since you're the help, you won't mind watching her while I go do the interview with your boyfriend."

I accept Annabelle and he walks out without me saying a word. Damn, why can't I think of a comeback? Boyfriend? Does he think Gavin is my boyfriend? And if he was, what is it to him?

I look down to find Annabelle's eyes studying me. "Your daddy is a complicated man."

She smiles at me as though she understands, and I can't help but wonder what it's like when it's just the two of them hanging out.

Not wanting to interrupt the interview, I quietly go down half the stairs and sit with Annabelle in my arms. Her eyes are slowly drifting closed. She's surely tired from all the chaos of the photo shoot. I should probably go place her in her crib, but she's so sweet and cuddly I decide to stay where I am.

Gavin asks Ford, "How did you feel that day when you got the letter?"

Ford chuckles. "I can see we're not going to ease into this."

"Well, the article *is* about you being a single dad."

"My first thought was that now I don't have to share holidays." Ford's voice is even keeled, no emotion. Although I've learned his dry sense of humor since I started working with the Jacobs family, even I can't figure out how he's feeling right now.

I never did find out who leaked the existence of a letter to the press, but I suppose that's neither here nor there at this point.

"That's a joke," he says. "I think my exact words were, what the fuck?"

There's the Ford I know.

"I don't blame you. Have you heard from her?" Gavin asks.

"Her letter was pretty clear. I don't anticipate that I will."

"Sometimes parenthood can feel overwhelming. Maybe she'll return at some point."

"Are you a parent?" Ford asks. I imagine him on the couch, one arm slung across the back cushions, his ankle resting on his knee.

"No."

"Then don't make excuses for her. She abandoned her daughter."

"Is that how you see it?" Gavin asks.

I throw my head back and look at the ceiling. He can't even handle a bloody interview.

Standing, I step down the stairs and Ford's eyes narrow on me. "I think Ford meant—"

Ford holds up his hand. "I meant what I said. She abandoned Annabelle, and yeah, parenthood is fucking overwhelming. I'm barely sleeping, barely have time to make exercise and healthy eating a priority like I used to, but I wouldn't fucking leave her. Not for anything. Especially with someone like me. She knows nothing about me, except the size of my dick and my bank account."

The bitterness in his tone surprises me, maybe because he seems as though he's taken this all in stride.

"Don't print that, Gavin," I say.

Ford's gaze narrows on me. "With all due respect, Lena, this isn't about my family. This is my daughter and me. I don't remember hiring *you* to do *my* PR."

"Don't talk to her like that," Gavin says. "Why do you think you can talk to her like that?"

He stands and so does Ford.

How have I lost control of this situation? I step closer

to them. "I'm sorry, but you're a Jacobs and your dad hired me on your behalf. This interview is to calm down rumors that you can't handle being a single father. So please, let's keep Britney out of this and just stick to the fact that you're handling it like a pro and doing an amazing job with Annabelle. Look at her."

I glance down to see her asleep in my arms and discover I'm rocking back and forth. Where did I learn that?

The fury on Ford's face falls away and one side of his lips tips up. "You think I'm doing an amazing job?"

I blow out a breath.

Gavin looks back and forth between the two of us. "Is there something going on between you guys?"

We turn to him and say in unison, "No."

Ford steps over to me and we transition Annabelle out of my arms, his one hand brushing against my breast. A million little nerve endings go off in my body as though I'm thirteen and got felt up for the first time.

Thank goodness I go home tonight.

CHAPTER 5

"Two months."

Ford

Who knew seventeen-year-old babysitters were so unpredictable? I got a last-minute call that something came up.

Now I'm in the locker room, having had no choice but to ask Lena to watch Annabelle. And of course Gavin said he'd love to go to a game and get pictures of Annabelle watching me play. That it'd really show how I make it all work. As though I don't know that he just wanted to tag along to be with Lena.

Thankfully, our goalie, Roadie, had some ear protector headphone things from one of his kids handy that I could borrow, so I left Annabelle in the hands of who I think is a competent person. My dad cares about nothing more than the Jacobs' family image, and since he's entrusted that to Lena, I figure she can sit with my baby strapped on her chest for a couple hours and return her safe and sound. And yes, strapped because she insisted on stopping on the way to buy one of those things Gavin mentioned earlier.

At least I got them front row seats so I can keep an eye on Annabelle during the game.

"So now you're making her babysit your kid?" Aiden asks.

"What choice did I have? I can't miss the game. Especially since we're playing Langley."

"As if anyone forgot." Aiden rolls his eyes.

"I get anxious when we play him," Maksim admits, sitting on the bench wearing only his jock strap.

"Seriously, put that shit away. I'm sick of seeing your monster cock."

Maksim smiles, stands, and dances like a damn Chippendale dancer. Tweetie joins in because the two of them are never shy about what's between their legs. Aiden ignores them, shaking his head.

I crack my neck, hoping to relieve some of the stress that's building. I wish I could get that compliment Lena gave me out of my head. She thinks I'm doing a good job with Annabelle when I feel like a failure every damn day.

Did that Gavin think I'd actually tell him my true feelings when I got that letter? Idiot. I don't know him, and I'm a damn hockey player. There's no reason for people to think I have a sentimental side, especially my opponents. I get enough shit for being Richie Rich as it is.

"Where are Saige and Paisley? I have Annabelle in the front row." I'm hoping they'll be sitting close by. Those two never miss a home game.

"They're with the wives and girlfriends," Maxsim says.

Fuck, I forgot about that.

"Want me to text Paisley and ask her to check in with Lena a few times and make sure Annabelle isn't chomping on a pretzel or something?" Maxsim finally gets suited up.

Aiden laughs. "I'd trust Lena with my kid. She looks… motherly."

"Motherly? I'm not sure she'd see that as a compliment," I say.

Aiden bends down to tie his laces. "You know what I

mean. Like a multitasker. Responsible. The fact that she keeps you in line half the time is a good sign."

I think about the trouble I've given Lena and wonder why she grates on my nerves. But I know the answer, don't I? I feel like an asshole when I'm a jerk, but I hate how she's at my father's beck and call.

"I guess so, but it still makes me nervous." I don't really see the motherly side. Unless motherly means you hide what I'm pretty sure is a bangin' body under those pants and blouses. I'd love to see Lena in high heels and lingerie. Fuck. I shake my head to get rid of that image.

"Relax. You need your focus on the game," Aiden says.

"I'm gonna take a piss." Maksim walks by, fully dressed now, to go do his stupid superstition.

I finish lacing up my skates and stand to put my phone in the locker. I've kept it on me in case Lena had any questions she needed answered before the game started. I catch a text message from my mom.

Mom: *Good luck on the game. Thank you as always for taking one for your dad. The press will be good. You'll see. Love you.*

Always the peacemaker.

Me: *Thanks Mom. It's done and you're welcome.*

Mom: *<3 Score me one tonight.*

I give her the thumbs-up and tuck my phone in the locker, allowing the music beating in the room to wind its way into my veins, to get me excited. Because if anything, I want to mop the floor with Langley tonight.

Aiden comes over and pounds his fists on my shoulders. "Let's go!"

"Let's go!" I pound back and we grab our sticks, filing out to the hallway.

By the middle of the first period, I've had my eyes on Annabelle more than the puck.

"Get your head in the game or your ass is on the bench!" Coach screams when I come to the bench during a line change.

I'm not sure why I'm worried. Annabelle has her headphones on and she's fast asleep in the carrier I gave Lena. Gavin won't stop stealing Lena's attention away from the ice and my daughter, and I'm growing irritated.

"That her boyfriend?" Maksim asks.

"No, just a friend, I think. He's the writer for *Sports Illustrated*."

Maksim's eyes light up. "Why didn't you say so? I gotta up my game. Maybe get 'Play of the Week.'"

"That's ESPN, dipshit." I use a towel to wipe the sweat on my face.

"Still, if I impress, maybe I'll get an article for my actual talent. Not a PR piece because I have money."

I turn to Maksim, and he's smiling and laughing. If he wasn't my best friend, my fist would be in his face right now. But he and Aiden razz me all the time about my money. As if the two of them aren't making bank themselves. I get it though. My trust fund is probably more than the team's lifetime salary.

"Seriously, he hasn't stopped talking to her the entire game." Maksim nudges me with his elbow.

"I saw. They're both boring as fuck, so I guess it's a match."

Maksim raises his eyebrows but says nothing.

I point at him. "Get your head in the game. Langley still has two legs to skate on."

"I think I've lost my edge with Paisley. She's made me soft. The other day she asked me to paint her toenails."

"And?"

"I did it," Maksim says.

"You didn't."

"Hey, I got the best kind of thanks for doing it."

I shake my head.

He points at me. "One day."

"Mark my words, I'll never paint a woman's toenails." I concentrate back on the game.

"I'd make that bet, but the chance of you ever really falling for a woman is slim."

I tilt my head at him momentarily before concentrating on the game. "What does that mean?"

"You have daddy issues." I see him shrug in my peripheral vision.

"That's a term for a woman, not a man."

"You have daddy issues. Shit, if your dad told you to have sex with a hundred different women, you'd probably go celibate."

"Richie? Celibate? Yeah, right," Tweetie chimes in from the other side of me.

Maksim is still staring at me, waiting for me to negate what he's saying. But damn him, he's right. Whatever my dad wants me to do, I do the opposite. And I know for a fact he wants an heir. I'm the last of the Jacobs name right now, and since Annabelle is a girl, I'm pretty sure he'll pressure me at some point to have a boy.

"I could totally be celibate. I didn't have sex at all this week," I say.

"Because you're taking care of Annabelle, but you won't last a month." Tweetie chuckles just as the referee on the ice blows his whistle.

"Bullshit. My hand does a fine job."

Tweetie laughs, climbing over the boards to get on the ice.

"Jacobs!" Coach yells.

I scramble to get over the boards, tripping and losing my footing for a second before I recover and hope no one saw.

"Nice fall," Langley says, skating past me. That fucking prick.

"Shamrock, you think Richie can go a month without getting laid?" Tweetie asks.

"Find the puck and score for once instead of always slapping those gums together," I say.

And Tweetie wonders how he got his damn nickname. He's constantly talking on the ice. Chirping at the other team is one thing, but he'll have a full-on conversation out here with his teammates.

"I give him six weeks," Aiden answers, and my jaw falls open that my best friend doesn't have faith in me. "And that's being really generous."

The puck drops, and Aiden wins the draw and skates down the ice with it. Maksim is back in now, and Langley is flying down to catch up. Langley's definitely a beat off tonight.

"Six weeks?" I yell.

"I'm done with this topic of conversation." Just then Aiden scores.

While he's doing his celly, I tap my stick on the glass at Gavin. He looks up and I point at him. "Leave her the fuck alone. She's watching my baby."

Lena gives me her classic expression when it comes to me—exhaustion and annoyance. She shifts in her seat so I can see Annabelle's face, and I see that she's asleep in her carrier still. Then Lena shoos me off with her hand and the audience laughs. I turn around to find us on the

Jumbotron.

Coach has his hands on his hips, staring down the ice at me, so I skate away from the boards. I skate ahead and Tweetie slaps me on the back.

"Let's make a wager. I bet you fall for that one." He turns to skate backward, pointing down the ice toward Lena.

"That's never going to happen."

"You seem awfully concerned about that guy talking to her," he says before skating away from me.

"Just score a fucking goal," I yell after him.

He holds up his hands like, "Whatever, you know I'm telling the truth."

He doesn't know jack. "Tell him, Roadie."

"What?" He stretches after not getting a lot of action down by him. What's happened to Langley's team? They suck.

"Tell him how protective you are of your kids."

"You touch my kid and I kill you." He laughs. "In all seriousness, I get you're worried, but that PR girl could probably run a daycare. She's just got that look about her."

My eyebrows furrow. "What the hell does that mean?" And why does everyone keep saying that?

Aiden skates by me. "I thought we were actually playing a game here."

I skate after the opponent on Aiden's back and push him into the boards. "Happy?"

He shoots the puck at me. "Score for your daughter, shithead."

I smile and wink, taking the puck with my stick and circling past a defender. Tweetie, Aiden, and I get into our usual rhythm, and they get me the puck right as I skate past the goalie then around the net and score on the wrap around. The red light on top of the net comes on and the buzzer blares.

I glance over my shoulder and see Lena and Gavin in deep conversation, not even noticing I scored. Well, that was for Mom, I guess.

Tweetie laughs his ass off and points at me with his glove covered hand. "You're jealous. Damn, Ford Jacobs jealous. I never thought I'd see the day."

"I'm not fucking jealous."

Tweetie follows me off the ice. "Then let's make a bet. See how long you can hold out with no sex. I mean, if there's no one you're not actively going after, why not?" He gives me a shit-eating grin.

"What could you possibly bet me that I'd want?"

Both of our asses land on the bench with a thud.

"You get bragging rights and can say you won. Please, everyone knows there's nothing we have that you'd want."

I shrug because he's right.

"Unless you think you can't do it," Tweetie says.

"Don't try that reverse psychology shit on me. I can do it. There's no one I want to sleep with anyway." I'll be so busy with Annabelle, I won't have to deal with temptation, so this will be an easy win. "Okay, then six weeks."

"Two months," Tweetie ups it.

"Have you ever even gone two weeks without it?" I ask him.

He laughs. "Right now, Tedi's got me on a three-times-a-day schedule. She jokes that I'm her breakfast, lunch, and dinner."

Of course Tweetie gets a fucking nympho for a girl-friend. Bastard.

I take off my glove and put out my hand. Deal sealed.

As if the universe knows, the buzzer goes off and the period is over.

CHAPTER 6

"Nah, I got everything you need."

Lena

Thankfully, Gavin accepted my excuse to get out of dinner with him since I had Annabelle. He looked disappointed, but my plate is way too full right now to be dating anyone. It's just not a priority for me.

I find myself waiting with a bunch of fans and puck bunnies for the team to leave the arena. I'm so annoyed I have to be here, but I'm happy it's dark out so no one really notices the baby carrier I have. Especially since I purposely set myself to the back.

A few players come out, and I recognize Aiden and Maksim in the small group. They come over to me, a few bunnies annoyed that they don't give them the time of day.

"He'll be right out. Coach wanted to talk to him," Aiden says.

"Thanks."

They nod and continue toward their cars.

"Carmelo's?" Maksim asks.

"Fuck no. I'm gonna go bury myself in Saige tonight."

"Thanks for the TMI," Maxsim says.

Aiden laughs, sliding into his SUV, then drives out of the lot.

"Is that Ford Jacobs' baby?" A woman pulls my attention away from the parking lot.

I wrap my arms around the carrier and the baby inside. "Um…"

"It is!" The woman who's practically dressed like she's ready for the beach waves her friends over. "This woman has Ford Jacobs' baby!"

Before I can blink, a bunch of women swarm me.

I tightly hold the carrier, swatting away hands as they try to pull down the hood to get a look at her. "Stop it!" I will cut a bitch if they even think of touching Annabelle.

"Come on. He's been so hush-hush," another woman says.

"God, I wish I had his baby," one woman whines.

"What an idiot that baby mama is for running off," another says.

"Who would leave Ford fucking Jacobs?" a woman calls, trying to peek over all the women's heads.

"Listen—" I put up my hand.

"Are you dating him?" a woman asks and snaps a picture, blinding me momentarily.

"No. I'm his publicist and please step back. She's sleeping." I take a step farther back, but they just follow.

"Oh, how darling," one says and comes over to the side.

I whip around the carrier, putting a hand inside to keep Annabelle calm. "Please just go back to waiting for whoever you're waiting for."

"I had my eyes on Ford. I figured he'd need a nanny or two."

"Hell, I was going to apply for the job."

"And wear a slutty outfit every day," someone else says, and all the women laugh.

I get them wanting to sleep with Ford. I mean, my libido is off the charts every time he enters the room, but to wait outside for him to come out and hope he picks you out of a group of women? Have some self-respect, ladies. You deserve so much better than that.

"Sorry, I'm only taking one girl home tonight." Ford slides through the group and I swear the women's hands touch any part of him they can reach. He flawlessly leads me through the crowd with his hand on my lower back. "Let's go."

The minute we're clear of the group, women yell after him.

"Daddies need love too," one says.

"Don't you want company after she falls asleep?" says another.

Ford ignores them, walking us to a Mercedes I didn't know he owned. The only car I knew of him having in Florida is a restored Bronco.

When he clicks her into her car seat, Annabelle wails.

He looks over his shoulder at me, back at the women, and blows out a breath. "Do me a solid and sit in the back with her while I get us out of here?"

I nod and get in the back seat, running my knuckles down Annabelle's cheek, trying to calm her.

"Thanks." He buckles in the front.

The women have migrated away from the area where the players come out and are only inches away when he squeals his tires and leaves the parking lot. I refrain from mentioning anything about his driving with Annabelle in the car. He had to pick between two evils. Once we're on the highway, he slows.

"So, is that a usual occurrence?" I ask.

"The women?" His eyes catch mine in the rearview mirror.

"Mmmhmm."

"Yep."

Annabelle plays with the little stuffed cow hanging

from the top of the car seat while I stare out the window, not about to ask how many times he's partaken in those women.

"They're called puck bunnies, and they hang around wherever we are with the hopes they'll be picked up by one of us."

"I'm not an idiot. That was easy to figure out."

"And I bet you assume I pick one or two up a night."

"It's really none of my business," I say, wanting this conversation to end. He always beats me with his snappy comebacks and I'm not in the mood to second-guess everything I say on the plane ride home.

"Come on. Tell me. How many women do you think I bring home during the season?" He seems oddly amused by the blush filling my cheeks, and I really want to flip him off for getting off on making me uncomfortable.

I turn to look out the window. "I don't want to have this conversation."

"Come on. I can take it."

I shake my head.

"Are you a prude?"

"What are you, fourteen?" I scowl.

He shrugs. "Some people probably think my maturity level never developed past that age."

I tend to agree with them. "Just take me to the airport, then I'll be out of your hair for the moment. I'm sure you can't wait for that to happen."

He blows out a breath. "I can't believe you won't answer the question. This is your moment to tell me exactly what you think of me."

"You're my boss's son. I'm not going to degrade you."

"Degrade me? So you must think the number is high, huh?"

I shake my head. "The last I checked, cameras don't lie."

We both know I'm referring to all the pictures of him out and about with various women.

He laughs and points at me through the rearview mirror. "There you go. Keep going. Give me a number."

"I don't really care to."

"Sure you do."

"I really don't."

Silence commences for a moment, and I cross my fingers that he'll let the topic rest.

"Tell me your number if it makes you feel better." We're stopped at a light, so he looks directly at me through the mirror.

I hope the darkness of the interior hides the fact I'd never in a million years tell him my number. My mortification would be complete. "No."

"It's okay if it's low. Actually, most guys would prefer low."

I stare blankly at him. No way he just said that. First of all, why would it be cool if a guy has a high number and a girl doesn't? But more to the point… "Why do you assume my number is low?"

"Well, you're certainly not dressed like you want to have sex tonight."

"Because I don't." Okay, not entirely true. I can admit to thinking about what it would be like to sleep with Ford, but not in any *real* way. I must be losing it because I actually look down at myself to see what I'm wearing. A pair of pin-striped pants and a blouse. It's presentable and professional and there's nothing wrong with it. "Are you comparing me to your bunnies who dress like they're in the tropics regardless of the temperature outside?"

He laughs. It'd be interesting to know how he wants

Annabelle to dress when she's older. "I'm just saying, you never show your legs. It wouldn't kill you to show some cleavage now and then."

"For who? Do *you* want to see my cleavage?" I feel my body temperature rising. I hope we reach the private airport quickly. "Do you know how sexist you sound? Should I complain that you're not showing off your groin cleavage whenever I see you?"

"Groin cleavage?" His forehead wrinkles.

"You know, those hip indentations arrowing down toward your junk."

"Babe, what I have is not even close to being junk."

I clench my hands, wanting to scream. "Probably diamond-encrusted," I mumble to myself.

His laugh says he heard me. "I'm really enjoying you this trip."

"Wish I could say the same."

He turns into the small airport that his family jet flies in and out of. Thank goodness I'm seconds away from being out of this car before I go ballistic. Not that I think Mr. Jacobs would fire me. I've seen him go ballistic on his son quite often. Ford parks the car and my hand flies to the door handle.

"I'm just messing with you. Except the part about my dick not being junk. If I wasn't on a sex diet, I'd show you." He winks.

I shake my head and open the door. "You're unbelievable."

But as I stomp toward the small office where the pilot is supposed to be, Ford half exits his car. "I meant that as a compliment."

I raise my hand in a dismissive gesture. And I have to admit to being pretty proud of myself for not raising my middle finger.

When I step into the small airport office, the pilot isn't there. My shoulders slump and I pull out my phone, seeing a message from him. How did I miss his call? Quickly, I dial up my voice mail.

"Hey, Lena, I'm sorry, but there's a problem with the plane and the mechanic doesn't have the part, so we're here until tomorrow. I'll call as soon as I know something concrete."

I end the call and plop down onto a seat. I didn't even pack a bag because this has never happened before. Then I spring up out of my seat. Shit. I race out the door and see the taillights of Ford's Mercedes in the distance. I fumble with my phone to press on his name so I can catch him before he gets too far.

"Second thoughts? I suppose I can show you, but you can't touch." He laughs and my teeth clench.

"I need you," I say between gritted teeth.

"Say it a little breathier, more seductive."

"Ford!"

"Oh no. That makes it sound like you're going to bite my dick off. Not good."

My shoulders slump and I walk farther into the deserted parking lot. "Just please come back and get me. There's an issue with the plane and I can't leave until tomorrow."

"No need for excuses. You don't want to be far away from me. That's sweet." His brake lights flash right before he does a U-turn. "No worries, darling, your prince is on his way to rescue you."

I hang up on his laugh. The man is maddening.

I watch him come back and he unlocks the doors. I'm unsure if I should sit with Annabelle or in the front, so I hesitate.

He rolls down the window. "Do you need directions? Okay, you put your hand under the handle—"

"I got it." I open up the passenger side and climb onto the plush leather seat of the high-end car, the likes of which I'll most likely never own.

"Do you need me to buckle you in?"

"Just drive," I say.

"Whatever the madam wants, the madam gets." He pulls out of the airport.

I take my phone from my bag and search for a hotel, ignoring him.

"You can stay with me. I have more than enough rooms."

"That's okay." I continue to check, not finding a lot of vacancies unless I want to stay somewhere sketchy. Clearly something big is going on in Waterfall Springs.

"Unless you booked a room about a year ago, you're probably done for. It's Merfest weekend."

I turn to look at him. "Merfest?"

"Yep. I'd like to see you in a coconut bra."

I roll my eyes. "Seriously? A conference for mermaids?"

He holds up his finger. "And mermen. Men can have fins too, you know."

"Fine, can you stop at a Walgreens or something?" I shove my phone back in my bag.

"Nah, I got everything you need."

"I'm not using someone else's toothbrush."

He turns onto the highway back toward his house. I'm way too familiar with the route from the airport to his house, which says how much of a headache he's been since I started working for his family. "It's all new."

"You probably own stock in Oral-B."

"Proctor and Gamble, and yes, I do. My dad didn't like

them as an investment, so of course I bought a ton of shares. You're a smart cookie." He winks.

Before I know it, we're in front of his beach house.

Lord, help me get through this night. Surely he has an off switch when he's tired.

CHAPTER 7

"Lay her down."

Ford

As sad as it is to admit, I've had more fun messing with Lena tonight than if I went to Carmelo's with the guys. Once Annabelle is fed and put to bed for the three hours max that she'll sleep before she needs me, I go into my bathroom and grab Lena a toothbrush and a pair of my shorts and a T-shirt.

She's on the couch, sitting with her back ramrod straight and her feet on the floor, looking as if she's here for a confessional.

"Relax." I place the stuff on the table. "You can take your shoes off."

"Thank you for this. Hopefully I'm out of your hair first thing in the morning." She slips off her black flats and wiggles toes that sport a vibrant pink I'd never have imagined would be her style.

"No problem." I sit on the couch and blow out a breath. "You can take the guest room. Top of the stairs, straight ahead."

She nods and scoops up the things I gave her. "Thank you."

"Maybe I'm not the big bad wolf you assume." I eye her as she stops her retreat to the stairs.

"I don't think that."

"Are you hungry?" I ask. I know I should let her go up to her room and hide out while I do what I usually do, but I'm kind of sick of spending my nights alone.

"I'm fine."

"I mean, I'm starved, so I was going to make something. If you want to join me." I inch toward the end of the chair, about to get up.

"Well… I didn't eat at the game because I didn't want to disturb Annabelle."

I hold up my hand. "Then I'll make you a late dinner. Go change and come back down."

She doesn't say anything else, but heads over to the stairs and walks up them so quietly she could be a thief.

I stare at my contents in the fridge. Hummus, chicken breasts, vegetables. All healthy and none of it appealing right now. So I pick up the phone and call for Chinese since there aren't many places still open.

Unsure what Lena likes, I order a little bit of everything. I'll be paying for the sodium in two nights at my game, but so be it.

Sitting back down in the chair, I turn on the television, keeping the baby monitor at my side. There's a woman in my house and I'm not even thinking about sleeping with her. That's a scary thought. But then again, it's Lena. She despises me even if I don't exactly feel different about her. She's annoying as hell, but if I'm honest, there's something about her I find… intriguing.

I hear the stairs creak before she turns the corner wearing my T-shirt that's tied in the front and a pair of shorts that are rolled at least three times at the waist. Her sandy-blonde hair is thrown up in a messy ponytail, and her expression looks almost shy. Not at all like the spitfire who can spar with me.

There goes that whole thought about having a woman

in my house I don't want to sleep with. In fact, right now, I'm reliving that kiss on my family's plane on New Year's Eve.

"I ordered Chinese. I don't have anything worth eating," I say.

"Thanks."

"You can stop thanking me. I'm sure I've put you in enough shitty positions that I at least owe you dinner."

She shakes her head but smiles, insinuating I'm correct. Of course I am. I've given her so much shit since she started, but it's been more about my dad than her.

"If you want to go out, I'll watch Annabelle."

I rock my head back. "Oh, because I can't stay home?"

"No." Her eyes meet mine and there's genuine kindness there. "I just meant you've really adapted to this single dad role and probably haven't had time to do the kind of things you used to—"

"I never had to go out every night. I do enjoy staying in sometimes."

"I was merely suggesting—"

"I know what you were suggesting. That I'm a manwhore who wants to go back to the arena and pick up one of those bunnies."

She looks away from me and sits on the edge of the sofa. I have no idea why it's grating on my nerves that she can't allow herself to get comfortable. I'm not a monster.

"That's not it." Her voice is small.

"You think I'm a manwhore, right?" I shouldn't push this issue. Just eat the Chinese, go to bed, and when I wake up, she'll probably be gone.

"Can we please not?" Her gaze remains diverted away from me.

"Why? I won't get offended."

"Do you ever stop?" Her voice is louder now and her cheeks are turning light pink.

I'm starting to enjoy myself, just like in the car. "I'll stop when you answer."

She says nothing, and I catch her chewing on the inside of her cheek. Just when I'm about to press her again, she says, "I think you're a professional hockey player. I think you're Ford Jacobs, heir to Jacobs Enterprises. I think you've rarely gone without something you've wanted. I think that's just normal life for you."

"What's normal life for me?"

"The girls falling for you, for one. Let's not sit here and pretend you're not hot as hell. And that you have money and you're a professional athlete. You're like the horse that wins the Triple Crown of horse racing."

I tilt my head, intrigued that she paid me that compliment.

"I doubt you've been told no many times in your life."

"Once in the seventh grade, but I was going through my awkward phase." I wink to lighten the mood because although she's complimenting me, I hear resentment in her tone. "What about you? You enjoy telling me no."

"It's my job to tell you no."

All that comes to mind right now is when she didn't tell me no or push me away when I kissed her all those months ago. When my lips pressed to hers and a strangled moan sounded from her throat. She definitely wasn't saying no then. "True, but—"

"The kiss was just a New Year's tradition. If there had been other people there—"

"You would've kissed another guy?" I cover my heart with my hand and fall back into the plush chair. "You're killing me."

She stands from the couch. "I meant if there were

other girls, you'd have been kissing someone else. Let's remember I had to tear you away from a pair of women that night." She remains on her feet, standing at the end of the couch. "I'm just going to go to bed."

"Why are you always running away?"

Her footsteps stop.

The doorbell rings and I stand to go answer it, but on my way, I stop at Lena's back. My hand wraps around her wrist, my finger running a figure eight along the inside. "Trust me. I might not have been where I wanted to be that night, but I was with *who* I wanted to be with that night. Stay and eat something."

I inhale her scent, lavender and vanilla, and leave her standing there while I walk to the door before they ring the doorbell again and wake Annabelle.

After I pay the driver, I come back to find Lena still standing where she was, her cheeks pinker than I've ever seen. I'm not sure why I told her what I did, but I wanted her to know that I didn't kiss her on New Year's because she was the only woman there when the clock struck twelve. I kissed her because I wanted to. It's as simple as that.

"Why does it matter to you?" she asks, glancing at me.

I take the white boxes out of the brown paper bag. "What?"

She slowly walks toward me at the kitchen counter. "Why are you so hung up on what I think about you?"

"I just like fucking with you. That's all."

She nods, and our eyes meet for a second. She probably knows I'm lying. And that's exactly why I care. For some reason, Lena Boyd is the only woman who sees through me and the front I put up to my family, the world. And maybe that's why I've been pushing so hard for her to tell me what an asshole she thinks I am. That I'm not worthy of that kiss on New Year's. So I can hear what she really thinks of me and put her out of my mind. She's way too good for a guy like me.

***

*L*ight streams in my room and I squint, rolling on my sheets, exhausted and a little banged up from last night's game. Damn Langley and his laser focus on where I was every second. Even though he didn't play his best game last night, he's still a contender. I cringe, rising slowly until I remember Annabelle. I grab the monitor and see that it's off. Shit, did the power go out or something?

I run out of my room into Annabelle's. Her door is open, and I rush through to find Lena in the rocking chair, holding Annabelle and feeding her a bottle. Did Annabelle really sleep through the night?

Lena looks up and her gaze falls back down to my daughter. Her tongue slides out and licks her bottom lip. "I just thought as a thank you, I'd let you sleep in."

My heartbeat slows now that I know Annabelle is okay, and I rest my shoulder on the doorframe. "Thanks."

"No problem. That's a nasty bruise. Do you get hurt like that often?"

I look down at my stomach to see a black and blue bruise. "It's nothing."

Although that's obviously what's making me cringe when I move.

She places the empty bottle on the table, picks up Annabelle and puts her on her lap, then runs her hand in a circle on her back, patting lightly, holding my daughter as though she's a professional nanny. This is another layer of

Lena Boyd I had no idea about. I see what everyone means when they say she's motherly.

Annabelle lets out a huge burp, and we both laugh. Lena picks her up and stands. It's then I notice she's wearing my T-shirt still, but the shorts are gone. And I finally get my first look at Lena Boyd's legs. They're as good as I imagined—long, shapely, and perfect for wrapping around a man's waist. Or his head.

"Last night must've been a big night. She's sleepy." Lena smiles at Annabelle.

I give my head a shake to clear my thoughts. "Lay her down."

I watch Lena lean over the crib to place Annabelle inside. My shirt runs up, but it's so big on Lena, I only get a glimpse of her ass for a moment before she's standing back up.

Turning around, she stays by the crib, not coming toward me. Her gaze falls over my body, her tongue sliding out of her mouth again as though she has no control. There's a hunger in her eyes that makes my dick chub. Could we cross that line? Surely being my family's PR rep isn't her life goal.

"I should go." She walks toward me, but I don't move out of the doorway. When she realizes it, her gaze slowly meets mine. "Ford…"

It's not clear what she wants from me—for me to press her to do what I think she wants me to, or for me to pretend there isn't something that feels like it's tugging us together, even if I can't explain what that is or why.

"Lena," I say, mimicking her tone. I step closer, removing any distance between us. Her nipples poke through my shirt and brush along my chest. My arm winds around her, touching her waist, ready to hoist her up.

Her phone rings from her bedroom and Annabelle lets out a small cry, clearly not as asleep as we thought.

"That could be the pilot," she says and squeezes around me, brushing her entire body along mine.

"Yeah."

I watch Lena walk into the bedroom and shut the door. Fuck. I run my hand through my hair because there's no denying I almost lost all self-control and tried to sleep with her. It has to be because I need some female attention. God knows it's been too long at this point, even before I made that stupid fucking bet with Tweetie.

When I pick up Annabelle, she looks about a minute away from a tantrum and I realize I feel the same way. I need to get laid and I need it soon, before I end up fucking the last woman I should.

Sex diet be damned.

CHAPTER 8

Lena

hen the plane takes off, leaving the beaches of Florida behind, I finally release the breath I've been holding. I didn't spread my legs for Ford Jacobs. Mission accomplished.

Now if only I could stop replaying his intense stare or the feel of his arms around me in his daughter's nursery. Not that it's much of a nursery. A crib, a rocker. No decorations.

I was just doing him a favor with Annabelle. He let me stay the night with no notice, so I was being nice, like anyone would, right? He played a hard game the night before and we were up late, eating and chatting about all kinds of things—where to get the best egg rolls in New York City, how he first got into hockey. The topic of his playboy ways was put aside, and as much as I'm surprised, I actually enjoyed his company.

I couldn't figure out how to turn the monitor off in Annabelle's room because the main unit looks like something NASA would use on a space mission, so I opted to turn off the one in Ford's room. Going into his room to turn off the monitor, seeing him sprawled out in only his boxer briefs, wasn't part of the plan. I can't lie, I stood there for a few seconds, watching him sleep. I didn't lie last night. Lots of women see him as the Triple Crown. He's got it all. If I hadn't witnessed his turbulent relationship with his father, I'd say he was handed not only a silver spoon, but an entire silver platter. But I know his deciding to play hockey and not take over the business caused a rift in his family. One that has remained unfixable.

Still, I can't stop wondering, if the pilot hadn't called and my phone hadn't woken Annabelle, would Ford have taken me to bed? Would we have kissed only to realize it was a mistake, or would the lust coursing in that room have been enough to keep us going until we quenched our thirst for each other? Afterward, would I have hated myself and been discarded like all the other women in Ford's life?

The fact that I have all these questions makes it clear the right decision was made. I can't sleep with him, even if it is for only one night.

I open my laptop, seeing an email from Gavin. I go through what he's got so far for the story. The pictures turned out awesome. Sending an email back to him, I ask him to send me everything before it goes to print.

Then my eyelids fall closed as I lean my head back on the headrest, thinking that I probably need to get laid. It's been way too long, and if I can just sleep with someone, maybe all these thoughts about Ford will disappear.

I walk into the Jacobs' house, surprised to hear Mr. and Mrs. Jacobs arguing in his office. Usually, he'd be at the Jacobs Enterprises office at this time of day. But I tend to do most of my work here with Mrs. Jacobs. I thought it'd be a light day, especially since the whole Ford baby mama crisis is well on its way to being spun to show Ford as a glowing single dad.

Deciding to head to the kitchen and hopefully convince Bennie to make me a sandwich for lunch, I find Imogen, Morgan, and Bennie huddled around a plate of small triangle sandwiches.

"What's going on?" I ask.

"They're at it again," Imogen says. "Dad's birthday party."

His party isn't for two more weeks. Usually, Mrs. Jacobs does whatever she wants for their parties and Mr. Jacobs just shows up in whatever she tells him to wear.

"They're arguing about the agreement they made," Imogen says, taking a triangle sandwich.

Before I can ask what she's talking about, Bennie says, "Heard you got stranded in Florida." There's a hint of mischief in his eyes.

"I did." I pick up one of the sandwiches, starved from not eating anything on the plane.

"And?" Morgan asks.

I still with the sandwich halfway to my mouth. "And what?"

They all stare at me, then Imogen pulls out her phone, types out something, and slides it over to me. There's a picture of me with Annabelle on my chest and a suit-laden Ford walking to his car. The caption reads, "Ford Jacobs sports new car and new baby mama." I laugh and slide it back, not bothering to read the article.

"They don't know it's you. It was too dark. You're described as a sandy-blonde with a resting bitch face." Morgan laughs.

I take the phone back, more interested in the article now. "The puck bunnies took this?"

They all nod, even Bennie in his Hawaiian shirt. The man is always wearing Hawaiian shirts and complains all the time about how he's never been to Hawaii but how he's prepared in case anyone wants to have sympathy and take him. You'd think the Jacobs would at this point.

I shake my head. "People are the worst." I give the phone back after seeing the women said I was a bitch the entire time and wouldn't let them look at the baby.

"You took what they want," Imogen says with a smugness to her voice.

I scoff. "I don't want your brother."

Silence. No one says a word.

"What? I don't."

"Where did you stay last night?" Morgan asks with a shit-eating grin.

"There was a Merfest going on, so there weren't any hotel rooms available." My tone already sounds like I'm making excuses.

"Merfest?" Bennie asks. "There cannot be that many people who think they're mermaids."

Bennie might have a point. Especially since I didn't call every hotel before Ford offered up his place.

"I slept in my own room."

"Did you bring extra clothes?" Morgan asks.

"I borrowed a shirt and shorts to sleep in." I shrug, feigning nonchalance.

Morgan elbows Imogen. "Right out of a movie."

They both laugh. Bennie shakes his head and pulls a cake out of the oven. It's chocolate and it looks delicious. I knew I smelled something good when I came in here.

"It's not out of a movie. The plane needed a repair. I needed a place to stay, so I stayed at your brother's. You've seen us. We don't exactly see eye to eye on everything. On anything really."

"That's the point, darling," Bennie says. "All that animosity boils up until you can't control your hunger for one another."

I tilt my chin down and look at him from under my brows. "Okay, Bennie, put down the romance novels for a night. This was nothing of the sort."

A door slams from elsewhere in the penthouse and we all quiet for a moment to see what might follow, but don't hear anything else.

"I take offense to the romance novel comment." Bennie turns his head away from me as if he's mad.

"I'm sorry, it's just…"

"What?" Morgan asks.

"I don't like your brother!"

"Well, that's clear, but those pictures are incriminating," Mrs. Jacobs comes into the kitchen. "Oh, are you doing the practice cakes for the party in a couple of weeks?"

"Sure am," Bennie says with a smile.

"This is the chocolate, right?" she asks.

Bennie nods. "Mr. Jacobs doesn't eat chocolate though?"

Mrs. Jacobs waves him off. "He won't even eat the cake. The majority of people like chocolate, so that's what we're having."

Morgan walks over to her mom and lays her head on her shoulder. "Are you and Daddy getting a divorce?" Morgan has a personality much like her brother—not much is ever taken seriously.

"He's trying to go back on his word. He told me that at sixty, he'd retire. We're still young enough to travel and see the parts of the world that don't have anything to do with Jacobs Enterprises." She takes a sandwich from the tray and bites off a piece of it.

"He's retiring?" I ask. If he retires, the family might not need a full-time PR person, which means I would be out of a job. The familiar anxiety about how I might shelter and feed myself makes my chest tighten and my breath come out shallow.

Mrs. Jacobs blows out a breath. "The man will probably never retire. I told him I'm going to start going away without him. Said I'd go to Africa on one of those safaris where there's hardly any signal. He told me that if I didn't have such an ungrateful son, he could've retired three years ago."

"Once again, he has one child who's involved in the company." Imogen shakes her head.

Imogen works part time at Jacobs Enterprises, but her position isn't high up on the food chain. She has to finish graduate school this year first.

I don't say anything about how Imogen has confessed to me that she too wants nothing to do with the family legacy. I think she's just hurt that her dad doesn't see her as an option.

"Anyway, on to more important things, the plane, okay?" Mrs. Jacobs asks me.

I nod, swallowing my second small triangle sandwich. "Yeah, it's all good."

"I'm glad Ford took you in." She runs her hand down my arm.

Then Mr. Jacobs comes into the kitchen with a severe look on his face. "Fine, you can have your way, but I want six months to make the transition." He shoves his hands in his pockets.

This is the odd thing about my position with the family. I'm treated like one of their own. I've witnessed the girls' breakups, the fights between Mr. and Mrs. Jacobs, Bennie's breakdowns. They don't hold back with me. It's nice to be a part of a family after living life alone all these years.

I don't even really have a close girlfriend. Imogen is probably my closest friend. We go out for drinks and scope out guys, but we're not "telling each other all our deepest secrets" kind of friends. When you're responsible for making sure your dad gets to work after your mom dies at the age of seven you don't have a lot of time for kid stuff like making a BFF for life. I took on the role of caregiver for over fifteen years—until I couldn't do it anymore.

"I can do six months," Mrs. Jacobs says, smiling at her husband.

He shakes his head and looks around. When he finds me standing there, he studies me for a moment as though he has to find the words. "Lena, glad you're home safely." He nods and leaves before I can say anything.

If Mr. Jacobs retires, that could mean I'm out of a job. And if I'm out of a job, how will I pay for everything? I make really good money right now, and it's allowed me to live a lifestyle that I never could've imagined as a teenager —one with financial security. I don't have to wonder how I'll eat or whether I'll be kicked out of yet another shitty apartment. This job allows me to pay the facility that cares for my dad. And without that paycheck, I'm screwed.

"See, girls, don't let boys break promises. Your father promised me ages ago. I understand things haven't gone how he wanted, but that was our arrangement, and I wasn't going to let him get away with turning his back on it." Mrs. Jacobs takes another bite of her sandwich. "These are perfect, Bennie."

Bennie smiles wide, happy with himself. What does he have to worry about? The Jacobs will still need a cook. Maybe I can be his sous chef.

CHAPTER 9

"I wanted to celebrate."

Ford

I'm beckoned up to New York City by my father a week after the photo shoot. I can't help but wonder if this has something to do with the fact that every woman on the planet now thinks Lena's my girlfriend, thanks to that picture and the accompanying article. There went my idea of picking up a woman to get Lena Boyd out of my fucking head. Not that I have time with Annabelle. Or that most of the bunnies would mind. But I can't have some money hungry woman threatening to tell her story to the press because I'm "engaged" and slept with her.

Everyone thinks I have this whole single dad thing under control, but truth is, I'm tired as fuck and I'm going to have to break down and hire a nanny soon. The only good thing is that Annabelle's become an awesome sleeper over the past week, sleeping at least six hours a night, plus naps through the day. But I'm gonna need permanent help soon. Live-in help, rather than just a babysitter here and there.

The only good thing about my father demanding my presence is that I'll get to experience New York City in the fall. I made sure to bring Annabelle's stroller so I can give my little girl her first experience of walking through Central Park.

The elevator stops on the floor of my childhood penthouse, and I step through toward the round table adorning the foyer. Giant flowers fill a vase, as always. A new fondness for the place I've both loved and hated over the years drapes over me because Annabelle will be a part of this now. I take a moment to envision a year from now when she'll be walking into the penthouse on her own, searching for them.

"Ford." My mom comes around the corner, a smile on her lips. "Your father told me to stick around the house today. Where's my baby?"

She walks toward me, and I put down the carrier behind me and open my arms for her. Although she hugs me, she's laughing because we both know she meant Annabelle and not me.

"What's it like not to be the favorite anymore?" Imogen joins us, biting an apple and leaning on the wall.

"Nice to see you."

"Your girlfriend's in the kitchen." She tilts her head in that direction.

"We both know she's not my girlfriend."

My mom already has Annabelle out of the carrier.

I place Annabelle's bag on the foyer table. "What am I being summoned home for? His party isn't until next week. Oh, and don't forget, Mom, it's in and out for me since I have a game in Nashville the next day."

"We know." My mom rocks Annabelle.

Imogen walks over and kisses Annabelle's forehead. I love the way my daughter's getting doted on.

It's amazing how only months ago, I thought my life was over when I found out I was going to be a parent. Now, I can't imagine not having a daughter, even if I do sense myself losing who I was. That guy was kind of a prick anyway, so maybe it's for the best.

We all walk into the kitchen, because it's the place we seem to congregate when we're all home. Bennie's busy cooking, and Lena's on a stool with her legs crossed, a grape between her fingers as though she's ready to pop it into her mouth. She pauses when she sees me in the doorway, then her hand lowers.

"Ford." She nods.

"Now, is that anyway to greet your boyfriend?" my sister says.

"Cut it, Imogen," I say, but Lena's blush says these jokes have probably been going on nonstop in my absence. "Sorry about that. Puck bunnies can be kind of brutal."

"I'm a big girl," she says and finally places the grape in her mouth. She's in another pants-and-blouse set, hiding that rockin' body I saw a week ago.

"It seems to have died down."

"That's only because you haven't been seen together," Imogen chirps.

What do I have to do to get her to stop talking?

"Well, as long as I keep up my good guy act, we should be good." I wink, and Lena smiles.

My mom looks between us. "You guys are amicable?"

"They're screwing, so…"

My mom smacks Imogen on the back of the head. "The baby is here." She looks at Annabelle with a smile.

"She can't understand me." Imogen holds the back of her head and walks to the other side of the large island between Bennie and Lena. "And I liked it better when that move was only reserved for Ford."

"Bennie's making homemade baby food," my mom says.

"I thought you didn't know I was coming?"

She laughs. "Who runs this household?"

I nod, knowing it's her. "Where's Dad? I want to get

this over with so I can take Annabelle through Central Park."

"He's at the office," Lena says. "We're to go over there." She stands and straightens the paperwork she was going through, slipping into her flats that were resting next to her chair. Stealing one more grape, she packs up her bag.

"Why are you going?" I ask.

Her smile fades, and she inhales and exhales as though I'm trying her patience. "I was asked to go as well."

"But I haven't done shit. Hell, I'm asleep every night at eight unless I have a game." Anger simmers under the surface. I've been behaving myself and he's still got Lena up my ass?

"Whine much?" Imogen asks.

"Don't you have a job?" I snap.

"Well, I wasn't born with a dick, so…" She looks at the ceiling. "No."

"You do so, Imogen. Your father made a very nice position for you." My mom shakes her head at my sister while simultaneously making funny faces for Annabelle.

"A position that means shit, Mom. I literally have nothing to do. He makes me go to meetings to pretend that I'm 'important,' but we both know I'm not. I've decided to say screw it and go to Europe. Find myself."

My mom blows out a breath. "You already did that, it didn't take. We should all be happy you didn't come home with one of these." My mom nods to Annabelle.

"It wouldn't have mattered. Only the male heir means anything around here."

"That's not true." My mom shakes her head, but it was ingrained in us all when I was young that I'd be the one to take over. The firstborn male of the family has always taken the reins from the generation before. You'd think we're fucking royalty or something.

"Well, have fun in Europe," I say. "Don't get in too much trouble, otherwise Lena shows up at your door."

Lena scowls at me. "You act like I'm a bounty hunter or something."

"You're a fun-sucker." I cross my arms.

"Now, now, happy couple. No fighting." Imogen tries to pretend to make peace.

"Let's go." I tilt my head toward the door. We need to get this over with.

"I'm going to keep her," my mom says, nuzzling Annabelle.

"Okay, but don't take her to Central Park. That's my thing."

Everyone in the room laughs, but I'll be pissed if anyone takes that away from me.

Then Lena and I exit my parents' penthouse. Instead of driving my car, I hail a taxi, wanting to cut this as short as possible. I can't imagine what my dad has to say to me. It better not have anything to do with me taking over the company.

We arrive at Jacobs Enterprises, and I'm about to pass by security without telling them who I am until Lena stops walking and clears her throat.

"Hi, Rick, can I have a pass and one for Ford as well please?"

I groan and walk over to her.

"Ford Jacobs?" Rick asks.

I glare at Lena, annoyed.

"This is procedure. You don't want to be part of your

dad's company, you get cleared by security." She gives me a saccharine grin.

I arch an eyebrow. "You're feisty today."

"Do you think I want to be summoned to the office?"

"Aren't you always here?"

She balks. "You have no idea what I do, do you?"

"Here you go, Lena." Rick slides over an ID badge. "I'm going to need your driver's license," he says to me.

Again, my head twists toward Lena, who's biting her lip to stop from laughing. I look around as I pull out my wallet. "You honestly don't recognize me?"

Lena outright laughs. "You're mighty full of yourself today."

"I'm the son of the owner."

"The son of the owner who never comes here," she singsongs as I hand my ID to Rick.

"I never stop at the security desk when I'm here and no one ever says anything." But in all honesty, I haven't been to my dad's office in many years.

"Well, precautions. Never know what kinda crazy might pop in one day."

"Are you insinuating that I'm the crazy one?" I accept my ID back from Rick and stuff it back in my wallet.

"You do have some anger issues toward your dad."

I put up my hand and shake my head, looking at Rick. "How's it coming?"

"Just checking that he has you on his list of visitors today."

I grow irritated by the slowness with which Rick is working while Lena seems like she's enjoying it.

"Here you go," Rick says a minute later. "Stop back and return it on your way out so we know you've left the building."

"Sure, buddy," I say and stuff the guest pass in my pocket before heading toward the elevators.

"You're supposed to wear it. And maybe be nice to Rick. Your father's safety is in his hands."

I dramatically look back at Rick who, from a glance, I'd guess is probably in his early sixties and not at all in shape. This guy isn't chasing anyone down regardless of the threat they might pose. "Sure thing."

The elevator dings and I press the button to go up to the top floor. Lena rolls her head back, circling it as she stands in the opposite corner of the elevator. The urge to cage her in comes over me before I shake that thought out of my head pronto.

"Do you know what this is about?" I ask.

She shakes her head.

"Really?"

"Yes really. Do you think I'd let you be ambushed?"

I shrug one shoulder. "You do work for him, not me."

She blows out a breath. "You really need to get that chip off your shoulder. Your family is not out to get you."

"It's not my family I'm meeting, it's my father, and he wants me traveling up this elevator every damn day until I die of a heart attack at my desk. That's not the life I want."

Her plump lips say nothing, but her eyes speak volumes.

"What?"

She shrugs. "Nothing. It's none of my business."

"There are a lot of things that aren't your business that you make your business. Let's hear it."

"I'm just saying, a lot of people would love to be in your position. Take over a successful, established company? A corporation the size of this one, just handed to you? I can't even imagine."

Annoyance brims inside me. "So I'm the douchebag

because I don't want it? Another spoiled brat move by Richie Rich for telling his dad to fuck himself?"

She shakes her head. "That's not what I'm saying. I'm just saying understand where your dad is coming from. Understand that it's hard for him."

"You're unbelievable." I shake my head and look away from her.

"I could say the same."

I whip my head back in her direction. Our eyes meet and neither of us looks away as though we're in a staring contest and the first one to blink is the weakest.

"Let's just agree to disagree," I finally say.

Luckily, the elevator dings and I step forward before remembering that my mom would smack the back of my head if I didn't let Lena go first. So rather than stomp off angrily, I hold out my arm for her to go first.

She does with a smug look and whispers, "Smile. People are watching."

"You'd know," I grit out, smiling and waving to a few people who say my name.

"Ford!" My dad's assistant, Frida, rounds her desk and looks me up and down. "You're so big." She waves me forward. "Come down here, you're too tall."

"Hi, Frida." I give her a smile. It's been a long time since I saw her.

Lena sits on the couch, waiting to be called in.

"Hi, Lena dear. How nice to have Ford escort you here," Frida says.

I'm pretty sure Lena is probably choking on her tongue as she tries not to say what she's really thinking, and I chuckle.

"Yeah, it was a peachy ride," Lena says sarcastically.

Frida doesn't seem to hear it though, and her hands pinch my cheeks. "You used to have the chubbiest cheeks, but look at you now, all grown and handsome." She steps back and I stand straight, my back stretching. "Where's the baby?"

"With my mom," I answer, and she frowns.

The buzzer rings and my dad's voice comes through. "Send them in, Frida."

Her eyes open as though she forgot momentarily that she's working. She hurries around the desk and picks up the receiver, telling my dad we're coming as she shoos us with her hand to get in there as though we're late or something.

We both walk to the door until I realize again I need to let Lena go first, so I wave her in.

"Always the gentleman," Frida says, smiling at us.

Lena rolls her eyes and steps in.

"Close the door," my dad says, standing and rounding his desk. "Drink?"

Lena sits at one end of the couch, crossing her legs and sitting up straight. "No, I'm okay."

"I'm good," I say on the opposite side of the couch in a much more relaxed fashion.

My dad grabs a bottle of champagne and three glasses. Lena and I share a confused look, then look back at my dad.

"Thanks for coming down here today," he says.

"It was right around the corner from my place. Not inconvenient at all." I'm sarcastic.

My dad drills me with a disapproving look. "I'm sure the private plane was comfortable enough."

He always reminds me of what he still does for me. I nod. Okay, my dad kind of schooled me there.

"Is there something I'm not aware of, Mr. Jacobs? I felt like things were under control." Lena reaches into her bag and takes out a notepad and pen.

"It is, but I have some exciting news and I wanted to celebrate."

I glance at Lena, and she looks at me briefly before we both turn back to my dad.

"What's going on?" I ask.

"You two are getting married."

CHAPTER 10

"Deal."

Lena

y heartbeat hammers in my head and my pen drops to the floor, but it takes me a minute to reach for it because of the words that just left my boss's mouth.

"I'm sorry," I say, leaning forward like those men who can't hear out of one ear so they're always putting their good ear toward you. "I thought you just said Ford and I are getting married."

"I did." Mr. Jacobs leans forward and opens the champagne bottle. "It's like this… people have embraced Lena as the new woman in your life."

"Since when is being called a bitch embracing?" The words are out of my mouth before I can think better of it.

Ford snickers next to me.

"What I mean is that they were okay with another woman besides the baby's mother being in the picture. That got me thinking—"

"Why?" Ford asks, clearly not as baffled as I am as to why Mr. Jacobs would even suggest such a thing. "What's in it for you?"

Mr. Jacobs pours the champagne into three flutes and leans back. Ford is a mini version of his dad. Well, only mini because he's the younger version. They share the same blue eyes and darker blond hair, although Mr. Jacobs now has gray around his temples. Both of their bodies are strong and tall. And they both intimidate me.

Mr. Jacobs sets his gaze on his only son. "I'm assuming you still have no interest in running Jacobs Enterprises?"

I do not want to be here to listen to this conversation. I stand from the couch. "Maybe I should leave."

"Please sit," Mr. Jacobs says, his eyes never leaving Ford.

"You know I don't."

"Your mom wants me to slow down. To retire from running the day-to-day operations. The only way I can do that is if I sell someone controlling interest of the company and make sure I have a spot on the board. Since you're the next heir, you will also have a spot on the board."

"I don't want any of it."

Mr. Jacobs shakes his head. "It doesn't matter. You're already listed on all the paperwork. You're on the board. I have a very interested party, but not all men are as liberal as I am."

Ford cracks up. "Liberal?" He raises his brows.

"Some people are more conservative with their values, and having a son who blatantly picks up women, impregnates a one-night stand, and gets in bar brawls isn't considered trustworthy in a lot of circles."

"Why is where I put my dick any concern to your buyer?" Ford leans back in the couch, his ankle resting on his knee just like his dad is across from him, and they exchange an intense and challenging stare.

"I don't make the rules, but we do have to follow them. I need you to clean up your image for this deal to go through. And an engagement to a woman like Lena will go a long way toward doing that."

Ford stands and shakes his head, hands on his hips. "You're asking me to marry her?" He points at me.

I feel the sting of the incredulous way that sentence leaves his mouth.

"Excuse me, but I think you could do worse," I say.

Mr. Jacobs laughs. "I like the way you two challenge one another."

"I'm not doing it, Dad."

"Then you come home," he says matter-of-factly. "Come home and take over for me."

Ford scowls.

"That's what I thought. If I sell this company, all you have to do is hold a board position. You can play hockey until you retire, and after that, your life is yours. So I guess the question is how bad do you not want to run Jacobs Enterprises?" His dad stands, never looking at his son.

Meanwhile, Ford paces and runs his hand through his hair. I have so many thoughts running through my head that it's hard to make sense of them, but they all come down to one word—no.

No way can I marry Ford. Why would I? The only thing that could possibly happen is that one of us would kill the other or eventually we'd give in to temptation and I'd be left heartbroken. Because Ford Jacobs is not a forever kinda guy. No bueno. No way. Not gonna do it. I love working for the Jacobs family, they've been good to me, but this is asking too much. And it's definitely not part of my job description.

"I can't believe this. No one will believe it," Ford says.

I scowl at him. "I'm starting to take offense here."

Ford looks over and his gaze locks with mine. "I'm not saying it because of you. It's me. Who would believe that Ford Jacobs would fall to bended knee?"

"No one thought you could raise a daughter by yourself either," Mr. Jacobs say.

"I have to. I don't have a choice."

"You have enough money to hire full-time nanny service, yet you're with Annabelle every minute you can be."

"Careful, Dad, you almost sound proud of me," Ford says and leans on the edge of the desk, his head hanging down.

"Excuse me," I say, raising my hand. "You're all forgetting that I haven't agreed."

Mr. Jacobs looks at his son then at me. "Excuse us, Ford. I want to talk to Lena on her own."

Ford straightens from the desk. "Why? If I'm going to be her husband, I wanna know what you're offering her to marry me."

Mr. Jacobs sits in the chair he was in before. "No. It's a fake marriage. It's Lena's business and her decision to share it with you should she choose."

My stomach tightens. As ridiculous as this idea is, I'm afraid he's going to make it hard for me to say no.

"Whatever." Ford storms out of the office and slams the door.

"I apologize for my son," Mr. Jacobs says, a comment he's made plenty of times before.

"No need."

"Lena, I know your situation. I'm sure that takes you by surprise, but I vet all my people thoroughly before letting them into our lives. I know about your father. About your upbringing."

My heart drops into my stomach with a huge thud and lands there like lead. I suck in a breath, and tears of embarrassment prick my eyes.

He gives me a soft smile. "There's no reason to be

upset that I know. If anything, it only makes me respect the fine young woman you've turned into more. But if you agree to marry Ford for a small time, I'll offer you enough money to start your own **PR** firm, enough that you wouldn't have to worry about paying for your rent or your dad's facility for many years. Depending on how well you managed the money, you could set yourself up for a long time. I understand what I'm asking. My son isn't an easy man. You'll be obligated to show up at events together, but I'm willing to give you a third now and the rest after it's over."

I tear my gaze away and walk over to the window and stare at the streets of New York City. A city full of possibilities. A city where things can go downhill really fast and I could go back to living out of my car. "What happens to my position after you retire?"

"I think you know that we will no longer need your services." His voice is soft, as though he feels bad saying the words.

I nod, confirming what I already knew, and turn back to him.

"How much?" I hate asking, but I have to put a number to it. That's the only way to know if it's worth it.

He smiles, goes to his desk, and pulls out a pad of paper with his name on it. He scribbles a number and slides it across the desk.

I walk over and pick it up to read it. My eyes widen and I stare at the number for a moment, speechless. "This is too—"

"It's not. Ford won't make this easy even if he agrees to it. I want to make my wife happy, and to tell you the truth, I'm tired. Tired of fighting my son. Tired of it all. I want to spend whatever time I have left with my wife, traveling and experiencing the things I can afford to do but never had the time for. I honor my promises, and I promised my wife I would step aside when I was sixty. I had hopes my son would take over, but since that's not an option, I'm going to sell. Unfortunately, in this industry, there are a lot of conservative people who don't look kindly on a man raising his daughter alone after a one-night stand."

I set down the paper and walk back to the window. "You can't change that. They already know it."

"You know as well as I do Lena that business is all about perception. The minute your engagement is announced, as sad as it is, people will forget the past. Most people don't care if things are actually the way they seem, just that they seem the way they want them to. As long as you two look and act like a couple in love, the new narrative will be what a wonderful family you're going to make. I've been in these circles a long time. Trust me on this."

"But how would we get out of it?" I turn to face him again.

"I'll have that conversation with you and Ford, but first you have to agree." He nods toward the piece of paper on his desk. "Is that enough money?"

I'm sick at the idea of doing this for money, but why would I do it otherwise? Upend my life and play pretend, for what? And if I'm not going to be employed after he retires, this money will make sure I never have to live out of a car again. It will give me financial security I've never before had in my life. Something I desperately crave.

Sure, I'm in PR and I'm used to spinning a story. But an outright lie feels different. If people ever find out it was a sham they'll judge me, maybe think I have no integrity, no dignity. But those same people likely don't know what it's like to wonder where your next meal is going to come from or wonder whether today is the day you'll be evicted from your apartment.

Then there's the question of how people will perceive me. Will they think I stole Ford away from Annabelle's mother? That I broke up what could possibly be a happy family?

And finally, how do I pretend to marry a guy I want to have sex with? That's the real obstacle here. If I let myself fall for Ford, I'll be in worse shape after this charade is over and the money won't matter. But I have no choice. I can't take care of my dad on my own. He needs to remain in that facility.

I draw in a deep breath, hands on my tummy willing it to calm down. "I'm in."

A smile displays his perfect veneers. "Great news, Lena." He leans over his desk and presses the intercom button. "Send in Ford, Frida."

"Sure thing, Mr. Jacobs. I just have to find him…"

"Frida, Ford is there, right?"

"Um…"

"Frida!" Mr. Jacobs' voice is sterner now.

"I'm here, relax. I just went to the restroom," Ford says through the intercom, then the door bursts open. "I can't believe you. You're still trying to control me. Too bad I didn't come with robot mode when I was born." Ford's eyes blaze.

While I was processing and getting what I want out of this deal, anger was consuming him.

"It's a simple question. Do you want me to stop harassing you to take over the company? Do you want to finish out your hockey career without any pressure from me to do otherwise? I guess it comes down to how badly you want it."

"I think I should leave you two to talk." I grab my bags from the couch.

"Lena, sit down please."

I do as he says, and Ford joins me on the other end of the couch.

Mr. Jacobs sits across from us. "Just listen to the arrangement. You announce your engagement at my birthday party next week. You marry at the end of the season, then you give it at least six months as a married couple. At that point, the company will be purchased and all paperwork will have gone through, and you can both do what you like."

My eyes widen and I sit back. I didn't think this plan would consist of that long of a time frame, but I guess billion-dollar companies aren't bought in a day.

"We have to pretend to be in love for over a year?" Ford's voice hitches. "And I'm sure there are events we'll have to go to. Who plans the wedding? Why can't we just be engaged and then break up?"

"The wedding is a must. If we do it at the end of the season, it should be just as everything is coming through. You have to remember, I need to schmooze the guy. If he thinks I'm desperate, he'll lowball his offer and I won't let this company go for anything less than top dollar. This is a charade I'm asking the two of you to keep up with."

Ford leans forward, his forearms resting on his thighs, his head hanging low. Then he peeks at me. "Did you agree?"

I nod hesitantly. He rolls his eyes. That only infuriates me because he doesn't know why I need to say yes, and frankly, it's none of his business. He can judge me all he wants.

He looks at his dad. "No more comments. I'm a hockey player. Right wing for the Florida Fury. Not Ford Jacobs, heir to Jacobs Enterprises. No holding it over my head or making me feel guilty for years to come if you sell."

His dad nods. "I promise. But—"

"Here we go." Ford blows out a breath.

"Lena will move to Florida. You two will be photographed—often. I'm sure Lena can arrange things, and she knows how to spin it so people believe it. You two need to sell this."

"Great, so I'm marrying a world-class liar. Perfect." Ford shakes his head.

"You're going to need me on your side," I tell him.

"There will be events up here you'll have to come up for. Some with Annabelle and some not."

"My daughter will not be used as a pawn." Ford's tone brooks no argument.

"Okay, then bring Annabelle when you want."

Ford turns to me. "I'll remain Annabelle's primary caretaker. No need for her to get attached to you just for you to leave her after a year." There's a coldness I've never heard in his voice, and a chill runs up my spine.

"She's a baby," Mr. Jacobs says. "She won't even remember."

"Nonnegotiable," Ford says.

Mr. Jacobs nudges the champagne glasses between us. "Deal. So are congratulations in order?" He raises his glass.

I look at Ford and he looks at me, both of our eyes filled with doubt, but we pick up the glasses anyway.

"Deal," we say in unison.

CHAPTER 11

"No kiss goodbye, honey?"

Ford

Lena and I split after leaving Ford Enterprises. She takes her cab to who knows where and I climb into mine to head back to my parents' penthouse. I'm fairly sure I speak for both of us when I say we're in shock. Never did I imagine my dad would throw a fake marriage at me. Sure, it's just another way for him to control me, but sitting on a board is a helluva lot better than having him up my ass every damn day to take over the company. Something I was never going to do.

The elevator dings on my arrival at my parents' penthouse, and the silence makes me still for a moment. My eyes jolt to the spot where I left the baby stroller and I see that it's gone. Immediately, I pull out my phone and call my mom.

She answers and I hear Manhattan traffic in the background. "You're already back?"

"Did you know about this?"

She's silent for a moment. "I did."

"Mom!" I yell.

"Come meet me downstairs. I just took Annabelle for a walk around the block because she was getting cranky upstairs. But come down and we'll walk through Central

Park. Surely you don't mind your mother being part of the memory?"

I sigh. "Give me five."

I hang up and go to the bathroom. After I take a leak, I stare at myself in the mirror while washing my hands. Can I really go through with this? Lena practically hates me most of the time and now she'll be my roommate? Even if there is some kind of weird sexual tension between us, I'm still not on her list of top ten favorite people. Hell, I probably wouldn't even make the top one hundred.

I head down the elevator and find my mom talking with our doorwoman, Anessa. They're both gushing over Annabelle. That doesn't really get old—people loving on my daughter. She is the cutest baby in existence.

"Here he is," my mom says and gestures in my direction.

I nod a hello. "Anessa."

"I saw the magazines, but I didn't believe it until your mother told me. Congratulations." Anessa beams at me.

She's been the doorwoman since I was in high school. The condo committee didn't want a woman outside the building, but my mom took her side and fought to make it happen.

"Yep, I'm a father now."

"And you'll make a good one." She winks as though we share a secret.

We do. We're both unsure if I can handle this new venture. Anessa saw me in my glory days when my parents were traveling for my dad's work and I was partying.

"Thanks." I nod and smile.

We stand there for a moment until my mom says, "We should get going. Give this little one her first stroll through Central Park." My mom covers up the stroller to make sure Annabelle stays warm.

"Have fun, you two," Anessa says with a wave.

Since my parents' building is directly across from Central Park, we cross the first intersection and enter the park. The leaves have already begun to change into vibrant reds and oranges. A few are sprinkled on the ground. It's crazy to think that in only a few short weeks, the trees will be bare.

"She's never going to remember this," I mumble, staring at the trees and stuffing my hands in my pockets to warm them.

"No, but you will. And you can tell her all about it one day. It's a special time for you."

Ever since my mom beat cancer seven years ago, her attitude on life has changed. I don't know for sure, but I'd bet that was when my parents made the agreement about when my dad would retire. I guess maybe that's why he's been pressuring me so hard the past few years to take over the company. Mom's diagnosis shook our family. Although she survived it after a grueling year, we all realized she's the glue that holds us all together.

"I can't believe you didn't warn me."

She glances at me, guilt in her eyes. "I'm sorry. I know it was a shock to you and Lena. Your father asked me to keep it quiet. I wanted to warn you before you went to his office, but I promised him. I wasn't happy with the suggestion at first either. I worried that you'd run, and I'd never see my granddaughter."

I swing my arm over her shoulders, "I'd never take her away from you."

She nods. "This is the kind of peace I need in my life." She glances up again, tears in her eyes. "You and your father have been at odds for so long. Now that you have Annabelle, I want it to stop. I don't want her to grow up witnessing the arguing and the fighting. You two can barely be in the same room right now."

"He's stubborn."

She huffs and swipes at her eyes. "So are you."

I take over pushing the stroller, needing something to do. "I don't want the same thing he does," I explain for what feels like the billionth time. "I worked hard to get where I am and I'm not going to throw it all away to work in an office every day until I die."

"I know. I know."

For a moment, all I hear are the leaves crunching under our feet and traffic off in the distance.

"I know your father's suggestion isn't ideal, but it's an end. Otis Sandersville has traditional family values, and appearance is important to him. All we have to do is convince enough people you and Lena are happily engaged, and eventually people will forget about the past and focus on the amazing future you're building for yourself and your daughter."

"And if Britney comes back?" I ask the one question that sometimes keeps me up at night. Because how will I handle not having Annabelle with me all the time now that I'm used to being her number one? How will I feel if the mother who abandoned her pops back up in her life?

I understand how tired Britney was. How much taking care of a baby sucks out of you. Especially since before Annabelle came along, we both lived the opposite of how a responsible parent probably should. But she abandoned her daughter. Still, she could have doubts about her decision and return, want partial custody back.

"Well, that could potentially pose a problem with the plan, but at the same time, it would be good for Annabelle. I guess we play it by ear."

Would it be good for Annabelle? I honestly don't know.

I guess if she were back for good. But having a parent pop in and out of her life like a Whack-A-Mole can't be good for a child.

We walk a little longer and eventually sit on a bench by the small lake in the park. Ducks gliding across the water leave small wakes behind them.

"Lena hates me." I voice the biggest reason I'm not sure this will work.

"She doesn't hate you. You aggravate her, for certain. You egg her on all the time. The two of you banter too much."

I refrain from telling my mom how turned on our banter gets me. There are some things you don't tell your mother.

"Listen." She places her hand on my thigh. "This plan is one right out of the movies or something, but I'm sure we're not the first. It's not as though wealthy families haven't based marriages on strategic alliances before. And who knows? Maybe something will come of it." Her eyebrows rise to her hairline.

"Don't go thinking Lena is going to change me. I'm not the happily-ever-after type, Mom. You know that."

She laughs and puts her head on my shoulder. "One day, every playboy has to retire. Sooner or later, you'll be too old. I don't want you to die alone."

"Jeez, knife me in the heart, why don't you? I'm just not looking for an exclusive relationship right now."

"And sooner or later, ten years will have passed and you still won't be committed to anyone. Have you ever thought about what will happen if Britney doesn't return? Where that leaves Annabelle? I'm sure Imogen and Morgan will help and you'll always have me, but don't you want Annabelle to grow up with a mother?" She squeezes my knee.

"I'm not saying never, but we both know it's rare for relationships to make it when one of them is a professional athlete. You saw what those bunnies did and said with Lena."

"Your two best friends seem to be doing pretty well so far."

I shake my head. "We both know how different I am from them."

"All I'm saying is you have a daughter now. Whether you like it or not, it changes things."

"Well, for the next year, I'm already spoken for, so…" I shrug and she laughs. "I just hope Annabelle doesn't get too attached and has to adjust when things end."

My mom's smile dims. Making her upset pierces my heart. I really hope she doesn't cry when Lena and I get divorced. That this isn't her way of getting me to commit to someone.

"Well, she's young. And you and Lena might come out of this as friends. I don't see Lena just leaving Annabelle high and dry once this is over."

I nod because my mom makes sense.

"But I want my family back, and I'm sorry that it means putting you in a temporarily uncomfortable position, but I'm your mother, so my happiness trumps all." She laughs and stands. Mom pulls Annabelle out of the stroller with the blanket, rocking her in her arms while showing her the ducks.

I watch the two of them together. If not just for myself, I'll do this for my mom so she can get what she wants.

"Lena!"

The sound of my soon-to-be fiancée's name pulls me from my thoughts. I look over to see her walking toward us.

"Hi." She waves. She must've come here right from the meeting with my dad. Her eyes are red-rimmed, but she smacks on a pretend smile as she approaches my mom and Annabelle, who are watching the ducks and smiling. "Wait until she can feed them."

"I can't wait. I don't want to rush it, because this age is precious too, but I can't wait until she's walking and talking," my mom says.

Lena smiles at my mom. "It'll be sooner than you think."

They both look at my daughter, love lining my mom's eyes and adoration in Lena's. At least she likes my daughter.

"You know what? Her hands are probably cold. I'm going to take her back home." I move to stand, but my mom shoos me down.

"You two stay here. We're perfectly capable of making it back on our own." Mom runs her nose along Annabelle's. "Isn't that right?"

"Mom," I say.

She places Annabelle back in the stroller. "You two have plenty to talk about. See you at home."

I watch my mom walk away as Lena comes over, sitting on the edge of the bench as though she's afraid of me or something. We sit in silence and watch the ducks. There's a mom and three kids a little ways down. One boy chases the ducks while the mom scolds him to stop. I feel a kinship with that kid. God, if Annabelle pays me back for all the shitty things I did to my parents growing up, I'm gonna have my hands full.

"So how are you feeling about this?" Lena asks.

"I don't really know yet, but I don't have a choice. You?"

She nods. "I'm going to go through with it, but I'm worried."

"Can I ask you a question?" It's been on my mind ever since my dad sent me out of his office.

"Sure."

"Does my dad have something he's hanging over your head? Is that why you agreed to this?"

She slides back on the bench, crossing her legs. The heel of one of her sensible flats pops off her foot, dangling from her toes. All I can imagine are those pink toes underneath curling in pleasure. I mentally chastise myself. This could be bad if I don't get my desire under control.

She shakes her head. "No, he doesn't have anything on me."

"Are you sure? Because for the life of me, I can't imagine why you'd agree to this."

She turns to me. "I could say the same about you."

"I'm doing it so he'll get off my back and to make my mother happy."

"Well, let's just say I need what your dad is offering."

"Money?" I say derisively.

She whips her head in my direction. "You know what I find funny about you, Ford?"

"What's that?" I press my lips together.

"That you have all this money and you're not embarrassed to spend it, but you judge others for wanting it. It doesn't matter what your dad is doing for me. I didn't grow up like you. If your dad retires, I'm out of a job, and I know it's no concern of yours, but jobs aren't always easy to find. At least well-paying ones aren't. I have expenses, so I'm agreeing to marry you in order to have those expenses paid."

I'm thrown for a moment, speechless because I feel like a prick. She's right. I can't judge her when money has never been an issue for me. I don't know what that feels like. "You're completely right. I apologize."

She raises both eyebrows in surprise. "Don't play nice. We can't pretend this is going to be anything but horrible. We'll count it down like a prison sentence." She stands. "See you later and we can talk logistics."

I nod. "No kiss goodbye, honey?"

She narrows her eyes.

"What do you want your pet name to be? Babe, baby, honey? I'm not sure I can pull off darlin', but I can try."

"You can call me Lena," she says with a straight face.

"What's the fun in that?"

She blows out a breath like a teacher who's on her last ounce of patience for the day. "There's no fun between us. Welcome to hell, Ford."

She turns and walks away, and I'm not ashamed that I notice my soon-to-be wife has a killer ass.

CHAPTER 12

"Clearly you don't like my dress."

Lena

I slide the tape over the last box I have to pack and stare at the room filled with cardboard rectangles. I toyed with keeping the condo, but it seemed ludicrous to pay for an apartment I'll never be in. After our divorce, I'll find a new place to live.

I'd like to say these walls have stories, that they hold memories I'll never forget, but other than the comfort and safety this place supplied me, the only memories I have are of me coming home, snuggling on the couch, and watching movies by myself. Making dinner for myself. Cleaning the condo by myself.

Sure, I've had a few dates here or there, but my job with the Jacobses is demanding and things change at the last minute all the time. Eventually I just kind of stopped trying to find dates and figured if I meet someone, I meet someone and if not, oh well.

The movers are coming in the morning, after Mr. Jacobs' birthday celebration tonight where my engagement to Ford will be announced. He'll fly out for his next game, and we'll use the excuse of me moving as the reason why I'm not tagging along. I'll have to go to most of his games once I'm settled, especially the ones in the Fury arena, but I don't really mind that part.

I go into my bedroom, wondering who I'll be a year from now. Will I even want these things in these boxes? Part of me feels as though I should take a hiatus afterward and go find myself in Europe, South America, or Australia. That sounds nice in principle, but not at all like something I would actually do. I'll put the money in the bank, earn some interest, maybe look for some really conservative investments to make even more money to ensure I won't ever find myself without again. But boy, it sure is nice to dream about what I could do with that money if I splurged.

My dress for tonight hangs in my empty closet. The heels I bought with Imogen two days ago rest on the floor below the garment. I'm so nervous to step out into their world on Ford's arm. I haven't heard from my fiancé in the past week, which doesn't surprise me. We both had our fair share of things to take care of in preparation for tonight.

A knock on my door surprises me, and I go to answer it. The eighteen-year-old doorman in training, Ricky, stands there holding a box. His cheeks appear red, and the way his gaze keeps darting away from me, I think he's nervous. He always seems nervous whenever I address him.

"Hey, Ricky," I say.

He holds the box out to me. "This was delivered for you just now."

I accept the box, surprised since I purposely didn't order anything because I won't be here much longer. I grab some cash from my purse for a tip and hand it over. "Thank you."

He nods. "Have a good evening, Miss Boyd."

"You too, thanks again."

He stays in place, and after an awkward moment, he turns to go to the elevator. The kid looks intimidated every time I have an encounter with him.

I carry the box to the kitchen counter and open it. The outside just has my name, and the return address is one I don't recognize. I must've forgotten about something I ordered.

Inside the outer box is a smaller *Fleur du Mal* box. This has to be a joke. I don't spend this type of money on underwear. Opening the box, I find a note.

It all starts with what you're wearing underneath. ~ Ford

He did not get me lingerie. I carefully open up the tissue paper to see in fact, yes, he did. A black pair of cheeky lace underwear and a matching bra that will barely contain my nipples rests inside. They're both sexy and gorgeous.

As though he knew the package just got delivered, my phone dings and I pull it out of my back pocket to see Ford's name.

Ford: *Your doorman doesn't have any fetishes, does he?*

I chuckle.

Me: *He probably likes black lacy things.*

Ford: *I take it you got the package?*

Me: *I did and it was unnecessary. And probably inappropriate.*

Ford: *If we were really together and getting married I'd be buying you lingerie. Trust me. Besides, this is all about appearances.*

I ignore the way his comment makes me feel. I've never had a man send me a package before, let alone undergarments. There's something weird about him knowing what I'm wearing under my dress tonight. I grab the box and head back down the hall.

Me: *No one is going to see me in this. Including you. I'm not sure why it matters.*

Ford: *Because you'll feel more confident.*

I can't really argue with him. It's hard to look at these two pieces and imagine not feeling that way.

Me: *Thank you, nonetheless.*

Ford: *I'll pick you up in an hour.*

That's unexpected. I figured I'd catch a ride over there myself. Mrs. Jacobs is having the party at their penthouse and I assumed Ford was staying there.

Me: *No worries. I'll catch a cab.*

The three dots appear immediately and I sit on the edge of my bed, waiting for his response.

Ford: *You're the future Mrs. Ford Jacobs. We don't do cabs in a cocktail dress. See you in an hour.*

This man… he could put it a lot less smugly.

Me: *I'm actually going to be Ms. Lena Boyd-Jacobs. And sorry. I didn't think people would care about my transportation.*

I set the phone on the bed and stand because my blood

pressure is rising and I no longer feel as though I can sit still. How am I going to live with this man for a year? As I head into the bathroom to turn on the water for my shower, I hear my phone go off again.

Ford: *I would never allow my soon-to-be wife to meet me at a party. Especially one hosted by my parents.*

My hand squeezes the phone before hammering out a message.

Me: *Fine. See you in an hour. I'll be waiting downstairs in my lobby.*

I figured that would end our conversation, but the three dots appear again. I can't imagine what else he has to say now.

Ford: *Do you take me for a schmuck? I'll come up.*

Me: *No need.*

Ford: *It's going to be a long year if you fight me on everything.*

Me: *Fine. Do whatever. But I have to go if I'm going to be ready in time.*

Ford: *You might want to dig deeper into that box. If you were mine, you'd show up with a glow that shows you're a very satisfied woman.*

I drop the phone and ruffle through the tissue paper, finding a box with a vibrator inside.

Ford: *I'll take your silence as another thank you. See you in an hour.*

I don't bother responding, staring at this unusual gift from a man who barely knows me. How will I get through this year without sleeping with him? Ford is a gorgeous hockey player who obviously has more game than I gave him credit for. It's almost as though I can feel the first fracture of my heart, knowing our breakup is inevitable.

I've just finished putting on my lipstick when my phone goes off. Shit, I forgot to tell Ricky that Ford is okay to come up.

I rush into my bedroom, answer the phone, and tell Ricky to send him up. Then I open the door and use the dead bolt to keep it slightly ajar so I can finish getting ready. As I'm switching a few things out in my purse, I hear Ford curse.

"You live in New York City, you do realize that?" A second later, the door shuts and the lock clicks into place.

"You were on your way up," I say, coming out of my room carrying my shoes and handbag. "Just think, if something should happen to me, then you're off the hook. You could mourn my death for the next year."

"Morbid much?" he mumbles.

I emerge around the corner and stop so I can catch my breath. Ford stands in a suit that fits him like a glove. I've seen Ford in a suit plenty of times. After a hockey game where he didn't take the time to blow-dry his hair, so it's still a little damp on the edges. At functions or charity events with his family. He knows how to pull one off, but there's something different about it tonight.

The suit is black, which is more conservative than he normally wears. He doesn't wear a tie, but the top two buttons are undone with a suit jacket over top, buttoned at his waist. The gel in his hair shows off his golden tips.

"So she has legs," he says, pulling me out of my stupor.

I look down at my burgundy dress that has long sleeves and bells out at my waist over my thighs. "Is that a compliment?"

"Sure, if you weren't my date. Remind me next time to send a dress." He walks around my apartment, his fingers brushing along the boxes.

Having him in my space is uncomfortable. His presence seems to fill the whole apartment. Although my apartment is nicer than I think I deserve to spend on myself, it probably looks like a shack to him.

"You're not bringing all of this to Florida?"

Disregarding his question and his insults to my attire for the evening, I sit on the edge of a chair to put on my heels.

"Now those I could get on board with. Wear those and just those panties I got you." He shifts. "I'm already half hard."

"Good to know I don't completely repulse you," I say, standing and grabbing my handbag.

"Repulse me? Where did you get that idea?" He follows me to the door, reaching around me to grab the knob before I have a chance. His mouth is at my ear. "Remember, I'm your fiancé. You wait for me to open doors for you now."

I close my eyes briefly from the rush of his hot breath on my neck and the shiver that courses through me. We file out of the condo and I lock up while he waits. We head down the hall, and every step he's next to me feels weird somehow. I feel more aware of his presence than I ever have.

"Let's circle back to the repulsive comment?" Ford

says, reaching ahead of me again to push the elevator button, purposely giving me a stare.

There's no one around. I don't know why he cares right now.

"Clearly you don't like my dress."

His gaze sweeps over me. "I like the dress if we were going to church. You should show off your legs more often, cleavage would be nice, and in all honesty, shorter sleeves." His nose scrunches. "Give a man a reason to give you his coat."

I look into his eyes, lost for a moment in thought of us walking the streets of New York City and having him shrug out of his jacket and place it over my shoulders. Damn my unrealistic romantic side. "So you don't like my dress. Like I said."

We step into the elevator. I wait this time, allowing him to press the button for the bottom floor and he smiles at me as though I'm a quick study. Makes me want to knee him in the nuts.

He steps in front of me, barricading me against the wall of the elevator, caging me in with both hands on either side of me. I swallow past the dryness that coats my throat.

Then he inches even closer and lowers his voice. "You're mistaking what I meant. You look gorgeous and I bet you look even more stunning in the lingerie I sent you, but it's for selfish reasons that I want to send you a dress. I want the tease of a slit up your thigh or a deep V that shows just enough cleavage to drive me wild. It's purely self-serving that I want you to show off what you have, rather than hiding it. Believe me, when you walked down that hall, I was anything but repulsed."

Ding.

The elevator doors open and Ford's fingers run down

the length of my arm, securing my hand in his. We exit the elevator and I'm sure I must be as red as a tomato. All I can think of is that I want to hear what comes out of his mouth next.

"Have a great night, Miss Boyd." Ricky waves at us.

"Thank you," I mumble, offering him a smile.

The next thing I know, Ford is leading me into the back of a black SUV and it's time for the show to begin.

But if that wasn't part of the show, what the hell was it?

CHAPTER 13

Ford

I file out of the black SUV and hold my hand out for Lena. There are no obvious witnesses, but being a Jacobs my entire life, I know eyes are everywhere.

Her legs emerge, and damn, I just can't get enough of them. I always thought I was an ass man, but all I envision when I see her bare legs are them wrapped around me as I have her pinned to the wall.

Her soft hand slides into mine, and I help her out of the car and off the curb. I tell the driver I'll call when we're ready to leave.

"I'll just get a c—"

I put my finger to her lips, leaning forward. "You're forgetting already," I whisper. "I'm not going to allow my fiancée to get in a cab at the end of the evening and go home to a dark apartment by herself."

She lets out a breath. The same one she did in the elevator when I told her exactly what I thought about her dress and her in it.

This won't be an easy night for Lena. She's essentially going from being on the payroll to being one of us, even if my family already kind of treated her as one of their own. There will be a whole new level of scrutiny now. Women will judge her, and men will wonder what makes her so special to be the one who finally claimed me. She's going to be cornered, sneered at, questioned, and talked about behind her back. I grew up with it, so my skin has toughened over the years, but Lena is like a freshly healed wound, her skin still thin and fragile.

"Mr. Jacobs." Anessa nods at us, opening the door. "Miss Boyd, you look spectacular tonight." Anessa winks at me, and I shake my head, leading Lena to the elevators.

"Hi, Anessa," Lena says, stopping me with a firm tug on my hand. "What is Libby going as for Halloween?"

She knows her daughter, Libby?

Anessa smiles, looking both ways before allowing the door to close and turning to us. "A unicorn. She loves them."

"Who doesn't?" Lena says. "I can't wait to see the pictures."

"I'll make sure to grab lots. Have a good night, you two. I heard congratulations are in order." Her gaze shoots to Lena's left hand, who quickly slides it to her back.

Shit, I forgot earlier.

"Thank you. You know my dad, we better get up there." I nod toward the elevators.

"Go. Enjoy your night." She smiles as though nothing is amiss, but Anessa makes her living off of knowing what people want before they want it. Her attention to detail is the reason she's the best doorperson in Manhattan.

"You too," Lena says, waving with her hand that holds no engagement ring. Yet.

Once we're secure in the elevator, I slide my hand into my pocket and pull out the ring I meant to give her at her apartment. Before I got distracted by imagining her in those heels with the bra and panty set I sent over. Her using the vibrator I sent along with it. Shit, I shake my head before my mind goes there again.

I take her left hand, resting my fingers lightly on her ring finger. "Lena Boyd, will you marry me?"

Her impatient gaze shoots to where the elevator is counting up the floors. "Just put the ring on."

"Hey, I'm trying to be a gentleman here." I place the ring at the tip of her finger.

She glances to the floor we're on again. "Let's not pretend this is anything but fake."

"You're no fun." I slide on the ring.

Damn, that three-carat cushion-cut diamond looks good on her. I would've gone bigger, but my gut told me she would think anything larger was too ostentatious. She admires it for a second, and I relish her smile as she watches it sparkle under the lights. If this wasn't fake, I would have pinned her to the wall by now.

"You didn't have to get anything so big. Now I'm scared I'll lose it."

I shake my head. "Would Ford Jacobs get his soon-to-be wife a chip of a diamond? Hell no. And it's insured."

She nods. "Thank you."

I bring my hand down to rest on the small of her back, stepping into her. She tries to shift away, but my hand molds to her hip, tightening to keep her in place. The elevator dings and the doors slide open. Moving my mouth by her ear, I whisper, "Showtime, wifey."

We step off and I straighten my back. Hell, I could pull this off in my sleep, but Lena looks pale and about ready to vomit.

"Trust me." I take her hand and walk us into the wolf's den.

All eyes shoot to us. I expected this, so I usher Lena casually to the bar.

"She'll have an Aperol spritz, and I'll have a whiskey neat."

The bartender nods and I grab a tip from my pocket, ready to put it in the jar.

"How did you know?" she asks.

I chuckle. "There isn't much I don't notice, Lena."

In all truth, I'm lying. Imogen told me how much they've been enjoying them lately.

"Bullshit," she says. "I've never had one around you before."

"Are you sure about that?" I tilt my head.

Then she does the cutest thing ever. She nibbles on her bottom lip while her eyes squint as though she's going over all the times we've been around each other.

The bartender puts the Aperol spritz down in front of her as Imogen walks up to join us.

"Good choice." Imogen holds up her own drink that matches Lena's to cheers her.

Lena looks at me and shakes her head.

"I can't tell you all my ways," I say, shrugging and accepting my whiskey before putting money in the glass jar. "What's up, little sis? Who's this?"

I eye the guy next to her like any big brother would. Tattoos up his neck, piercing in his lip, and he's dressed in a leather jacket and black combat boots. Not a bad-looking guy though.

"This is Jay. He's an artist." She smiles widely.

I sip my whiskey and nod. "Nice to meet you. I'm Ford."

Imogen puts her arm through Jay's and points. "This is my older brother. He plays on the Florida Fury."

The guy looks unimpressed, but I'm gonna take a guess that he doesn't follow hockey.

"And this is his fiancée, Lena. But they're announcing it tonight, so shh."

His eyes fall over Lena so intently she shifts her body closer to me. I switch my drink into my other hand and put my arm around her. She stiffens before she relaxes in my hold.

"Nice to meet you," I say, not really meaning it.

Jay looks around. "Nice place. A little stuffy."

"I'll be sure to tell my parents." I eye Imogen with a bored expression because we both know she's using this guy to get attention from my father. She's always had middle child syndrome. Thought she was the forgotten child. She says she wants to take over Jacobs Enterprises, but I know my sister—she doesn't. She just doesn't know what she wants to do with her life yet. She got access to her trust fund when she graduated college. She has money and time on her side, so why rush?

"Who's that handsome young man?" My Aunt Claudia comes over, kissing me on the cheek. She eyes Lena. "Are you going to introduce me to your friend?"

"This is Lena Boyd."

Unfortunately, my great-aunt Claudia is starting to forget things, so her forehead wrinkles as though she's never seen Lena before.

"You know her, Aunt Claudia, she's our family PR rep," Imogen says.

Lena offers her hand. "It's okay, I think I've only met you once or twice. Pleasure to see you again."

They shake hands, then Aunt Claudia looks at me. "Girlfriend?" she mouths as though no one else can see her.

"Yeah." If I tell my aunt now that Lena is my fiancée she'll have the news spread throughout the party in two minutes flat and my dad won't get his big moment to announce it to everyone.

A huge smile lands on her lips. "I knew you'd come

back from the dark side. Your mom says the baby is with a nanny tonight?"

I nod. "She is."

"You need to come home."

"Or you come down to Florida," I say with a wink.

She waves me off. "The heat makes me sweat under my boobs."

I guess it's clear I get my sense of humor from my mom's side.

Lena chokes but recovers. "Sorry, went down the wrong pipe."

"Aunt Claudia!" Imogen exclaims.

"I like her. My ballsac gets all sweaty in the heat too," Jay adds, and I catch Lena cringe.

"Well, I guess I've just gotten used to it." I shrug, wanting to move on.

She smiles and glances at Imogen and Jay. Her eyes narrow. "Imogen, you need to grow up." And she walks away.

Imogen balks. "I hate this family."

"You know you don't." I give her a light shove on the shoulder.

Just as I see the trace of a smile, my dad approaches.

"Don't you two look happy," Dad says, ruining my mood. "I think we'll make the announcement now. People are asking a lot of questions."

"Happy Birthday, Mr. Jacobs." Lena smiles at him.

"Thank you, Lena, but it will be Eli from here on out. You're going to be family, after all."

He ushers us to the center of the room, then grabs a fork from the appetizer display and taps his glass that holds the same drink as mine. What can I say? The apple fell close to the tree, then rolled away.

The waitstaff appears with glasses of champagne, handing every guest a flute.

"I have an announcement to share. Tonight, I'm blessed with the best birthday gift." My dad's voice carries through the large room.

I tense, every muscle from my neck down to my toes tightening. After this, there's no going back. I look at Lena and she's staring at the floor, shifting her stance.

Lowering so my lips reach her ear, I say, "Own this. Sell our happiness. Hand on my chest." I put my arm around her waist, tugging her toward me.

She's just as stiff as I am, but there's no going back now. She tentatively puts her hand on my stomach, over my suit jacket.

"Ford not only blessed me with a grandchild this year, but he's giving me another daughter. They've been sneaking around for a while behind our backs."

My jaw clenches through my father's lie.

"But Ford has proposed and Lena has accepted his hand in marriage. A wedding is on the horizon." Dad raises his flute in the air. "To the happy couple. Welcome to the family, Lena."

He holds out his arms and Lena steps away from me and into his. Then my mom comes over and gives us fake congratulations. Morgan, Imogen, and Jay follow shortly before all the party guests line up to offer their best wishes.

Once it's over, my breathing finally slows, as though the moment of impact is over and it's all smooth sailing from here. That is, until my dad taps his glass with that damn fork again and everyone in the room starts in on a "kiss, kiss, kiss" chant.

A strangled cry comes from Lena next to me, but as I told myself this afternoon, we're selling this because we have no other option. I tug her toward me with force so that her hands land on my chest. She really is the perfect fit. I put my finger under her chin, inching it up to look at me, then I bend and capture her lips.

When she doesn't move, I murmur, "Open for me."

Her lips soften, and I lick the seam. Her hands slide up my chest and wrap around my neck, bringing her breasts flush against me. Our kiss is languid and lulling and heart-thumping goodness. She tastes like citrus and I find that I can't get enough.

Her tongue grazes mine and passion threatens to over-flow from inside me. To take her, to have her, to claim her. By the time we stop, I think we're both mystified as to what just happened, but we smack on our smiles at the applause in the room.

Yep, I'm royally fucked.

CHAPTER 14

"I can't not do it."

Lena

Florida couldn't be more different from New York City. It's been a week since I moved down here and I've rarely seen Ford. He signed him and Annabelle up for some daddy and me things on the days he doesn't have games. Or he's training, but he always has the babysitter here for Annabelle. I know he said he didn't want me to care for her but it feels insulting—as though he doesn't trust me to watch her. Whatever connection I felt with him in New York City vanished the minute the party was over. Isn't that the point though? I keep forgetting the word fake between the words Ford and fiancé.

I head downstairs late morning. I slept in because I don't have much to do. Turns out all the Jacobs have been behaving themselves recently.

There's coffee in the pot, so I pour myself a cup, happy it's still hot. Which means Ford and Annabelle didn't leave that long ago. I'm starting to feel lonely. Not that I had a ton of friends back in the city, but I had places I knew and liked to visit. Maybe it's because I'm not that familiar with the area.

Ford said I could drive his Bronco while I'm here since he's usually in his Mercedes with Annabelle. He's not risking her traveling in a truck without a top. I glance at the keys in the dish next to the landline phone. Who has a landline anymore?

Screw this. I dump my coffee in the sink and head upstairs to get dressed for the day. After putting on my bikini with a pair of cut-off jean shorts and a tank top, I pack a towel, sunscreen, and the book I've been reading off and on lately. Back in the kitchen, I jot down a quick note for Ford to tell him where I am. No sense texting him because I know he doesn't care. But in the strange event he is wondering when he gets home, there you go.

I lock up and leave the house, then I'm standing beside the vehicle. The Bronco is all custom done with a shiny navy blue paint job and brown leather seats adorned with white stitching. Then my gaze falls to the stick shift. He didn't say anything about that. Good thing I was forced to learn to drive my dad's car when I was far too young, so I know I've got this. I hop inside, press on the clutch and brake, insert the key, and start it up.

I close my eyes. The sun beats on my head and the humidity soaks into my skin. This is awesome. I can't believe it took me a week to get out of the house. Sure, there's a beach at Ford's place—and a pool—but there are no other people. And I just need to be around people today.

I ease off the clutch and give it some gas. The Bronco sputters for a second before kicking into gear, then it's smooth sailing and I'm rolling down Ford's street. When I reach the stop sign, I glance at the radio to see that of course Ford has it set to play from his phone.

Pulling out my phone, I plug it in the jack and switch on Blondie. My dad had such a crush on her when I was growing up that he played her nonstop. Now I love her too.

I stop to get a smoothie, then I park the Bronco by a long pier and explore the small downtown area of Waterfall Springs. About fifteen minutes into my exploration, a man's voice says my name. I turn away from the window of the cute beach shop that sells jewelry and sundresses to find Tripp Newton, Florida Fury's PR representative.

"Hi, Tripp," I say, smiling. I've had to converse with him a lot due to Ford's antics in the past.

"I just heard the news. I'm surprised, to say the least." His hand lands on my hip and he draws me close, pressing a kiss to my cheek. The exchange is friendlier than we've ever been, but I guess this is more social than work related right now.

"What happened?" I ask. What PR nightmare has Ford started now, and how am I not in the know? A million possibilities run through my mind.

Tripp tilts his head, his gaze moving to my left hand and my empty ring finger.

I clutch my hand. "Oh yeah. Big news, right? I'm not wearing my ring because I was afraid to lose it in the sand. Can you imagine?"

Truthfully, it's in a jewelry box in the bedroom I'm staying in. I can't wear it. I feel anxious the entire time it's on my finger.

"From the picture I saw, it's quite the ring." Tripp rocks back on his heels. He's wearing board shorts and a cut muscle tee that shows his lean arms and biceps. "I was just headed to play beach volleyball. Do you want to join me?"

I sip my smoothie, not sure what to say.

"It's just me and a few friends who get together every weekend to play. Super chill." He points.

I follow the direction of his finger and see two sand volleyball nets set up on the other side of the road. At least Tripp Newton wants my company. "Sure."

"Cool. Let's go. I'll make sure to tell all the guys you're

taken." He winks. "But you gotta tell me, when did you and Ford start dating?"

"Remember New Year's?" I ask. Ford and I decided to pretend our relationship started when I had to drag him out of the party because his dad insisted on seeing him. The night we kissed for the first time.

"Oh, you two left…" He nods.

"Yeah, so we were in hiding for quite a while. Especially with the whole Annabelle thing."

He nods. "Makes sense. Where is he now?"

We cross the street. "He's with Annabelle at a daddy and me class."

He chuckles. "I gotta say, I'm shocked at the way he's taken on the role of daddy so well. I hope he takes on the husband role with the same ferocity."

"I'm sure he will." I smile.

Lies. All lies. The more I have to lie to people, the more the fact that I'm doing this for money leaves a sour taste in my mouth.

We approach the volleyball courts, and the warm sand feels good in my sandals but makes it harder to walk. Tripp puts his hand on the small of my back, presenting me to his friends, who are all men. I raise a hand to wave hello when the sound of a car squealing to a stop jars me. Cars honk and we all turn to see what's going on.

That's when I see Ford in his Mercedes with the window rolled down and his sunglasses tipped to the edge of his nose, staring at where I am. It's clear he doesn't like what he sees.

I narrow my eyes at him. What does he care? He's left me alone the entire time I've been here.

"Shit, he doesn't look happy," Tripp mumbles from behind me.

Ford pulls into a parking spot clearly marked with a no

parking sign and files out of the car in a pair of shorts and a shirt that shows off his big biceps and the strength of his shoulders.

"Tripp." Ford smacks on a smile and walks over with his arm outstretched. "I see you ran into Lena." They shake hands, then Ford comes over to me, putting his arm around my waist. He presses a chaste kiss to my cheek. "You heard the news, right?"

"Where's Annabelle?" I ask.

"She's at Aiden and Saige's. They want to pretend to be parents or some shit." He straightens and eyes the rest of the guys. "Are we playing volleyball?"

"Well, I was…" Tripp says.

"I'm game. You playing, sweetie?" He looks back at me. "Want to be on the same team?"

"I was actually going to finish my smoothie." I hold it up in front of me.

Ford lets his grip on me go and holds out his hand for the volleyball. "Cool. Let's play."

Tripp appears tongue-tied but heads over to the court. Meanwhile, I can't strip my eyes off of Ford after he acted so protective and possessive over me. It shouldn't turn me on, but damn, who thought he cared so much? Certainly not me.

I sit on the cement ledge that separates the beach and the small row of parking before the street. Ford takes charge, dictating how the game will go and who is on whose team. He puts Tripp on the other team, which I assume was on purpose.

There's burning anger in Ford's eyes that's so hot, I grow wet. Damn, I can't get turned on by him going caveman just because I was conversing with a man we both know. What does that say about me?

The game starts and Ford is all over the place, barely

allowing any of his teammates to handle the ball. He spikes it on Tripp, and Tripp ends up sprawled out in the sand. Ford doesn't glance my way at all during the match.

This continues over and over until finally one of the other guys steps in and they lose the serve. Mid-game, I'm way too hot in this sun, so I take off my tank top and pull out my sunscreen. I'm spreading the lotion on my chest when I glance up and see Ford's hooded eyes set on me. My skin comes alive with awareness and my heart pounds. I have to bury this want I have for this man. I have to.

"Ford," one of the other guys says.

Ford dives to the ground, hitting the ball with his fist to get it up in the air. A puff of sand floats up, and when he stands, he's covered.

Is there anything he's not good at?

"I'm going down to the beach," I announce, taking my small bag and heading in that direction. I'm done with his alpha side and him trying to show that he owns me. We both know he doesn't own me, doesn't even want to.

"Wait for me. We're almost finished," Ford calls.

I don't stop, and the squawk of a police car grabs all of our attention.

"Looks like you have more important things to take care of." I point to where the cop has pulled up behind Ford's Mercedes.

He runs over, already explaining the situation before he reaches the police officer.

No doubt he'll get off because of who he is.

"Nice to see you, Tripp." I shoot him an apologetic look.

"Don't look like that. I kind of like the jealousy thing. Makes those doubts I had about you two disappear."

I should be offended, but I shrug and head down to the beach. Stopping a few steps from the water, I take off my sandals and jean shorts and shove them into my bag. Walking along the shoreline, I dodge small kids running back and forth to the water. Some people are building sandcastles and others are just lying out, allowing their skin to soak up the sun.

"We need to talk," Ford says, suddenly alongside me and breathless.

I roll my eyes and walk closer to the water, but he only follows me.

"Is that Ford Jacobs?" a man says.

"No shit!" someone else says.

Before I blink, Ford takes my bag off my shoulder, drops it in a dry spot in the sand, and places his hands on my hips, ushering me into the water.

"I'm not swimming," I say, trying to turn around.

"Just go. I'm not in the mood to sign any fucking autographs. And we need to settle some business."

"Why do I have to go into the water? You can't drown me in broad daylight." I turn and place my hands on his sandy chest. Jeez, it's way too muscular for me to be expected to think straight when I'm touching it.

His face twists. "What the hell are you talking about? Just keep walking."

Then his arms wrap around my waist and he tugs me toward him, pushing us fully into the water.

I take a mouthful of saltwater before I emerge to the surface. "Jesus, Ford!"

"Sorry, but you refuse to listen to me."

"In case you forgot," I say, looking around and lowering my voice, "we're not actually engaged."

"You need to start believing we are because your behavior and attitude are convincing people we aren't."

"Are you talking about Tripp?" A wave washes up and our bodies rise and fall. "Give me a break."

He lifts my hand. "You have to wear the ring."

I tear my hand away. "I don't want to. It's too expensive."

He groans and eyes the area around us. "You understand that I can afford to replace it?"

"So what? That doesn't mean you should have to."

A couple slowly make their way closer, obviously recognizing Ford from the man's creepy smile. Ford nods, giving him the look to say, "Hi, but now isn't the time." His hands reach for my waist and he pushes me the other way again, but I lose my footing and a wave comes, leaving me no choice but to wrap my legs around his waist to stay afloat.

"Now you got the idea," he says.

I still because either I've caught a sea cucumber between us, or there's something very hard between his legs. Could he want me like I want him?

I blink a few times before I recover. "You don't own me and I don't appreciate the jealousy act." I'm lying about the jealousy thing.

"Sorry, but it pissed me off. He had his hand on the small of your back. That part of your body is mine until this is over."

I laugh and rock my head back, trying to unhook my legs until I find he's taken us even deeper. There's no hope that I can stand here, which leaves me no choice but to stay glued to him. Short girl problems.

"Stop playing games. We know exactly what this is." Unable to stop myself, I grind along his length and he tugs me even closer, raising his hips to thrust into me. "It's all fake."

"There's nothing fake about what's happening right now." He pulls me closer, his hand that faces away from the beach reaching down. His knuckle grazes my nipple.

It pebbles and I resist a full-body shiver, my eyes closing. "We can't do this."

His lips hover over my neck right under my ear. "I'm sorry, but you in that bikini…" He groans and I feel that groan centered between my legs. "I can't not do it."

I run my core along him, needing a release from being wound so tight. "If we cross the line now, how will we survive an entire year?"

His lips press to my neck, his tongue traveling up my ear. "Don't you ever want to say fuck it all and just do what you want?"

Um, yeah. Like right now. Right now, I'd love to, but it doesn't change the fact that we have to get through an entire year. I'm not sure I can have him once and never again, because Ford is a chaser. I'm only tempting if he can't have me.

"We can't," I say, my voice strong, firm this time.

He grunts, stripping his body off of me. As we emerge from the water, I catch a few people with phones out. We've floated down the beach from where my bag is, so I wait patiently as Ford signs autographs and people wish us congratulations. Once the crowd disperses and we head toward my bag, it's clear that Ford Jacobs is mad at me.

CHAPTER 15

Ford

I'm in the locker room, getting dressed for the game.

"You're quiet tonight," Maksim says.

I shrug. "I'm fine."

"Fuck you. This is exactly how you were when you found out Britney was pregnant." Aiden eyes me from across the room.

He's right, and I hate that my first reaction at the news I was having a kid was depression. Especially now that I can't imagine my life without Annabelle.

"Your fiancée not doing it for you?" Maksim asks.

There are a few lingering stares from some of our other teammates, and I scold Maksim with a look. Of course I didn't keep the truth from my friends, but I know they'll keep their mouths shut.

"Just think of the outcome," Maksim whispers. "He's off your back for good."

And that is some great fucking news, but it would be a helluva lot better if I didn't actually want my fake fiancée. I almost took her in an ocean. With spectators. If she would've let me, I probably would've let it happen, bet with Tweetie or not.

"The pictures look like you're enjoying your fiancée," Tweetie chimes in, coming to stand in front of me.

"What's not to enjoy?" I say and adjust my pads.

He has a smug smile. "Guess you lost the bet."

"Guess again."

His eyebrows rise into his hairline. "You're telling me you just got engaged and you're not hitting that? No fucking way."

I shrug then stand. "You know how competitive I am." I grip his shoulder. "She's tried a few times, but I just keep reminding her how good it'll be in a few weeks."

He rolls his eyes and shakes his head before he walks back over to his area, but he must believe me because he doesn't argue the point further.

Of course, pictures emerged of Lena and me in the ocean. My dad thought it was a great PR move and called to applaud her over the whole thing. She sheepishly thanked him, but we both know what transpired in that water. The minute she found me rock hard at her core, she ground all over me. All my dick could think about was sliding into her wet pussy.

It's been two days and my body still aches from not having her. She turned me down, which was the smart decision. The right one. She's a hundred times smarter than me because while all I thought about was how I could have sex with her in an ocean without people realizing, she was thinking of the long year ahead of us.

Someone turns on the music and everyone runs through their superstitions before the game. Maksim goes to take a leak, and I sit down across from Aiden.

He's eyeing me. "Want to talk?"

I shake my head.

"You sure?"

"I can handle my shit."

"I know you can. But you're not used to catching feelings."

I glance up to see Aiden's raised eyebrow. The one to suggest he sees right through me. But he's wrong. There are no feelings, it's pure lust involved.

"It's just attraction, and anyway it's probably because she's the only woman on this earth that I can't fuck right now. That's the only reason I have blue balls." I basically just repeat what Lena said to me.

He nods. "Like a chastity belt, huh?" He laughs.

I finish tying my skate and stand. "Fuck off, Shamrock, I'm serious."

"How bad you want your dad off your back?"

"You know I want him to piss off about the whole business thing and just let me play hockey in peace."

He lifts his shoulders. "Then just beat off to the image of her. Or fuck someone else discreetly. Or go celibate for the next year. But you cannot let this thing explode, and if the two of you sleep together, that's exactly what's gonna happen. It's gonna end before you reach the altar."

I knew Aiden would make sense, and that's why I didn't want his opinion. Always the voice of reason. I wanted to hear it from Tweetie, who would've said fuck her and deal with repercussions after.

"Let's go," I say.

Aiden allows me to go first, and we all cheer our captain on when he joins us in the hallway and we head toward the ice.

On the ice, Aiden skates toward me. "One thing you need to do is get her ass to your games. She needs to be here, cheering you on."

I nod. He's right. If we're supposed to be in love, she should be here, but I hate asking her to do anything she doesn't want to do. Hell, I know what that feels like because it's practically been my entire life with my father. But if we're going to own this, we have to sell it.

I drop my bag in the foyer when I get home. Annabelle's babysitter, Rylee, is on the couch with the monitor next to her.

"Hey, Rylee, how was she?"

She stands, and since she's only seventeen, she always looks intimidated when I arrive home. I've been dragging my feet on having in-house help because there's no way I can hire someone who could report I'm in a sham of an engagement.

"Great as usual, although she didn't want the bottle, so Miss Boyd came down and she got her to take the bottle before bed."

I nod. "Okay, thanks." I dig out cash for her and walk her to the door. "I have a game tomorrow night. You available?"

She nods. "I'll be here at the same time."

"Perfect. Thanks."

As I shut the door, the stairs creak and I don't have to turn around to know she's standing there. I turn around and there she is on the stairs in a pair of sweats and a half shirt that shows her stomach. Her nipples poke through the fabric and my mouth salivates at the thought of her nipple on my tongue.

"Hey, wifey." I walk across the room and put my bag in the closet.

"Did Rylee tell you about Annabelle? The bottle?"

She joins me in the kitchen, and the open floor plan does nothing to diminish the sexual tension. I loosen my tie, but I still feel as if I'm suffocating.

"She did. Thank you for your help, but you don't need to do that."

"I want to," she says, and something in her tone has me looking her way.

"Maybe we should establish some rules," I mumble, my eyes diverting to her flattened stomach. I shrug off my jacket and place it on the counter, folded in half.

"Rules? What are you going to say? I can't come down when Rylee is here? The fact that she comes at all when I'm home is already offensive enough, just so you know. Rylee probably thinks I'm some bitch who won't take care of your baby."

The anger in her voice surprises me. I was giving her an out.

"You don't have to take care of my baby because you're not really my fiancée."

"Aren't you always saying we have to sell it? Well, we aren't selling it to Rylee, and just so you know, a seventeen-year-old girl has a shit ton of power on social media." She goes to the fridge and takes out the leftover Thai food she got delivered last night.

"Well, you're not coming to my games." I sound like a whining seven-year-old complaining to his parents about them not coming to see me play.

She stops with the silverware drawer half open. "Do you want me to come to your games?"

"I'm just suggesting that you should be with the wives and girlfriends."

She shuts the drawer and puts the takeout container on the counter, along with a fork. "Answer the question, Ford."

I stare at her, distracted because of how much I want to see those pink lips swollen red from my kiss. I blink. "I can't."

I step away, taking off my tie and unbuttoning the top few buttons of my shirt. There's no fucking air in here.

"Can't what? Be civil? I knew this would be hard because we don't see eye to eye on much, but am I that unbearable to live with? To be around, so that you have to always be gone with Annabelle?" She raises her hands and I'm rewarded with a glimpse of her underboob.

"I'm not used to it, okay? Give me some time."

Her shoulders fall and she stares at me until I have no choice but to look at her. "Maybe we should scrap this whole thing. Your dad can find someone else. Someone you'd rather—"

"No," I bite out.

Her hands go up in the air, and once again, underboob is all I can focus on. "Then what do you want? I can't live like this anymore."

"I want to fuck you, okay!" I sit in the chair, staring at the monitor on the table for a moment to make sure I didn't wake Annabelle. "I can't see straight when you're around." I nearly whisper the words.

"Oh. I thought you hated me."

I glance up. "My dick definitely doesn't hate you."

She bites her lip and her eyes squint as though she's thinking. Just one of her many habits that turns me on so fucking bad. "Well, we can't."

"I know that. And stop biting your lip."

She frees her lip, and her eyes widen. "Sorry."

"Don't apologize," I say.

"Okay, I take it back."

"Good. Fine." I stand. "Whatever. I'm going to bed."

"Okay," she says, her hands locked behind her on the counter, her tits pushed out almost as an offering.

I close my eyes briefly so I can get my jacket. "Good night."

"Good night, Ford," she whispers. I hear her staggered breathing when I lean around her to get my jacket and tie. "It was a good game."

"It was a shit game. I played like a fucking rookie." All I could think about was her and what it would be like if she were there with Annabelle in her arms. To look up and see someone was there for me.

"I thought you played well."

"You watched?" I ask, pausing in front of her.

She leans back and our eyes lock. She bites her lip again and nods.

"What did I say about the lip?"

Releasing it, she's quick to say, "I'm sorry."

We stay like that for a moment, my willpower draining with every second. "God, I want you so bad."

"It's only because I'm the one thing you can't have," she says.

It's like someone has sliced me open. "What?"

"It's easy to figure out why you want me." She slides away from me—whether it's from the displeasure I'm sure is flaring in my eyes or she just needs space, I can't say. "You can't have me, so you want me. It's going to eat away at you. But we'll get through it. Want me to tell you a million bad things about myself? Your desire will wane, I promise."

I lean my hip along the edge of the counter. "Is that what you think? That I want you only because I can't have you?"

She shrugs and picks up her Thai food. "Name one other thing you've never been able to have?" She sits on the couch, crosses her legs, and buries her head in the noodles.

For fuck's sake, she's right. That must be it. "Okay, tell me something bad about yourself."

She laughs, but there's something in her eyes that I can't read—disappointment, maybe. "I rarely shave my legs in the winter. As soon as cold weather hits, I don't bother unless I have a date, which is hardly ever."

"But you'd shave if you were dating someone?" I ask, sitting on the chair.

"Sure, but not my armpits." She laughs, giving away that she's kidding.

I shake my head, but maybe this will help me get her out of my system. She's just the carrot hanging in front of a bunny, or the steak in front of a dog. I have to avoid temptation until someone comes around who I *can* have. This is easy. I got this.

CHAPTER 16

"We're not even close to done."

Lena

Based on the other night, Ford wants me to attend his game. So I pay Rylee for her time after she arrives—since I don't have her contact information—grab Annabelle, and bundle her up in her car seat with her ear protectors. Once I've packed her bottle and snacks, along with a few stuffed animals, we head out to the arena.

Thankfully, Paisley and Saige were willing to help me out by getting me tickets.

By the time I reach the seats with Paisley and Saige, my arm is on fire. They introduce me to Saige's best friend, Tedi, who I've heard a lot about but haven't met yet.

Once I set the carrier on the seat beside me, I let my arm sag in relief. "How do moms do this?"

I look at the two of them. They both shrug because they're not moms.

"I think moms have superhuman strength," Tedi says. "I'm one of five and my mom made us walk behind her with a rope and each of us had a handle to hold on to."

"That explains your fuck-it bucket list," Saige jokes with her friend-slash-assistant. She nods to me when I look surprised. "But the joke is on her. She screwed Tweetie as part of her fuck-it bucket list and now they're the hottest couple… well, besides you and Ford."

A few heads turn in my direction. The other wives and girlfriends. A few whisper or smile with a knowing look like I won't be here long. They're right, I'll be here for about a year.

"Shut up. We aren't serious." Tedi shakes her head and waves Saige off.

"Says the woman in the girlfriend and wives section." Paisley is giving her shit now. Then she puts her hand on Tedi's shoulder. "I'm totally kidding. God knows I never thought I'd be here."

"Me either," Saige agrees.

"So I'm not the only one then? How many women has Ford had sit here?" I eye the women in front of us.

Saige waves me off. "Don't worry about it. You're here now and that's all that matters. But since I've been coming, just Britney, and all she did was hand Annabelle to Paisley."

They all give me reassuring smiles, and I reach into the carrier to check on Annabelle. She's still asleep. I'm nervous about Ford's reaction when he finds out I'm here. I really hope this is a good surprise.

Tedi announces that she's heading up to the concession stand, and as soon as she's out of earshot, the other two women turn in my direction.

"So tell us what's going on with you guys," Paisley says.

A few rows separate us from the other wives and girl-friends. Because of my circumstances growing up, I never had a girlfriend I trusted to have my back. But these women know the truth of my situation and are with the men Ford trusts with every fiber of his being. Surely they'll understand if I tell them about last night.

"Can I ask you a question?" I look around again and

they huddle together. "Ford told me last night that he wants to sleep with me," I whisper.

"Oh." Paisley nods. Clearly her psychology degree gives her some insight I don't have.

"And?" Saige asks.

"I said that he only wanted to sleep with me because I'm the one thing he can't have."

Paisley smiles.

"Do you think I was right?" I ask her.

"I think that it's your choice. But I understand why you would think that. This is a long-term arrangement, you don't want to mess it up."

Saige is quiet, so I set my eyes on her. "What?"

She shakes her head.

"Come on. I'm dying to figure this out, and other than Imogen and Morgan, you two are the only women I can talk to who might understand. And they're his sisters so…"

Saige exhales. "It's just… I'm a lot like you. I was terrified of crossing the line and getting hurt. God knows I'm not sure there's a woman who would vouch for Ford Jacobs, but I held myself back from Aiden for a long time, and now I think to myself… why?"

"I'm sure you had reasons," Paisley says.

"I had fear. Fear ruled my decisions. And when it didn't, things worked out. We're really happy. But what if it hadn't worked out?"

"You could have been hurt?" I fill in.

She nods. "True. But I see now that I would have healed. Eventually. Never ever would I ever date any professional athlete after that, but I would've recovered." She straightens and leans closer. "The two of you are in unusual circumstances. Neither of you can sleep with anyone else while you're pretending, so why not have fun? One thing I'm almost certain of is that Ford is good in bed." She holds up her hands. "Not from personal experience. At some point, Ford is going to fall for someone, and who's to say that woman can't be you?" She places her hand on my knee. "Maybe there's something underneath the lust. But you'll never discover it if you don't quench the lust first."

I blow out a breath and the lights dim in the arena.

"It's a big decision. Good thing you have a year to make it." Paisley tilts her head supportively. "Just make sure you're clear about what you want from it and your expectations afterward if you do cross that line. That should help keep anyone from getting hurt. Communication is key."

Everything they've said makes sense, but my biggest concern isn't being hurt. I am concerned, but more than that, I don't want to live uncomfortably for the rest of the year. I thought maybe we'd develop a friendship, but clearly if we keep dodging one another because we're lusting for each other, we'll never even get there.

When the announcer introduces the players, I get up from my seat. I see Ford notice me and he stops skating for a moment, a slow smile spreading across his lips.

Yeah, who am I kidding? This has gone way beyond lust for me.

Figuring I should stop and talk to Ford after the game, I wait with the other puck bunnies outside once again. At least Saige, Paisley, and Tedi are with me this time. Annabelle did awesome throughout the game, but right now she's in Saige's arms because she needs to get to bed and found comfort there. Saige is very maternal, so I understand why.

This time, no one talks to us, and when the players emerge from the arena, Tweetie comes out first. Tedi runs up to him, jumps in his arms, and kisses him as though it's the end of a movie. She's really staking her claim. Everyone in her life except her seems to know those two will have marriage bells one day.

"Great score in the second," she says.

"Thanks, babe." He lowers her to the ground, taking her hand and winding through the throngs of fans over to us. He bows his head in greeting. "Ladies."

"Tweetie," we all say in unison.

"Have a good night."

"Try not to break anything tonight," Saige says, and we all laugh.

"Don't be jealous. Tell Shamrock to up his game if you're not breaking furniture," he calls behind us.

"Hey, my woman is satisfied." Aiden sneaks out and moves to capture Saige in a hug, stopping cold. "What did I miss?"

"I had a baby while you were playing." She offers him Annabelle and he stares at her for a moment.

Moving in close, he whispers loud enough for us to hear, "Three goals. You know what that means." He winks.

"Ew," Paisley says. "Give me the baby. Innocent ears."

Saige hands Annabelle to Paisley. "See you guys later."

They leave, which means it's just Paisley and me.

"Ever wonder what takes them so long?" she asks, rocking Annabelle.

"Gossip," I say.

She chuckles. "Probably."

Annabelle grows fussy, so I offer my arms and Paisley hands her over before digging into the bag for one of her pacifiers. It truly takes a village to handle her while Ford can do it all himself.

"Fuck that." Ford's voice pulls my attention away.

I look up to see him and Maksim coming our way. Ford glances up from the ground and stops in his tracks. Our gazes fix on one another and I think adoration fills his.

"Come on, *kotik*, let's leave the happy couple alone," Maksim says to Paisley.

"Bye, Lena." Paisley squeezes my shoulder, then they leave.

One of the puck bunnies comes up to Ford's side, but he steps forward, his eyes on me. He bends down and kisses Annabelle's forehead. "Is she okay?"

I nod. "Just cranky and past her bedtime. I hope—"

"It's great. I'm glad you came."

I've never seen Ford so earnest. So willing not to crack a joke about how I invited myself along. Another sign that things are turning, our road maneuvering into foreign territory.

"I'm going to kiss you," he whispers before his lips press to mine.

It's only a quick peck on the lips, but I feel as if I licked the end of a battery. I'm tingling everywhere. I love this look when he's in his suit, but his hair is still slightly damp and he smells like clean sheets. It's hard not to get lost in him.

"Let's go home." He raises his voice so the people around us can hear.

Maybe that was all part of the act. Maybe I just can't figure out what's real and pretend anymore. I suppose a kiss gives the appearance that we're a couple, but he could have taken my hand or even grabbed Annabelle.

He picks up her carrier and we walk toward his Mercedes. "Did you bring a car?"

"I had an Uber drive us." Which I will never again do

with the car seat situation. Not having a base to snap it into is beyond annoying.

"Next time I'll get you a car service, okay? We should get you a car while you're here."

I wave him off. "The Bronco is fine. I just know how you feel about Annabelle riding in it."

He turns with the back passenger door open, holding his arms out for Annabelle. I pass her over, and he nuzzles his head into her neck. It's the most tender moment I've seen him share with her. He gets her in the carrier and snaps it into place.

After shutting the door quietly, he opens the passenger door for me. "It really means a lot to me that you came."

"I got the idea you wanted us here. I would've come to earlier games, but I didn't want to step on toes."

He blows out a breath. No sharp comebacks on his tongue. "Never."

Something about the way he says it has me leaning forward to press my lips to his and slide my tongue into his mouth. His hand wraps around my head, holding me to him. Our tongues slide and graze, and moans erupt from deep in our throats. The kiss is consuming and intense and a throbbing pulse lands right between my legs. I want this man.

He presses me into the hollow car door opening, and I slide my hand down the front of him until my fingers anchor into the waistband of his slacks. I'm starved for this man. Saige is right—someone has to get him, it might as well be me.

A few whistles call out from somewhere behind us, but Ford doesn't stop, his mouth unrelenting.

I finally pull away, my cheeks heating from our witnesses. "Maybe we should cool it."

He rests his forehead on my shoulder with a groan.

"That did nothing to quench my thirst for you, Lena. I hope you know that we're not even close to done."

I inhale and make the decision to step off the ledge. Whatever happens, happens. I relinquish control because I'm taking something for me this time. "Who said I wanted to be done?"

"Fuck, you might be the death of me." He captures my mouth in a soft, quick kiss, steps back, and waits for me to slide in the front seat.

Once I'm secure, he rounds the hood of the car and folds himself into his seat. He shoots me a look that I can only see thanks to the glow of the parking light above, but I interpret it as a promise. I clench my thighs together with the thought of what he's going to do to me once we're alone and how long I've waited to find out.

CHAPTER 17

"I need some space."

Ford

I drive out of the parking lot. She finally made the move and I'm going to take advantage no matter if it's a bonehead decision. I want her and lately I feel like I can't breathe around her.

"You gotta hold that thought for about twenty minutes. Think of nothing else but that kiss and where it might've gone if we were alone."

"And your daughter in the back seat?" she says with a laugh.

I ease off the gas. "Yes, God, I hope she goes down easy tonight."

Lena squirms in her seat. I really hope she's thinking about having me inside her, what my hands will feel like on her skin.

The drive to my house seems as though it takes about an hour longer than it does, but when I pull in the driveway and park my Mercedes next to the Bronco, the rush of passion recedes for a moment and I decide I need to really make sure this is what she wants.

But the minute the garage door shuts behind the car and I glance at her, she leans in and crushes her lips to mine. My hands land on each side of her face, not wanting her to go anywhere. Our tongues rush into one another's mouth, and we collide with a force so strong, I know I've never wanted anyone like I want Lena.

The question plagues me though. Do I only want her because she's forbidden? I really hope that's not it and I don't wake up tomorrow thinking my dick made a mistake again. Wouldn't be the first time.

I tear my lips off hers, and her swollen red lips glisten, making me go rock hard. "I need you now. Let me get Annabelle to bed."

I open the door, head to the back, and grab Annabelle. Meanwhile, Lena slowly climbs out of the passenger seat, following us inside.

"How about I make the bottle while you change her?" Lena offers as I take Annabelle out of the car seat.

"I think I want to kiss you again," I say, leaning into her as she pulls the formula from the cabinet.

Over Annabelle, I kiss the living shit out of Lena. *Sorry, little girl, but you'll never remember this anyway.*

"Hurry," I say.

"Just go and worry about yourself." She chuckles.

I walk upstairs to Annabelle's room and change her diaper, then I put on the onesie she's slept the longest in with the hope that she sleeps through the night again. I'm not even done when Lena's leaning on the doorframe.

"I guess I'm faster," she says with a coy smile.

"You don't need to worry about me being fast." I wink and sit in the rocker.

Lena hands me the bottle before sitting on the floor. Her legs are propped up with her arms around them as she looks around the room. "You really need to decorate this room. Make it hers. She's getting older."

"Have at it," I tell her. "She has what she needs."

She shakes her head. "Men."

I poke her side with my foot. "What does that mean?"

"It means your attention to detail sucks. She needs pretty things in here. And look at her closet." She rises and I'm rewarded with her perfect ass in a pair of jeans. I can't wait to spank it. "Half of these have tags. You need to dress her in more than just onesies."

"Because my mom bought most of them. I'm not putting her in a dress every day. And shoes? Explain why she needs shoes."

She laughs and comes back over. "Still, paint the room. She's growing every day, and pretty soon she'll need a space that feels like hers." She leans over me and watches Annabelle, who is unusually fussy with the bottle, taking more breaks than usual and squirming in my arms. "Is she okay?"

It's then I notice the sweat along Annabelle's hairline. "Do me a favor, can you get the thermometer in my bathroom?"

Lena's face turns serious and she heads into my bathroom, returning a minute later with my thermometer. "You know this isn't accurate for a baby, right?"

I take it from her and scan Annabelle's forehead. It says she's just over one hundred. What the hell? She's been healthy since birth. "What do we do?"

Lena smiles at me. "We need a real thermometer, and babies run hotter anyway. I'm taking it you don't have the old-school kind?"

"The ear thing? The nurse told me to get this when I had strep last year." I hold up the thermometer.

"Strep, huh?"

I tilt my head. "I have big tonsils."

She laughs and goes to the large closet where I stuffed most of the things people have bought for Annabelle. "Big tonsils. That's interesting."

"It's not the only big thing of mine."

She bends down, digging through items. I don't remember anyone giving me a thermometer. I got a lot of clothes and shampoo. Enough shampoo to last Annabelle's entire life. "Do you often compare your member to others?"

I pick up Annabelle to burp her since she's not eating. "Might only be Maksim who beats me. But Maksim beats everyone."

She glances at me over her shoulder. "I do not need to know that."

"Well, if things go the way we want tonight, it was a warning to prepare yourself."

She pulls out a box and sets it on the changing table, looking at me before opening it. "Prepare myself? Should I do some Kegel exercises?"

"It wouldn't hurt."

Her head is buried in the box, so I have no idea what reaction my comment earned, but she pulls out a thin thermometer. "Thank you"—she turns over the box—"Aunt Claudia."

"The only practical one in my family."

Annabelle lets out a huge burp and we both freeze because she's never sounded like that before—like a grown man who just did a keg stand.

Then I feel warmth on my back, and the rancid smell of vomit fills the room. When I pull her away from my chest, I see that she looks flushed and sweaty. "I think she's sick."

"Let's take her temperature, and after, you should call the doctor." Lena reaches for Annabelle, so I pass her over. "Go change and I'll get her out of the onesie to prepare her for you to take her temperature."

I stop, unbuttoning my shirt. "What do you mean, prepare?"

"We have to take a rectal temperature."

My eyes widen. "Rectal?"

"In her anus."

I want to cover my ears and scream. "Anus and my daughter should never be used in the same sentence."

She laughs and wipes Annabelle's mouth with a wet wipe.

"How do you know so much?"

"I used to nanny through my summers in college."

It makes sense now how she takes everything with Annabelle in stride.

"You can do it. Let me know what it is." I start to walk away, but she keeps one hand on Annabelle and grabs my wrist to stop me.

"You're her father. You have to learn and I'll teach you."

I shiver all over, unwinding myself from Lena's grip to go change. The entire time I'm changing, I can't stop thinking about putting something in my baby girl's butt. How uncomfortable for her and ugh, I just can't do it. A man has his limits.

Minutes later, I'm in a T-shirt and sweats. Lena looks me up and down as though she'd like to eat me up with a spoon. Twenty minutes ago, I was game for it, but now I'm thinking about all the times I've had anal sex with someone else's daughter.

"I don't think I can do it," I say with a pleading look.

"Yes, you can." She tugs me closer. "I'm going to put her on her stomach and arch her up. We'll put the thermometer in some Vaseline then gently insert it in her bum."

"Fuck, stop saying shit like that. Just be vague." I reach for the thermometer and retract my hand with a full-body shiver before I touch it, fully aware that I'm acting immature. This is my daughter, and she needs me. I've been put in more uncomfortable situations since she's been born than my entire life before she existed.

This is your daughter and she needs you, I repeat in my head, then pick up the thermometer slowly.

"Okay. Okay." She places her hand over mine. "We'll do this together."

She dips the thermometer in the Vaseline and raises it up, moving it toward Annabelle's little bottom. I want to close my eyes, but Lena's staring at me, not Annabelle. "You can do this."

"I know I can. I just don't want to."

Slowly, we insert the thermometer and Annabelle doesn't even flinch.

"Now we just wait a minute." She raises her wrist to look at her watch.

"A minute?" I groan and rock my head back and forth. "What if she's sick?"

"Then we call the doctor."

"Then we go to the hospital," I say definitively.

"No, we'll call the doctor and go from there."

She's insane. I'm not taking any chances at this time of the night. She might think I'm crazy, but we're going to the hospital.

Finally, a minute goes by and we retract the thermome-ter. She raises it up to the light. I have no idea how she's even reading the fucking thing, it's so small.

"She's one-oh-four," Lena says and bites her lip, diverting eye contact.

"Let's get her dressed, we're going."

"Don't be ridiculous, Ford."

"Lena," I bite out, panicked for my daughter.

She shrugs. "Fine. But—" She must see something in

my expression because she cuts herself off from the fight she wants to give me.

I put on Annabelle's diaper and a new onesie, taking her downstairs to her carrier. Lena comes down with her computer and a sweatshirt.

"By all means, anything else you'd like to grab?"

"We're going to be there a while. The emergency room at this time of night will be busy."

"You don't have to come," I say.

She stops and glares at me. "I'm coming."

"Fine then, let's go."

I'm anxious and angry and lashing out, I know, but I can't help myself.

We file into the Mercedes and Lena puts on her seat belt while I get Annabelle in the back.

"You drive. I'm sitting back here with her," I say.

She chuckles and climbs out, rounding the car and accepting the keys over her shoulder once she's in the driver's seat.

"I don't understand why this is so funny," I say while she pulls out of my garage and reverses down the driveway.

"Because you're overreacting like a first-time parent."

"I *am* a first-time parent." My anger is apparent in my tone. "She probably caught something at the game. You shouldn't have taken her."

"It wouldn't have happened that quick and now you're blaming me?" She turns out of my neighborhood.

"I'm just saying. She's a baby."

"And you've had me take her before." Her eyes are narrowed in the rearview mirror. "I thought you wanted us to be there."

I run a hand through my hair. "Not now that she's sick."

"It's not from the game. She caught a bug. I'm sure she's okay."

"Did I miss you going through med school?"

She drives in silence.

Of course, I can't control my anger. I hate having no control over this situation right now. "What is this, *Driving Miss Daisy*? Hit the gas."

She blows out a breath and accelerates.

"It's not *The Fast and the Furious* either," I bite out.

"What the fuck do you want?" she yells, and I'm taken aback by her anger. "I'm about to pull over and you can handle this yourself while I hitchhike back to the house."

"Hitchhike? No one hitchhikes anymore. Might as well just cut off your own head."

I notice her hands tighten on the steering wheel and she pushes back in the driver's seat.

Thankfully, the hospital signs come into view. I touch Annabelle's forehead, which is still hot and sweaty. Lena pulls into the emergency area and puts the car in park.

"What, are you not coming inside?" I ask, getting out and unhooking Annabelle from the carrier base.

"I need some space. I'll see you in there."

We're barely out of the car, the door not even shut, when she slams on the gas and drives away.

I guess I'm not getting laid tonight. Just as well. I probably dodged a bullet.

Annabelle squawks and I look at her. "You're my number one anyway."

CHAPTER 18

"Can I ask you a question?"

Lena

I want to drive away and leave him on his own because of the ass he's being. Blaming me for taking his daughter to the game and getting her sick? Screw him.

But instead of leaving, I park in a spot and think. We were this close to having sex. Maybe this is yet another sign from the universe that we need to keep our distance from one another in that respect.

With a sigh, I get out of the car, grabbing my computer bag and sweatshirt. I want to hear it from the doctor's mouth when they say what's wrong with her. Although I think it's a bug of some sort and she'll recover with some Tylenol, fluids, and sleep, I could be wrong. Ford's right, I'm not a doctor.

When I enter through the emergency room doors, I find Ford arguing with the nurse that this is an emergency and his daughter needs to be seen as soon as possible. I walk over to see that Annabelle has thrown up again.

I take the carrier, but Ford grips it harder until he sees that it's me, then he loosens his grip, an apologetic expression on his face. Getting some wipes from the diaper bag, I clean Annabelle, but her bottom lip trembles and she cries softly. I pull her out of the carrier, not caring that she's covered in vomit. Holding her, I continue to clean her up as I rock her.

"Is this the mother?" the nurse asks with a nod in my direction.

Ford looks at me for a moment, his back stiff. "Yes."

I try not to act surprised he said that.

"Let me get a nurse." The woman leaves the desk and heads into the back.

Ford comes over to me. "They wouldn't have allowed you in otherwise."

I nod, but in this moment, I feel a seed of something that's been planted inside me. To have this man as my husband and Annabelle be our baby… what would that life look like? Shaking my head, I try to decipher when my brain changed its mind about Ford Jacobs. When did he turn into a man I'm envisioning as my husband and not the spoiled prick who makes me nutty?

He comes toward me, taking over the cleaning while I hold Annabelle, and I know from the outside that we look like the real thing. "I just want to find out what's wrong with her. What if it's something serious?"

I don't say anything, allowing the anger between us to disperse a little. This is his daughter. Of course he's protective of her, and if it makes him feel better to bring her here, then what really is the harm? "Hopefully it's just a cold."

He throws away a handful of wipes. "Want me to take her?"

I hand her over because she is his after all. I take the diaper bag and lean along the wall, watching him with her. He's kissing her forehead and murmuring to her. I'm not close enough to hear, but I've never seen this look on his face before. It takes me a while to piece it all together, but it's a look of love and concern. When you think you might lose something you can't live without. Seeing that facial expression on Ford sears my heart. Yeah, I think maybe he could be someone's husband and a damn good one at that. But I'm not sure that's something he wants.

The nurse comes out from the back. "Okay, Mr. Jacobs. Come with me."

We file through the doors and are ushered to a room with a small bassinet. The nurse takes Annabelle from Ford's hands, placing her in the bassinet.

"She's thrown up, what, three times?" He looks at me. "And her fever is one hundred and four. We took it the right way."

The nurse looks at him in question, taking the stethoscope from around her neck.

"You know." Ford moves his ass out and points.

I bite my lip to stop from laughing.

"Rectal?" she asks.

He cringes. "Yes."

"Okay. That's good. Let me get her vitals and we'll go from there. You two sit down and relax."

I sit. Ford paces.

After the nurse listens to Annabelle's heart and lungs, she touches her forehead, putting the thermometer in the armpit. Ford shoots me a glare and I shrug.

"She is running hot," she confirms. "Her lungs and heart sound great though. I'm going to talk to the doctor, and we'll see where he wants to go from there. Let's just keep her in her diaper for the meantime."

"How long will that take?" Ford asks.

She smiles at me as though she understands what I deal with when in reality, I don't know this version of this man who cares about someone who's not himself. "Not long."

"That's not really an answer…"

"Ford, just relax."

He looks at me and I square my shoulders. Better for me to take his wrath than the nurse.

The nurse leaves and he sits on the doctor's stool, wheeling it over to Annabelle who seems as though she's slowly falling asleep.

And so we sit in silence, waiting for answers.

*L*ess than an hour later, we're told that Annabelle is being given some Tylenol and being admitted for a one-night stay, leaving the ER to go to the pediatric wing. They're concerned with how high her fever is and the fact that she's a little dehydrated. It takes a half hour before we're situated in her room. Annabelle sleeps peacefully in a thinner onesie the hospital supplied and is hooked up to a bunch of monitors.

I'm curled into a chair in the corner of the room. "I'm sorry. I shouldn't have questioned you about bringing Annabelle here. You're her father."

Ford tears his eyes away from his daughter. "No, I'm sorry. I shouldn't have blamed you."

A few beats of uncomfortable silence pass.

"I hate hospitals," I admit, pain in my voice. "Maybe that's why I was reluctant to admit this is where she needed to be, I don't know."

"Why?" he asks, turning his chair to face me with his hand still on Annabelle.

"Don't you ever think about the dead bodies in the morgue or the fact that someone could be dying in this building right now?"

His eyebrows rise. "Pretty morbid. Babies get born here and people cheat death here too. Survivors."

I nod. "I guess I never saw the good. I saw the fixing. But it was always temporary."

"Why were you in a hospital so much?"

Now I have to decide if I want to tell him the truth, the most personal part of my life. As I look at him, I can tell that he genuinely wants to know, so I tell him. "Because of my dad."

"I'm sorry," he says, voice rough.

I shake my head. "He's alive."

"So he's the survivor?" he asks with hope in his voice.

"He was an alcoholic. I had to bring him to have his stomach pumped a few times."

"Jesus, I'm sorry, Lena."

"Don't be."

"Where is he now? And your mom? You never talk about them."

I tighten my arms around my legs. "My mom passed away when I was seven. My dad is in Tall Trees Assisted Living Facility back in New York. He lives there because he got drunk one night and went the wrong way on the interstate. Got into an accident and now he's brain damaged. Doesn't even really know who I am anymore."

Admitting the truth is painful, but at the same time, it feels almost as though I've set down a heavy sack that I've been carrying around everywhere.

His mouth hangs open. "Lena…"

His tone tells me he's figured out that my dad's situation has something to do with why I agreed to this entire ruse between the two of us in the first place.

"Your dad is paying me a large sum of money." I wipe the tears escaping, feeling ashamed of what he'll think of me. A man who's never wanted for anything other than to play hockey.

He says nothing.

"I know what you must think—"

"Don't go assuming you know what's in my head. It's a complicated place." One side of his lips tilt up.

"It's expensive. The home he's in. Sure, Medicare takes care of some things, but he needs more than the bare bones care, and in order to pay for that plus my own expenses…"

"I get it. I already knew you were doing it for money. But now I feel like maybe you felt like you *had* to do it. Like you had no choice."

"If your dad retires and your family doesn't need me anymore—"

"Lena," he says, and I stop talking. "You don't have to justify your reasoning to me."

"I just don't want you to think…" I look at him and his eyes are on me.

He glances at Annabelle, then stalks over to me and slides into the chair next to me. "Since when do you care what I think?"

I don't tear my gaze away from his. "I have no idea." Another tear slips, and he catches it with his thumb. "But I'm not a gold digger, and I know you deal with a lot of women like that. I'm afraid that's what you'll think of me."

His hand cradles my head, making sure our eyes don't leave one another. "Well, you did agree to marry me for money."

I try to shift my head to the right, but he holds it tight.

"That was a joke. I don't think that of you."

I nod and he releases my cheek, coolness seeping in after the warmth of his hand. "What do you think of me?"

He stretches his legs out in front of him, crossing his arms. "I think I can't get you out of my head and it scares me."

I shove him with my shoulder. "I meant about me

taking money from your dad."

"I think you're smart. You're right. You have expenses and he's using you to get the most he can for his company, so why shouldn't you get your share? I knew you didn't agree because you've been hot for me and wanted to marry me."

"I might not have been hot for you then, but I am now."

His head slowly turns toward me, a smoldering haze of want filling his blue eyes. "What exactly are we doing?"

I shake my head, gaze remaining fixed on his face. "I have no clue, but it could go south."

"I know." He places his hand on my thigh, running it up and down. Need throbs between my thighs. "But I'm not sure I can be in close proximity and control myself."

"You hate me."

He scowls. "I never hated you. I teased you."

I tilt my head at him incredulously.

"Well, you did strip the fun out of my life."

I chuckle. "Can I ask you a question?"

"Sure."

"Why did you kiss me on New Year's Eve?"

He blows out a breath. "You're the complete opposite of any girl I've ever been with, and I think because you despised me, I thought it would be fun. That I'd make you uncomfortable and then maybe you'd avoid me at all costs. I hated how you were always entangled in my business, but then…"

I kind of know what he's going to say, but I don't fill in the blank for him.

"Then that one small kiss sprouted this need inside me and I wanted you. Hell, I would've taken you right there on the plane if I thought you'd be into it," he says.

"But…"

"Then the news about Annabelle came and I couldn't make sense of where my life was going. People act like I don't know what they think of me. And having a child as a result of a one-night stand doesn't disprove their theories. All the girls, the parties, the fights—the more it pissed off my dad, the more I did it, as immature as that sounds. I think… no, I know that I always felt like my dad was going to find a way to get me out of hockey. That he'd manipulate or use leverage in some way to get me to work at Jacobs Enterprises. I wanted to live it up every second before the inevitable happened."

"And now?"

He stares at Annabelle, a soft smile on his face. "I don't want Annabelle growing up thinking her dad's a sleazy guy. That he sleeps with women and discards them. Don't get me wrong, most of the women know what they're getting into, but I want to set an example for my daughter on how she should be treated. I don't mind coming home after the games and taking care of her. Believe me, I'm just as surprised as everyone else."

"Funny, right?"

"What?"

"That you got the opposite of what you thought you wanted and it's been good for you. You're happy."

He nods. "But, Lena, that doesn't mean I'm a great guy. I'm scared to sleep with you because I'm scared that once I've had you, I'm going to bolt and ruin this whole situation."

His honesty strikes me hard. It's my fear as well. I haven't been in a ton of relationships, but I'm not the girl who sleeps with random people either.

"I know," I say softly.

We both sit straight, our eyes on Annabelle. We're in a crap situation with no clear way out.

CHAPTER 19

"Relax. It's just an orgy."

Lena

Two days after Annabelle has a day without a fever and seems to be recovered, we're on the Jacobs' private plane, heading to Manhattan to attend a party with Otis Sandersville. As Mr. Jacobs informed Ford and me on a mutual speaker call, this is it and we better sell our happy engagement.

Morgan will stay back and watch Annabelle at the Jacobs' penthouse, which leaves no buffer between us.

At the hospital, we were honest with one another. We're both fearful of crossing the line, but we'll never know if we don't. Annabelle being sick has been something we can focus on and put all those issues to the side. But tonight, we have to sell this relationship, and if we feel uncomfortable or awkward, someone is bound to notice.

Ford leaves me in the foyer, dropping our bags and saying he has to run out. Mrs. Jacobs takes Annabelle immediately, baby-talking with her about being sick.

Bennie's in the kitchen making everyone lunch, so I go visit with him. "Hey, Bennie."

He hugs me, kissing my temple like a father would. "How are the beaches?"

"Good, but I missed the first snowfall, right?"

He nods. "A week ago, and it was beautiful."

"It's all melted now." I pout, upset to miss the first snowfall of the year in New York City since I've been born.

"I heard you're coming for Christmas. A photo shoot has been scheduled." His eyebrows waggle as though it's big doings.

"I know. I booked it." I chuckle. "It's good PR to show a happy family."

He pushes a cup of his homemade salsa and a bowl of chips my way, knowing that's my favorite. "I suppose so, but things are good?"

I'm fairly sure Bennie knows about the deal. He's heard me complain about Ford enough to know I wouldn't just fall head over heels and accept an engagement, but I tread lightly anyway. "They're great. But weird."

"Weird?" he asks, peeling some apples. No doubt making homemade baby food for Annabelle.

"Things are developing."

"How so?"

Oh, screw it. "Do you ever feel like…" I lean over and whisper, "The help?"

He chuckles. "Hello." He runs his hands down his Hawaiian shirt. "I've been wearing these as a hint and never been invited once."

In their defense, the Jacobs go to Europe way more often than Hawaii.

"I think I'm falling for him." I bite my lip.

"Shouldn't you have fallen before accepting that three-carat ring?" He glances down.

I look and see my ring isn't on my finger. Shit, I need it tonight. I'm so bad at wearing it, Ford's always giving me shit, but that's some high-priced jewelry.

"Bennie," I say, insinuating he understands.

"Okay. So what if you are?"

"I don't come from this. I'm supposed to work *for* them,

not be one *of* them." It's just another one of my fears where Ford and I are concerned. That even if Ford and I make it past day one post-sex, he could wake up one day and realize I'm not the kind of woman he's supposed to be with.

"Says who?"

I blow out a breath, dipping a chip into the salsa. "The world. It's just the way it is."

He shakes his head, dropping some apples into the blender. "That's nonsense and you shouldn't think that. You're both the same species."

"Species?" I chuckle.

"The heart doesn't care about money or status or the hierarchy of the wealthy. That's why there are fairy tales."

I dip another chip in the salsa. "There are fairy tales so the poor can have hope. And why do people think the prince is all that?"

"You're confusing me now, because from what you're saying, you're smitten with the prince."

I clench my fists on the counter. He's right. "I can't help it. I've always been a self-confident person, you know, but why do I allow money to intimidate me?"

He leaves the blender and sits on the stool next to me, taking my hands. "Because it's something you lacked. The security money gives people isn't something you've ever had. They have the one thing you were always working for, so in essence, you feel as though they're more successful than you. I can't speak for the other generations, but Ford was born with that money. He didn't earn it."

"He is now," I say.

"Yeah, and believe me, that kid worked hard to be where he is. No one handed him that hockey contract. He fought for it just like you did to get through college and get out of your car. You two are a lot more alike than you think." He pats my hands and goes back to his task. "At some point in every rich family's story, there was someone poor who had a dream. Remember that. So take that money you're getting and build your own empire."

He smiles at me, making it clear that he knows the arrangement. I shouldn't be surprised he knows the specifics. He knows everything that goes down in the Jacobs household.

"Thank you," I say, feeling so much better.

He winks. "That's what I do. I give pep talks. Imogen was just here…" He stops talking and looks at me with that smile that suggests that what happens in the kitchen, stays in the kitchen.

I'm getting ready in one of the guest rooms when a knock lands on the door.

I open it and see a box with a bow lying on the floor. Excitement bubbles in my stomach. Taking the box into the room, I open it. The note on top of the tissue paper is in Ford's scrawling script.

You didn't think I'd forget, did you? If you'll allow me, I'd love the honor of sliding this off your body later tonight. ~ Ford

I undo the tissue paper to discover a champagne-colored dress with a slit high up the one side, just like he wanted. The dip in the fabric for my cleavage is equal on the front and the back. I've never in my life worn something this elegant or this revealing. My excitement turns to nausea, wondering whether I can pull this off.

Digging in farther, I find another item wrapped in tissue paper with a note.

. . .

'm going to be thinking about you wearing this all night. Torment me. ~ Ford

blow out a breath, and sure enough, there's a pair of panties that are barely there, merely a square of fabric. There's no bra, but he did include little sticky things for my nipples. Does he go to these stores or do they just package it all for him?

I lay it all out on the bed and head into the shower, where I shave and lotion every inch of my body.

When it's time to put the dress on, I step into it as there's a knock on the door.

"Hold on," I say, holding together the back of my dress.

I open the door to find Ford in a tuxedo. He looks phenomenal, as though he belongs in a men's cologne ad. "I was going to send my sister to zip you up, but I want to do it."

I laugh as he slides into the room, shutting the door and locking it.

"Now that's a dress." He stays a foot away, his gaze soaking me in. "Damn, don't leave my side tonight."

I'm hyperaware of his gaze running all over my body. Unsure where we stand, I take his notes and behavior to mean that he wants to try again to have our night together, that after reflecting since Annabelle's illness, he still wants to cross the line.

He raises his finger and twirls it. I turn around. Stepping up behind me, Ford zips the dress but doesn't pull away. I'm positioned in front of the mirror and he towers over me so it's easy to catch a glimpse of us. A couple. An engaged couple.

"Beautiful," he whispers, staring into the mirror.

I swallow hard and lock eyes with him in the mirror. "Yes." But I'm talking about us, or even just him.

"Did you like my gifts?"

"I did. Thank you."

"You're missing one thing." He puts his hand in his pocket and holds my engagement ring in front of me. "If I find you without this again, I'm going to spank you."

My eyes flare because I can tell from his voice that he's serious. My panties grow wet with the thought of being bent over his lap in my thong. "I…"

He kisses the nape of my neck and I close my eyes. The scent of his expensive cologne and the waft of heat from his body on my bare back add to the sensation.

"We need to go now before we don't make it to the party. Let's go, beautiful." His fingers brush a path down my arm until his hand locks with mine.

I grab my clutch and we leave the confines of the bedroom, stepping out into the world as the soon-to-be Mr. and Mrs. Ford Jacobs. I repeat to myself that I can do this. And for some reason, with Ford at my side, I believe I can.

We stop in the foyer, where Morgan is holding Annabelle. She's getting so big, you can practically hold her on your hip now. She smiles and runs her hand down Ford's face.

"Love you, baby girl. Be good for your aunt and make sure she's not doing anything naughty like having boys over." Ford looks at his sister with a stern expression.

Morgan rolls her eyes. "Give me some credit."

I say goodbye to Annabelle with a kiss to the top of her head and she reaches for my hair. I'm able to sneak away before she gets a hold of it though because if she did, we'd be here a while.

"Call me if you need me? Call 911 if it's really bad. Don't wait for me," Ford says. I gently nudge him toward the elevator, but he whirls around. "And no boys. Or friends. Or parties." He points, but I give one last little shove and he stumbles into the elevator.

"Relax. It's just an orgy." Morgan laughs, giving him a small wave as the elevator doors slide shut.

"She's kidding," I say.

He squeezes the bridge of his nose. "She's only eighteen."

"And fully able to watch Annabelle. She'll be asleep in an hour."

He blows out a breath.

It's endearing that he doesn't want to leave Annabelle. I know she's not actually mine, but I'm kind of ready for an adult night out, even if I'm pretending to be someone I'm not. There'll be no interruptions tonight. As Ford places his hand on the small of my back when we reach the lobby, I wonder whether that's a good or a bad thing.

CHAPTER 20

Ford

We walk into the party and all eyes turn toward us. Lena tenses next to me. I bend down and whisper in her ear, "Relax."

She doesn't though. I'd thought about reminding her to use the toy I bought her the first time to relax her. Then when I went into her room to zip up her dress, I thought I could do it for her—slip my hand under the slit of her dress, slide the thong over, and watch her come on my hand. But it just didn't feel right. Then again, I've been waiting a fucking lifetime for it to feel right.

There's too much at stake. I don't want to just take her, I want to have her. And more than once.

We check our coats and I slip the ticket into the pocket of my slacks. Grabbing two champagne flutes off a server's tray, I hand her one. "This will relax you."

She sips it and smiles at me.

I take the opportunity to kiss her on her cheek because she's so cute. "Save the blushing for after."

"I'm curious, how do you think we're going to have sex with Annabelle there?" she asks, because I haven't filled her in on my plans for after we ditch this party.

"We're not going back to my parents' place, we're going to a hotel. A suite."

The flute almost slips out of her hand, but her grip tightens. "No. Don't waste money like that."

"Believe me, it's gonna be the best money I've spent in months, maybe years."

"That's a lot of pressure."

"Let me add that we do nothing if you don't want to. It's completely up to you." But I really hope she wants to. I mean, she did kiss the living shit out of me after the game. I see her clench her thighs sometimes and I wonder if it's to soothe an ache I've caused.

She finishes her champagne, puts the flute on a table, and wraps her arms around my neck, pushing her body into mine. "I want to."

And damn, my dick chubs.

"Then let's get this party over with."

"Ford." My dad's voice is like razor blades on my balls, ruining my moment with Lena.

"Be nice," Lena whispers, linking her hand in mine as though we're a united front.

We both turn and see my father standing with a short-statured balding man. I assume he must be Otis Sandersville. A petite brunette next to him has her hair in a bun and a dress similar to the one Lena wore to my dad's birthday party, aka hiding every inch of skin.

"Dad," I say, holding out my hand to shake his. I see my mom escaped and I wonder how she managed that.

"Hi, Eli," Lena says, hugging my dad as though they really are more than employee and boss.

"Lena, you look stunning."

She blushes. "Thank you. Ford surprised me with the dress." She winds her arm through mine and rests her head on my shoulder.

"He always does surprise me with the interests he

pursues. I'm not sure Gabi would like it if I tried to pick out her dress." My dad laughs.

We all carry on as though it's funny when he really just insulted me. I bite back my reply because Otis is here.

"May I see?" the woman next to who I'm still assuming is Otis asks, holding out her hand to Lena.

Lena stares for a moment, clearly not understanding the question.

"The ring, darling," the woman says.

"Oh. Yes. Of course." Lena holds out her hand, and the woman comes so close to the ring I'm surprised she doesn't have one of those magnifying glasses like at the jeweler's.

"Very pretty. And expensive." She nods to me as though complimenting my good taste.

"Let me introduce you." My dad looks at Otis. "This is Otis Sandersville and his wife, Penny." Then he gestures to me. "My oldest, Ford, and his fiancée, Lena Boyd."

We all shake hands, and Otis sets his gaze on me. "You've made the magazines and newspapers a lot of money."

I nod. "I think the internet more."

We both laugh.

"You like to be the center of attention?" he asks.

Lena stands like a statue next to me.

"I'll admit I was a bit wild when I was younger, but Lena's shown me a new way of life." I look down at her, and she forces a smile.

"And, Lena, taking care of a child that isn't yours? Commendable," Penny says.

Lena looks at Penny instead of Otis. "No child should be motherless."

Penny nods and glances at Otis with a soft smile.

"Won't it be hard knowing she came from Ford being with another woman?"

"I—" I'm ready to dive in and save her. She's not supposed to be raked over the coals, I am.

But Lena places her perfectly manicured hand on my arm, softly implying she has this. "It was before Ford and I truly got together. Sure, there was a kiss at midnight on New Year's Eve." She glimpses at me with love-filled eyes. "But it was complicated, what with me working with the Jacobses. We had to tread carefully. Like you, I'm familiar with the unknown, of not knowing when my next meal would be, and I couldn't risk my job."

I freeze. Where the hell is she going with this? This man might be richer than my father. Certainly they're on the same level at least.

My dad glares at Lena, then at me. Questions in his gaze. Questions I have no answers for.

"I see you've done your research." Mr. Sandersville smiles at Lena. "I guess I assumed you came from the same mold as the Jacobses."

Lena shakes her head. "No, that's why I keep taking this ring off. I'm afraid to lose it. Too expensive." She holds it out again and Penny holds out her own hand, where there's a simple gold band.

It's then I take in their clothing. Penny is in a presentable dress, but nothing like I'm used to seeing women in high society wear. Otis is in a suit, but it's not Armani or perfectly tailored to his body. These are frugal people who don't show off the amount of money they have.

"I'd want it locked to my hand." Penny laughs, and Lena joins in. "We tend to stick to core values. Money is security and nothing more."

Lena's smile could light up the room.

"I told Otis I thought you must be a saint. Taking on Ford alone is a big feat." She looks at me. "No offense."

I hold up my hand that I take none, even though I do.

"And then his sweet daughter. We've seen a few articles with the three of you, and you make a beautiful family. And you're right about no child being motherless. We ourselves have adopted two children of dear friends of ours who unexpectedly passed."

"That's so very kind of you," Lena says.

"Turns out maybe I was wrong about you." Otis turns to me while I'm still processing this whole exchange between Lena and Penny. "You know, they say the worth of a man is in the woman he chooses."

"Can't say I've ever heard that before, but it's the truth. This woman has changed me." I wrap my arm around Lena's waist. I mean every word. I'm not acting, although Lena probably assumes I am.

"Do you smoke cigars? Come join me on the balcony," Otis suggests.

"This is where we part." Penny squeezes Otis's arm.

"I'll be back in no time," he says.

I bend down and give Lena a kiss on the cheek. "You made me hard," I whisper in her ear.

The soft moan my words elicit only makes me think of when we leave here and whether we'll even make it back to the hotel room.

"Don't be too long," she says. Her touch lingers on my arm as I walk away with my dad and Otis.

"Never." I wink and catch her hand falling to her stomach.

"Oh, he is a charmer and very handsome," Penny tells Lena, but I'm out of earshot before her answer.

We file out to the balcony where my dad and Otis say hello to certain people they're used to doing business with.

Standing around a tall table, Otis pulls the cigars out of his pocket, handing us each one. We pass around the cutter and lighter until we're all situated. I stop a waitress to ask for a whiskey.

"I know we've been in talks about me buying a majority stake in Jacobs Enterprises." Otis is the first to breach the subject as to why we're all here.

A topic I don't want to be a part of. It's not like I don't feel any guilt over my dad selling what my ancestors built. I do. But I can't bring myself to want the life my dad wants for me. I would if I could.

"We'd remain forty-nine percent stakeholders and hold positions on the board, but you'd have majority ownership, yes." I can't tell from my dad's tone whether he's upset with me still or if he really is okay with letting part of the company go so he can travel with my mom.

"Is there something I don't know?" He sucks in smoke and billows it out into the crisp night air.

"Not at all. Why do you ask?" my dad says.

"Because from what I understand, your business isn't in jeopardy. Quite the contrary. You've brought it back better than ever after your father tanked it."

My dad's hands tense on his glass of whiskey, and I worry for a moment that his anger about Otis talking badly about my grandfather will undo this entire situation.

"I have no one to hand it down to, and I promised Gabi that once our kids were grown, I'd step away. Unfortunately, my son has more love for a puck and a stick than a boardroom and an office and my two daughters aren't interested. That leaves me no option but to sell." My dad briefly looks in my direction.

"You could remain owner. Hire someone you trust to run the day-to-day," Otis says, and I can't help the chuckle that escapes me. Otis raises an eyebrow in my direction.

"If my father still had controlling interest, there's no way he'd be able to keep his hands off of it. He's a bit of a control freak." I glance at my dad. "Sorry, Dad, but it's true."

He gives me a terse nod.

"I understand. Not sure I could do it either," Otis says. "The temptation to pop in the office would always be there."

"Exactly," my dad says with a satisfied smile.

Otis puffs away on his cigar for a moment. "And you both want to sit on the board. That's part of the deal?"

We both nod.

"And you, Ford, you've cleaned up your act? I don't want any bad press. I don't want to have to be putting out press releases because you've had an orgy with fifteen women or something."

My eyes widen. I guess my dad was right to assume we needed this fake engagement.

"You just saw him with Lena. They're in love. A wedding is in the works for the end of the hockey season."

"That so?" Otis poses his question to me.

I nod. "Yes."

"Okay, we'll sign the papers the day of the marriage."

"Seriously?" I ask, and my dad's hand lands on my shoulder. "I mean—"

"No." Otis laughs. "The day after, but I do want to ensure that you are marrying her. You've done a one-eighty in a short amount of time, Ford. Some leopards never change their spots."

"I assure you, I do… did."

He smiles and nods. "Can't wait to get the invitation in the mail. In the meantime, Eli, let's put a meeting on the books after the holidays. We can work out some more details, then let the lawyers do their thing." Otis raises his cigar, puffs another billow of smoke, and leaves the patio.

My dad turns to me. "I told you the man is inflexible. How the hell did Lena know about them not having any money when they started out?"

I shrug. "How am I supposed to know?"

My dad gives me a look and rejoins the party.

I do the same for a bit, making the rounds and schmoozing with everyone like I'm expected to. I receive the many congratulations on my engagement with a smile and tell them what a lucky man I am.

Finally, I've had enough so I seek out my *fiancée*. I spot Lena talking to a group of women, including my mom. I come at Lena from behind, surprising her, which makes all the older women smile.

"You ready?" I whisper, and the fact that she steps back into my embrace I take as a yes. "Can you all excuse me while I have a moment with my fiancée?"

My mom smiles at us. "Go, Ford. You two never get a night alone. We've got Annabelle tonight."

I kiss my mom's cheek and Lena hugs her, saying how nice it was to meet everyone.

We leave the room with my mom bragging about Annabelle and how in love Lena and I are.

"Are you sure we should leave?" Lena asks me as the elevator doors shut.

I backstep her into the elevator wall and my fingers graze the side of her tit. "You're so fucking amazing."

"Well, thank you. And I haven't even sucked your dick yet." She grins and laughs. I like this side of her.

"You're good at everything else. I'm sure you'll rock that too." Our eyes meet and I inch closer.

"Get me to the hotel and you can find out for yourself." Her voice is breathy.

"Fuck." I take her hand and bring it down between my legs. "Look what you did. I've been walking around with a fucking hard-on since you put on that dress. Since I know what little lingerie is on under it, I'm dying."

When the elevator doors open, I yank her out of the confined space before I end up taking her up against the wall. Tonight, I'm having Lena Boyd regardless of any repercussions.

CHAPTER 21

Lena

I slide over to the far side in the SUV, but Ford sits right next to me, his thigh pressed to mine.

"Don't go running on me," he whispers in my ear, his hot breath on my neck and his hand sliding around my waist and up my torso. Again, his knuckles graze down the side of my breast and goose bumps cover my body.

"I was simply leaving you room," I say.

He chuckles softly in my ear. "I don't need that much room."

His mouth covers my earlobe, and he sucks it, his tongue toying with it. My eyes close and I relish his undivided attention. I'm finally going to have him.

His fingers travel down the side of my body, past my waist to my leg, and slide under the slit of my dress. "See why this dress is so much better?" His breath tickles my neck, and he bites my earlobe.

A long exhale expels from my mouth when his hand brushes along my core, over my damp thong.

I put my hand on his. "Ford…"

He draws back and looks into my eyes. The darkness of the interior doesn't hide the fire raging inside me and he sees it. There's a cocky smirk on his face, then he's back to nuzzling my neck. He shifts my panties over, his finger swiping through the wetness at my core. He draws in a deep breath when he finds me soaked.

The SUV pulls along the curb outside the hotel and I lightly push Ford off me, my cheeks hot. But before we come to a complete stop, Ford brings his finger to his mouth and sucks my essence off of it. I clench my thighs, hoping to stop the impending orgasm he's brought to the surface.

I've never had a partner who was so comfortable with sex. The guys I've been with before have always been more conservative. The same moves over and over—kiss my lips, travel to my neck, hands to my breasts. A man has never been so blatant about how much he wants me. And I can't say I hate it.

"Thank you," he says, his voice groggy.

He slides out the door to the curb, holding his hand out to me. Of course, the hotel is one of the nicest in Manhattan. The doorman opens the door and Ford tips him as we head to our room. Even in the elevator, we have a man who presses the buttons to our floor, but Ford puts his hand on my ass and squeezes, gripping the thin fabric of my dress as though he wants to rip it off my body.

After we step off the elevator and walk down the hall to our room, we're silent, and I wonder if he's second-guessing his decision.

He pulls out the key card and unlocks the door, but he looks at me for a moment before he goes inside. "Remember, this is your decision. What do you want?"

I nod, grab his lapels, and step into the room with my back pushing the door open, pulling him along. "I want you."

"Thank God." He grunts and his mouth slams down on mine. The hotel room door shuts and he quickly turns me around, pushing my back into the door. "All night, I've been thinking of all the things I want to do to you, but one thing specifically kept resurfacing in my mind."

He kisses me, shoving off his tuxedo jacket and tossing it on the floor. Then he falls to his knees, his hands on each one of my legs, pushing my dress out of his way.

"Then I tasted you and all my willpower cracked." He slides over my panties and swings one leg over his shoulder. Without any preamble, he buries his head between my legs.

One swipe of his tongue and I'm done. He owns me. My head falls back to the door with a thud, and I jut my hips out to meet his mouth. The man is talented beyond belief, starting slow, the tip of his tongue circling my clit. His huge hands are on my ass, squeezing and tugging me closer, but keeping me steady. I let out a breathy whimper when he licks me wide and sucks my clit.

My fingers dive into his hair, clutching, needing something to anchor me. He stops and my gaze shoots to his, the devilish glint staring right back at me. Never pulling his gaze away, he pushes a finger inside me, and my back arches from the door. Then he adds another one, never tearing his gaze from mine.

"Tell me," he murmurs. "Tell me what you want."

"I want you to fuck me," I say, and he shakes his head slowly.

"Be specific."

"Don't stop," I say, my eyelids falling from the pure pleasure coursing through my veins. I should've known he'd be as talented in the bedroom as he is on the ice.

"You're so tight." He groans as if this knowledge is torturous for him. I clench down on his fingers and a groan falls from his lips. "Goddamn, I'm not going to be able to control myself in a minute."

My hands fall to his face. "Don't. I don't want you to

control yourself. Show me, Ford. Show me how much you want me."

He unbuckles his belt, opening his slacks with his free hand. While his fingers manipulate me into ecstasy, he strokes himself. My eyelids flutter from the stretch of him thrusting his fingers in and out.

A strangled moan slips from my lips and my hands splay against the door. His mouth lands on my clit again and his tongue works me into a frenzy before I'm grinding on him. When he curves his fingers in a come-hither motion, my climax hits me like a train, bulldozing me over. I quake around him until finally he pulls away and my back slides down the door until my ass hits the floor.

His hand runs along my cheek. "You're fucking beautiful when you come."

It's then I process that he's still stroking himself, so I get up on my hands and knees, one arm reaching out and taking the weight of him in my palm. He props himself along the wall and I pump him a few times before taking him in my mouth. I twirl my tongue around his tip and his hands reach to my back, unzipping my dress and allowing the fabric to fall forward and show off my breasts.

He takes my breasts in his hands, his thumbs toying with my nipples and sending signals straight to my center. The more he plays, the more turned on I become as I suck him off.

"Damn, you have a talented mouth."

His compliment only spurs me to increase my pace and efforts. To make him become as unglued as I just was. But he tears me off of him when I think he's close.

"I have to be inside you." He climbs up, pushing his slacks down, toeing out of his shoes, and taking off his socks.

As he undresses, I sit on the floor and admire his rock-hard abs and chiseled V torso. From head to toe, he's the most magnificent man. When he holds out his hand, I accept, and he pulls me to my feet. My dress pools around my waist. He nudges it down the rest of the way, leaving me in my thong and my heels. He admires me, stepping back as though committing it to memory.

I bite my lip from the nervousness of being under his scrutiny. Not that he's ever given me reason to think I'm not beautiful.

"I can't believe you've been hiding this body under those baggy clothes."

"Baggy clothes?"

"It was a compliment," he says, stepping into me, his hands around my waist and his face in my neck. "You're so goddamn hot and I'm gonna fuck you with only that thong and heels on."

Although I'm caught up on the baggy clothes comment, it's soon forgotten when he licks my neck up to my earlobe and his hot breath once again makes goose bumps shoot up my spine. That spot is surely a new erogenous zone for me.

He sweeps me up and I wrap my legs around his narrow waist. Then I'm falling to the mattress. He wastes no time climbing on top of me, the tip of his dick at my opening.

"Condom," I say and his eyes sparkle.

Reaching over to the nightstand, he grabs the box that's sitting there.

"Aren't you a Boy Scout?" I laugh.

He tears open the foil packet, takes out the condom, and rolls it down his length. My mouth salivates the entire time. He glances at me. "I wrote out a checklist for tonight because I didn't want anything to go wrong."

My heart flips with his confession, but I don't have any

time to process that he planned tonight to be perfect because he widens my legs with his thighs, baring me to him. He locks his eyes with mine, slides my thong over, and inches inside me slowly. I accept him inch by inch with our gazes glued to each other's. Ford grabs a hold of my hips, and once he's fully inside me, my eyes close from the feeling of being so full. He's the biggest I've ever had and whoever said size doesn't matter can go to hell, because it sooo matters.

"You good?" he asks, his voice gruff as though he's holding himself back.

Never in a million years would I have thought Ford would be a caring and considerate lover. I want to ask if this is his usual MO or special just for me, but a small part of me doesn't want to know the answer. I want to believe this is especially for me. That I pull out a different Ford than the other girls before me.

"Perfect," I say.

He smiles, circling his hips inside me. Slowly, he slides out of me before thrusting himself back in. Oh my god, that felt so damn good. He continues the pace, never getting as deep as he did the first time. I thrust, hoping to break him, to make him dig into me, give me everything he has, but of course, Ford has other plans.

"I'm not going to beg," I say in a begging tone.

He laughs, awarding me with a thrust that hits me so deep and hard, I cry out.

"Is that what you want?" he asks.

I reach out, wanting him to lie down on me, but he stays upright, moving in and out of me in a teasing fashion.

"Again," I moan.

"That sounds like begging," he says, and I shake my head.

"I can get out of this bed and get myself off," I tell him.

"Baby, after I'm finished here, you'll never be satisfied with your own fingers again."

And I know he's right because he already feels more incredible than anything I've ever experienced.

Then he falls forward, pushing into me. "This what you want?"

I dig my fingernails into his shoulder blades. "God, yes."

Finally, he fucks me. Hard, fast, and thorough. Sweat beads along our bodies. My legs wrap around his waist, and he drills inside me like I wanted.

"Fuck," he says, smashing his lips to mine.

It becomes a frenzy of touches, caresses, grabs, squeezes. We can't get enough of one another, each of us right at the end of our willpower. He takes my nipple into his mouth and I drown in my orgasm, free-falling into an open pool of water and sinking into its depths.

Another two thrusts and he stills inside me, coming right after.

We hold one another for what seems like a lifetime. I don't want to move and I don't want him to move. Maybe because we're both scared of what will come now that we've quenched our desire for each other.

Ford slowly withdraws from me and I want to pull him back in, but I don't. He slithers down my body, sliding the thong down my legs. I help him get it off and he drops it onto the floor. He unbuckles my heels and slowly removes each one from my feet, allowing them to fall to the floor with a thud.

That's all it takes for me to know I've fallen for Ford Jacobs.

CHAPTER 22

"What are you really afraid of?"

Ford

I never imagined Lena Boyd would be a nympho, but we've barely caught our breath from round one and she's rubbing her pussy along my thigh. This is the first time I've ever cuddled after sex, and I have to say, I'm not hating it. I actually kind of like it.

She props her chin up on my arm. "So?"

"So what?" I ask, looking at her.

"Do you want to run?" She doesn't divert her eyes, waiting for my answer.

"No. I don't."

She straddles me, her bare pussy teasing my half-hard dick. "So once wasn't enough?"

I grip her hips, moving her back and forth, the slickness of her pussy warming my cock. "Not even close."

She bends down, but I urge her up, taking one of her nipples into my mouth. Stilling in place, she groans. I won't admit it to her right now, but I'm not sure I'll ever feel like I've had her enough times.

"Can you even?" she asks through labored breaths.

My mouth pops off her tit. "Are you questioning my ability to fuck you multiple times?"

I feel her chest vibrate with laughter as I cast kisses there. "Did I offend you?"

I grab a condom and have it on in record time, then lower her to my now-erect cock.

"Oh." She gasps.

"Oh is right. Don't doubt me again. You'll be begging for mercy before I can't go again."

"That sounds like a challenge." She takes me in her hand and slides the tip of my dick along her folds. Fuck, the slickness makes me throb.

"Take it as you will."

Then she sinks down on me. "How about I take control this time? You can reserve your energy because I bet you I'll still be like the Energizer Bunny while you're passed out."

"You know I don't back away from a bet."

Just the word bet reminds me of the one I have with Tweetie. I try to figure out if enough time has passed for me to win, but Lena circling her hips distracts me. Fuck it, even if I end up losing, this was worth it.

"Do your worst."

She shakes her head, a smile tipping her lips, and for a moment, I think this must be what Aiden and Maksim love so much with their women. Times when you really feel like you know the person. Because I've grown to know Lena pretty damn well and the fact that we can communicate with just expressions is awesome as hell.

She rocks along my length and my hands slide up to her tits, taking one in each hand. "I do love these big soft tits."

Her hands fall back on my thighs when she arches her back. "I love your cock." I raise my hips up off the mattress and she squeezes in with her knees. "I'm in control. Remember?"

I dramatically put my hands behind my head. "If you say so."

Her back arches more, her tits begging for my attention while she moves me in and out of her. I fixate on where we're joined. It's hot as hell watching my glistening cock sink into her over and over again. I glance up to see she's watching as well.

"Ford." She's breathless already. My name on her lips does something to me. "Touch me."

"You said you're in control," I joke.

Her eyes close and she rocks faster. "Please."

"Afraid not, baby."

She pops her eyes open. "Ford!"

I laugh and raise my hips off the mattress.

"Oh god, again."

I do it again, still keeping my hands entwined behind my head.

She falls forward, her hand on my pecs. "Touch my tits. Please."

"Can't."

Then she lies on me, her hands trying to get under my head to mine, but I'm stronger.

"Stop playing. I'm right there." She's needy and greedy and she sits back up, staring at me. "Then I'm going to touch myself." She holds up her hand in warning.

"I'd love to see you touch yourself." I give her a shit-eating grin.

"You don't want to be the one who gets me off?"

She stops moving and I take over thrusting up into her. "You're in control."

She slides her hand dramatically down the valley of her breasts, past her naval to the top of her trimmed pussy. My cock flexes inside her when she touches her clit. It's hot as fuck, but she's right—I want to be the one to make her come.

"Stop." I move her hand out from between her legs and take over.

She gives me a satisfied smile. Her hands are on my thighs again, and I lightly massage her clit until she's rocking so hard she might break my dick. I'm not complaining at all. Then I increase the pace and she whimpers, staring at me with hooded eyes like she can't take anymore or she's going to explode.

"Should I let you take over control again?" I ask.

She glares at me. "If you stop, I swear to God I will break your dick."

I laugh and her pace accelerates, sweat dripping down her body. All I want is to lick the salty sweat off her body. Her hands whip forward onto my hand manipulating her clit and she bolts forward, her orgasm hitting her. She shudders with small aftershocks until she opens her eyes and stares at me. With just-fucked hair and a face slack with satisfaction, she's fucking perfect.

"Now roll over and get on all fours. It's time for me to take control."

She manages to climb off my lap and props her ass up in the air. Without waiting, I grind into her, grabbing her hips and thrusting in and out. There's no better view than her ass in front of me, her pussy taking my dick again and again.

I run my hand over her ass. What I wouldn't do to make it pink, but she's losing steam, her body struggling to stay upright.

The tingling in my spine starts and my balls draw up before my orgasm hits me. I drill into her two more times before I fill the condom. Her body gives out, sprawling on the bed.

I fall down next to her. "How's that energy level now?"

She opens up one eye. "I'm good."

I laugh and get up to take off the condom. When I return, she's in the same spot.

I push the covers open. "Time for you to get some sleep."

"I don't need sleep. I'm ready to go again." She reaches between my legs for my dick that lies limp along my thigh.

"Somehow I doubt that." I kiss her temple. "Get some sleep."

Eventually her breathing evens out and she falls asleep, while I lie awake dissecting everything we just did, the chance we took. All I can think of is Annabelle and how much my actions affect her now. I can no longer act on temptation without thinking it through, even though I just did.

I'll give Lena one thing. She doesn't need a lot of sleep. I was about to fall asleep when she woke and stuck her ass in my direction. What was I supposed to do except take her from behind, raising her leg and pushing into her while I play with her tits? It's my favorite position and I think she's as big a fan as me now.

But that left us lying in bed with the television on but no sound.

"How did you know about the Sandersvilles?" I ask her.

She shrugs. "I did some research. Found out how they got to where they are."

"I know, but why? All you had to do was show up on my arm and convince them you loved me."

She laughs and shakes her head. "It's my job. I'm still the Jacobs family PR rep."

I take her hand, staring at the engagement ring. "Do you really not like it?"

"Like it?" She sits up and I find it hard to concentrate with her tits hanging out. "I love it."

She holds up her left hand and I think about what it means if this isn't just a "get it out of our systems" thing. I mean, we're supposed to marry and here we are sleeping together. I'd love for her to stare at that ring like I gave it to her out of love, but I didn't. What do we do—get married and divorced, only for me to ask her to marry me again at some point when the timing is right?

She nudges me out of my mindfuck. "What are you thinking about?"

I slide up to rest my back along the headboard. "Where do we go from here?"

She sits back on her ankles, looking deflated. "What do you mean?"

I take her hand again, moving the ring back and forth on her finger. It fits her so well, as if it was meant for her— which makes sense, because I was thinking about her when I bought it. I would've gotten her a bigger ring if I thought she'd let me, but I knew she isn't the type who would want to show off a huge diamond. "We're going to get fake married and we're embarking on a real relationship."

She straightens her legs out, sitting cross-legged and giving me a view of her pussy. All the blood rushes to my dick, when I really need my mind working on this one.

"Are we embarking on a relationship?" she asks softly.

I think, not wanting to say something I'd have to take back at some point, but I've spent the entire night with her and I don't want it to end. I find myself excited to see her after games, or when I pull into the garage and the Bronco is there, my stomach stirs knowing she's inside. Late at night, I wonder what she does in her room and hope that our paths collide at some point. All of this means something. One thing I know for sure is I don't want it to end. "I think so. You?"

She stares at her hands, twisting them for way too long. Her back straightens and her demeanor changes. "I don't know."

She slides off the bed and heads to the bathroom.

I look around the room as if someone will fill me in on what just happened. Getting out of bed myself, I stalk after her and rest my shoulder along the doorframe of the bathroom, watching her stare at herself in the mirror. "What am I missing?"

She slowly turns.

"Wait!" I hold up my hand, grabbing one of the complimentary robes and tossing it to her. "I can't concentrate while you're naked."

She puts it on and I feel slightly offended she can concentrate with my dick hanging out. "I don't know what to think. I mean you're Ford Jacobs. And…"

"And what?" I ask. "I thought we were on the same page here."

"We are. I mean, it's just that I didn't expect to feel…"

Anger percolates under the surface. "Feel what? Speak, Lena!"

"Don't yell at me." She covers her face with her hands. "I have to think." She looks at me as tears fill her eyes.

All I want to do is take her in my arms, but she's having doubts and I'm really pissed off about it. "What does the fact I'm Ford Jacobs have to do with us giving this a shot?"

She holds out her arms, her hands insinuating like I should know. "Because you're you."

"What the fuck does that mean?" She's talking in damn circles.

"You're not monogamous. You don't do candlelight

dinners or Netflix and chill. You live on the edge and I don't. You have all this money and want for nothing. I scrape by. We're total opposites. And I have more to lose than you do if we screw this up for your dad." She walks past me in the doorway.

"What are you really afraid of?" I ask.

She freezes with her back to me. I watch for an excruciating minute as she breathes heavily but doesn't face me.

"That I'm not good enough," she whispers. "That you'll want more."

Then she buries her head in her hands and cries.

I stand, unable to move my feet, not sure what the hell I should do. We just slept together and already there's fucking drama.

CHAPTER 23

Lena

I can't believe I admitted that to him, as though I want him to convince me I'm worthy. And maybe a part of me does. The feelings that have surfaced for Ford are all-consuming. I'm one hundred percent invested, but how can a man really change so quickly?

I hear him step forward, but I raise my hand. "I'm sorry. I'm sure you're like 'what the fuck?' I'm not being fair to you."

"I'm so fucking confused right now." There's some residual anger in his tone. Probably because he put himself out there and said he wanted this to go somewhere.

I turn, and god, he's so beautiful. Even now, when he looks pissed off, I want to run to him and wrap my arms around him. "I told you about my dad, right?"

He nods.

I go over to the bed and blow out a long breath before I plop myself down on the edge. "He'd always clean up his act for a while after something major happened, like he got picked up by the police for sleeping on the street, or the shelter caught him with alcohol. Or if I got on him about needing money and he needed to sober up and show up for work. For a few short months, he'd try. I have no idea if he was just hiding it or actually stopped drinking, but he'd secure a job and I'd think, *This is it. We're going to be okay.* Then I'd come home to whatever dump we were living in and he'd be passed out. It was a cruel cycle of hope and disappointment. He always promised he'd change, but it never lasted."

He sits down next to me. "So you think that's me?"

I bite my lip and look at him. "I think you had a daughter and it changed you. I think you want the new you to be you, but I don't know if it actually is you now. It's all happened so fast. I fear that one day it's all going to be too much. Becoming a parent when you weren't planning to is enough on its own, but add on the fact that now you're a single parent, and then think about if you added on your first ever real girlfriend… don't you worry that's a lot of change all at once to deal with?"

He seems to think for a moment. "I've been going through the motions. I'm not really thinking about all of it being new. All I know is I'm enjoying it." He bends forward, leaning his forearms on his thighs. "But I see your point."

As stupid as it is, since I raised the point, the fact that he understands crushes me. But I'd rather be crushed now than six months from now. "You do?"

He nods. "There's been a lot of change in my life."

I can't be upset that he's agreeing with me. I can't, but I am. "I know."

He turns his head in my direction. "How would we even manage this then? I mean, I really like you."

I smile. "I really like you too, but… *ugh!* Why do I have to be so sensible?"

"Yes, please tell me why. We could be fucking on this bed again right now." He stands, and the fact he's putting on his boxer briefs makes my breath falter.

"So you agree? We shouldn't pursue anything?" I ask.

He runs his hand through his hair. "I don't agree, but I understand. If it were up to me, I'd be fucking you five times a day every day, but I get your hesitation. I understand your worry. I know what kind of guy I am."

Since he's only thinking about fucking me, I'd say we're probably making the right decision. He's not saying he wants to get to know me better and spend more time with me. Wake up to me every day and fall asleep next to me every night. A relationship can't survive on lust alone.

"So where do we go from here?" I ask.

He moves to the couch area of the suite. "I'm going to get dressed and go back to my parents' penthouse. You're going to stay here and enjoy the suite. I'll swing by with Annabelle on the way to the airport to pick you up. We'll go to Florida, where we'll coexist until the arrangement is over."

In just this short time, he has it all figured out. "Can we coexist?"

He shrugs on his tuxedo slacks and buttons them. I commit every moment of him dressing to memory because he's rocking the just fucked half-dressed look and I won't be seeing it again.

"We can try. Who knows? Maybe you'll be the first girl I become friends with after I fucked her." He glances at me, and there's no heartbreak in his eyes. Maybe he truly is okay with this, whereas my heart is cracking.

"Friends would be nice."

"Sure." He pulls on his shirt and buttons it.

My body begs my brain to run to him and stop him from leaving. To take him to bed with me, forget all my doubts. For him to convince me he's different and has changed and there'll be no going back to the womanizing Ford who couldn't ever stay grounded.

He walks back to me and puts his finger on my chin, urging me to look at him. "One more."

He places his lips on mine softly. No tongue, just a press of his mouth to mine. Drawing back, he winks, turns around, swipes my thong off the floor, and shoves it in his pocket before walking out the door.

After it shuts, I sink to the floor and allow myself to cry for what I almost had but lost.

The next morning, a bellhop brings me my suitcase from the Jacobs' penthouse, allowing me to get dressed.

Ford texts me when he arrives and I tell him I'll meet him downstairs so he doesn't have to haul Annabelle out of the vehicle. I have no idea what his family must think. Us staying at a hotel was probably a sign that things were progressing with us. With him showing up in the middle of the night, it's clear we're back to the land of pretend.

I take the elevator down to the first floor, and the bellhop places my bag in the SUV Ford ordered to take us to the airport. Annabelle is in her carrier, smiling at me.

I tickle her belly and her smile only grows. "Good morning, sweet Annabelle."

"I think Morgan spiked her bottle. She's been this happy all morning." Ford glances up from his phone. He has dark bags under his eyes and doesn't look like he slept the entire night.

"If Annabelle's happy, everyone's happy," I say.

He chuckles lightly before burying his head in his phone again.

We ride to the airport in uncomfortable silence as I try

to interact with Annabelle, but a five-and-a-half-month-old can only do so much to break the ice.

Ford is the perfect gentleman, as he always is with me. Opening doors and directing me through the people until we're boarding the Jacobs' private jet.

The plane ride is more silence, him busy on his phone except for a brief twenty minutes when he fell asleep. I'm embarrassed to admit I watched him the entire time he slept. The way his mouth slowly parted, and his chest expanded when he inhaled. I memorized his chiseled jaw and sharp nose. The way his hair is always perfectly tousled. His broad shoulders straining his T-shirt and strong thighs are prominently on display through his worn jeans.

I can't believe I told him no. I should've lived it up for the moment and when he changed his mind, just moved on. But no, stupid me has to think years down the line. Sometimes I hate my fear of history repeating itself.

At least the sun is out when we land, and it brightens up the dark cloud over us.

We drive to Ford's house, and since Annabelle slept on the plane, she's awake.

"I can take care of her. You look like you need to sleep," I tell Ford, knowing he has a game tomorrow night.

"I'm good. You go." He nods upstairs, so I take my suitcase to my room and shut the door.

Collapsing on the bed, I stare at the ceiling and wonder if I'm one of those people who can't be happy. I had a great guy who did everything perfectly, and I ruined it because I'm afraid. Then again, he agreed with me, so he must not have been certain about his feelings for me.

After an hour of lying there doing nothing, I can't stand staying in this room any longer. Besides, I figure if we keep the friendliness going, we'll make it to the finish line a lot happier. So I head downstairs and find Annabelle asleep in Ford's arms. He's out cold.

I tiptoe over and pick up Annabelle. She transports well, so I take her upstairs to her crib and place her in it, then turn on the monitor. I go downstairs as quietly as I can and take the monitor with me to the beach.

Five minutes later, a deep voice announces his presence behind me. "Soaking up the rays?"

I glance up from the lawn chair I'm in. "The sunshine makes the day feel a little brighter."

"Glad it does for one of us." He picks up the monitor and heads back to the patio door. "Thanks for putting her down."

He's cordial, polite but cold. Clearly doesn't want me around his daughter anymore.

I sit out here for another hour because it's a lot warmer outside now than it is inside. Maybe that friendship thing is off the table.

CHAPTER 24

"Don't just admit defeat."

Ford

It's the last game before our short Christmas break.

"Congratulations," Tweetie says and puts his hand on my shoulder. "You fucking did it."

"Did what?" I ask, looking up from lacing my skates.

"You went two months without getting laid. I'm proud of you."

How did I forget that ridiculous bet? "Nah, I lost."

All movement in the locker room stops and everyone's eyes are on me.

"What?" Tweetie's mouth is hanging open.

"Yeah, couldn't do it." I did the math on the way home from New York after Lena. I knew I was shy of the deal, but I didn't care. I wanted her too badly, and if that meant I lost bragging rights, I didn't give a shit. Knowing what I know now, I should've kept my cock inside my pants. Now I just know what I'm missing and can't have again.

Tweetie laughs while Aiden and Maksim stare at me, questions on both of their faces.

"Damn, I wish I would have bet you, like, your fucking Bronco or house or some shit." Tweetie goes back to his locker and puts on his pads.

"Lena?" Aiden asks quietly.

Lucky for me, the locker room fills with music and voices again. I nod.

"And?"

"And she told me afterward that it was a mistake."

He slides over on the bench closer to me. "Mistake?"

"She worries a leopard doesn't change his spots. That in the long run, I'll find an excuse to leave her high and dry after she's got feelings for me. Pretty much thinks I'm in a funk in my life but one day that prick she used to hate will show back up and want to fuck other women." I hate the bitterness in my tone, but as the days go on, the more pissed I become with her assessment of me.

"And what did you say?"

"I told her she was right, and maybe we could be friends." At the time I meant it, since we have to be together for this pretend marriage thing, but I'm finding it really hard to be around her now.

"Why?" Maksim asks. "Why would you agree with her?"

I shrug. "You can't change someone's opinion once they've made up their mind about you. She thinks I'm a douche and nothing in the last two months has changed that, so nothing ever will."

"Are you going to marry her?" Aiden asks, looking at Maksim as if he can answer the question.

"I have to. But then we'll get divorced. It's fine." I stand. "It would never work out anyway." I head out to the hallway to wait for game time.

"Why would it not work out?" Aiden's right behind me.

No doubt Maksim went to take his superstition piss after he's geared up.

"Because she's right. I'm Ford Jacobs. I mean, come on. She's supposed to trust me after only two months?

She's got a point, and I care about her too much to hurt her."

He stands next to me. "So basically you agreed with her and now you two are living together and pretending you haven't had sex?"

I nod.

"Was the sex bad?" he asks.

I shake my head. "The best I've ever had."

I'm not going to go into detail with Aiden, but fuck, Lena gave me her body as though she trusted me with it. And I loved that she likes to joke when we're messing around. The best part was how insatiable she is. Damn, I'm going to miss all of that. One night wasn't nearly enough.

He puts his hand on my forehead. "Are you feeling okay?"

I pull away. "I'm fine."

"You gave up?" Maksim asks when he joins us.

"I didn't give up. She made her case and I can't argue it. I mean, I was a douche who couldn't commit to any woman before Annabelle was born. Lena has a right to question my intentions."

Aiden puts his finger on the bridge of his nose. "What the hell happened to the Ford Jacobs I know?"

"What does that mean?" I ask, narrowing my eyes at him.

"You just laid down like roadkill. Fight, motherfucker. If you like her and you think she's wrong, fight."

I put my hand on Aiden's shoulder. "That's the thing, I don't think she's wrong."

He and Maksim stare at one another as the rest of the team gets hyped to go out on the ice.

"I can't believe you're gonna give up," Maksim says.

"Give up what?" I shrug. "We never even were."

Both of them glance at one another, sharing a look of confusion.

"You're fucking with us, right?" Aiden asks.

The rest of the team heads to the ice, the three of us bringing up the rear.

I'm surprised when I spot Lena in the stands—without Annabelle this time. She doesn't meet my gaze, although from the way she's purposely dodging it, I'd say she feels my eyes on her. A boulder sinks deep into the pit of my stomach. I remember she was smiling and waving at me the last time she was here.

Aiden skates up to the line, ready to take some warm-up shots. "Ford, you can't just let it go. You've talked us off a lot of ledges, but you can't roll over and pretend it didn't happen."

"Nothing is gonna change. Sometimes a man just is who he is and can't change no matter how hard he tries."

We run our warm-up drills, leaving the conversation there. What do they want me to say? That I felt something different for Lena? So what if I did? It doesn't mean anything other than maybe I'm human. But eventually I probably would've gotten bored with her, so she's smart to have pointed it out.

---

*A*fter the game, I come out of the shower, looking at the fresh bruise on my arm. "Fuck, Maksim," I say, because it was his doing.

"I had hopes that it would knock some sense into you."

"I'm your teammate. Did you go color blind?" I strip off my towel and shove on a pair of boxer briefs.

"FYI, the ladies are going to your house to relieve the

babysitter and you're coming out with us." Aiden holds up his phone.

"I'm going home," I say, continuing to put on my suit.

"The deal's done, man. Consider this your sentence." Tweetie comes over, trying to put me in a headlock.

I maneuver out of it. "Why? You all have women to go home to."

"And you do too," Tweetie says.

"It's all a sham. For my dad," I confess and Tweetie stops drying himself off.

"No?" He looks at Aiden and Maksim.

They both nod.

"But we're pretty sure Richie Rich here found his heart." Aiden pats me where my heart would be and goes to his own locker to get dressed.

"Fuck off," I shout after him.

"I can't believe you fuckers left me out of the gossip. There can be four musketeers, you know that, right? We can be original like that."

I laugh at Tweetie's attempt to get in our circle. And he is in our circle, but he travels during the off-season when we're all hanging around here. He's my roommate on the road, so I consider him a great friend. We just haven't hung out as much as we used to since he's been in a relationship.

Tweetie pulls out his phone,—texting Tedi, no doubt. A minute later his phone dings and he looks upset and confused. "She already knew the plan. Said to make sure I have enough dollar bills?"

Aiden and Maksim laugh. "There's only one way for you to find out what you're made of."

Ugh. I know exactly what they're thinking. "I'm not going."

"You sure as shit are, so put on your makeup, sweetheart, you're getting a lap dance."

Thirty minutes later, we're filing out of Aiden's SUV into one of Florida's well-known higher-end strip clubs. I used to frequent this place when I was much younger. A lot of the guys still head here sometimes.

After we enter, I find out there's a reserved table right by the stage for us. Maksim shoves me in the chair on the outside and they all fill in around the table. He raises his hand and a pretty redhead comes over, asking if we want any drinks. Her tits are barely held up by a skimpy bra and her skirt is so short I'd see her ass if she wasn't wearing panties.

I order a whiskey, Maksim a vodka, and beers for both Aiden and Tweetie.

Aiden holds up a bill. I can't see how much, but he waves it and two girls come over, rubbing themselves on him.

"Oh no, that's our bachelor." He points the bill to me. "Give him everything you got."

I'm not gonna lie, there were days that I fucking loved strip places. And sure, I've taken a few women home from them. But right now, in the mood I'm in, I don't want anything to do with a lap dance.

Still, the music is going and she's grinding her hips in front of me.

"Are you hard yet?" Maksim asks.

I glare at him. "No, asshole."

"Because you're thinking of Lena," he says.

I don't respond.

"You're being a wimp," Aiden says.

"Nice word choice," I sneer as the two blondes kiss in front of me.

"Are you imagining one of them being Lena?" Maksim asks.

"Can we please stop talking about Lena?" I yell over the music.

One girl swings her leg over me, pushing her tits right in front of my face.

"No, because you need to believe you've changed before you try to convince her of it. We could sit you down, but you need to be shown with action, not words. Like a child." Maksim continues to insult me.

"No one needs to convince me of anything." I raise my hand, inches away from grabbing what's in front of me just to prove him wrong.

"Stop it, Ford, you're gonna throw away everything in your life," Aiden says.

"What?" My gaze moves to him and he legit looks pissed off.

"You know you like her. I saw the way you looked at her. The way you respected her. The way she won you over. And now she's scared, which"—he holds up his hand—"I would be too. Let me ask you a question, when she voiced her concerns, what was your first reaction?"

Rather than grabbing the woman straddled around me, I finish my whiskey and hold my hand up for the redhead to bring me another one. "I said fine and went back to my parents."

But that's a lie. My initial reaction was the squeezing of my chest and disappointment.

Aiden shakes his head.

"Listen." I turn away from the woman grinding on me. She's not even mildly titillating, and if I didn't think it would give credence to everything my friends are saying, I'd tell her to get off. "I'm not the noble guy like you, okay? I like to have fun. And I've fucked up enough already in my life. Hell, my daughter doesn't even have a mother. If Lena doesn't believe in me, then she's not fucking worth it."

The table goes silent for a moment. I grin, proud of myself and the point I made. It shut them up.

"Did you ever prove to her that you had?" Aiden asks. "The first sign of a problem and you shut down and ran."

Fuck Aiden. I fucking hate Aiden. Even if he is one of my best friends. I think about that night and the moment she ran out of bed and into the bathroom—my heart locked up tight and I turned stone cold to any emotion. Sure, I have feelings for Lena, I told her as much, but she's doubting me just like my dad always has.

"Words are words, man, actions are actions," Aiden says. "We could all sit here and be like we're gonna win the Cup this year and I'm gonna be lead scorer, but no one is gonna believe it unless we're training every fucking day and showing up out there on the ice. You want her to have faith, but let's remember, she's the one who got you out of most of the jams you put yourself in. She saw you with the women, saw your anger on all the videos from your brawls. She's already had to deal firsthand with the person you were."

I sulk back in my chair, feeling as though Aiden fucking scolded me like my father. Except he has a point.

"You've never had to fight for one damn thing except to play hockey," Maksim says. "And look, you're here. You did it. You proved your dad wrong."

I sip the new whiskey the redhead placed on the table and motion for the blonde to get up off of me.

"If you want Lena and a future, prove her wrong. Don't just admit defeat. Fight for her," Aiden says. "Show her you've changed with actions, not words."

Tweetie brushes his finger under his eyes as if tears

were shed. "Man, you guys are awesome. I'm inserting myself as the fourth whether you agree or not. Now, can I be next?" He raises his hand.

"Next for what?" I ask.

"Next to be told what the hell is wrong with me. Why am I afraid to propose to Tedi?"

We all crack up, but my friends' words have gotten me thinking. I proved my dad wrong once. Now I have to prove Lena wrong.

CHAPTER 25

"The truth."

Lena

’ve always dreaded Christmas. As soon as the songs hit the department stores after Halloween, my gut twists. The bells ringing, the families walking hand in hand downtown, people with arms overflowing with packages. It's great if you have family and money and security. Not so much when you're at a soup kitchen getting a coloring book and crayons. Once you're ten, that's about enough of that. You've figured out your lot in life.

On years my dad was sober, he'd always get me something. A shirt or sweater maybe. Always secondhand and usually not my taste, but it was fine. That's what I told him. And it was. The fact he spent any money on me made me feel guilty.

Now, I'm at the Jacobs' because we're one big happy family and stupid me planned the photo shoot before everything went down with Ford and me.

Their penthouse is overflowing with red and green. Gold and silver. Two trees. One in the family room and another on the terrace. I stare at the one in the family room in all its perfection. There are no family ornaments that have been handed down over the years. Mrs. Jacobs clearly had a design in mind with matching ornaments of a specific color scheme. It's beautiful, but I've always loved the trees filled with homemade ornaments that I saw in the movies. Probably because I never dreamed that anyone decorated trees like the department stores until I first came here.

"What happened to all the ornaments you made in school?" I ask Ford.

He's relaxed on the couch, dressed in the ivory cable-knit sweater I picked out and a pair of slacks. I'm in a simple green dress, and we put Annabelle in a red dress. The photographs will be taken here in the Jacobs' home.

"I don't know. Probably in the garbage." He sips his drink.

He's been odd this trip. Not too talkative, but not as cold as he was before.

"I guess both of ours are together somewhere." Mine would hang on the fridge or on the window until I eventually tore it down and threw it away myself. Or it got left behind when we got kicked out because my dad hadn't paid the rent.

"When is this guy coming and please tell me it's not that Gavin jackass again?" He tugs his collar. "I can't believe you convinced me to wear this."

"It is Gavin, and he's a friend who lets me spin things. And please, you've worn worse." I pick up the apple cider Bennie made. The man might love Hawaii, but he prepares the best cider and hot chocolate.

"You do know he likes you?"

I sit in the chair across from him as Morgan comes in with Annabelle. Her smiles are addictive nowadays. For a little girl growing up with two adults at odds, she's darn happy about it.

"She's getting mean with the hair pulling," Morgan says and hands her off to Ford.

"That's my girl." He gives Annabelle a high five,

although he has to actually lift her hand to do it. Still learning.

"I swear she got a chunk." Morgan scowls. "And she does not like the dress. Keeps pulling at it, just like her dad."

"The other day, one of my strands was wrapped around her finger and turning it purple. I check her every time I put her down for naps now."

Ford turns to me. "You didn't tell me that." He sounds offended.

"We're not usually together. And your hair is too short to wrap around her finger so…"

Morgan looks at us for a moment and I realize my misstep. "What do you mean you're not together? Like, physically you don't see one another?"

I look at Ford for him to answer. This is his family.

"Lena's giving me the cold shoulder," Ford says only to Annabelle.

I scoff. "Try the other way around."

"What do you expect?" Ford asks. "You made your point."

I head into the kitchen, not in the mood for his dramatics. But I'm only four footsteps away before two hands land on my hips and usher me out onto the side terrace. He shuts the door behind us.

I wheel around. "It's freezing."

"Your next job could be as a weather girl."

I narrow my eyes, wishing I could transport him to another planet. "Seriously, what is your problem? I thought we were on the same page."

"Well, we're not."

"What?" I wrap my arms around myself to warm up.

"We're not, okay?" He walks toward me, running a hand

through his hair. "I think you underestimate me, and it pisses me off. My father did it my entire life and the fact that the woman I… like is doing it now… it makes me mad, but…"

My heart lurches, wanting to jump out of my chest and rest in his hands. I wish I could trust what he's telling me. "But?"

"But I get it. I get you've seen me at my worst and to take me at my word wouldn't be wise." He puts his hands on my shoulders, stepping forward before dropping them. Then he pushes my chin up to look at him. "But I'm going to fight for you. I'm going to show you that I am a man worthy of you."

My breath catches in my throat. "Ford…"

"No, Lena. You're who I want."

"I want you too. It's not that I don't. At the same time, I'm so scared."

"Exactly. I'm going to prove to you that you don't have to be scared."

I shake my head. "You don't have to do that. I'm sure you'll find some other woman who won't have so many issues."

He laughs and bends forward. "Get ready, Lena Boyd, because I'm about to woo you."

Then he presses his lips to mine. I want to wrap my arms around his neck. Plaster my body to his and beg him to take me to his room. Or hell, take me right here on this snowy terrace. But he backs up.

"Don't start coming on to me." He smiles. "Trying to seduce me."

I open my mouth, but there's a knock. I glance over Ford's shoulders and see Gavin and Morgan, Annabelle in her arms, standing at the glass door.

"Showtime," I murmur.

"For you maybe. It's easy for me to show how much I want you."

We walk toward the door and he reaches around me to open it.

"Gavin, I'm so sorry. We were just discussing—" I start.

"You were kissing, and please tell me you don't have rules to not kiss in front of Annabelle. That's lame," Gavin says.

I laugh. "No, not at all. We just needed a moment."

Gavin doesn't smile as his eyes linger on our joined hands. Seriously, if this is about his crush again, he needs to stop.

"So I was thinking by the tree or the fireplace. Maybe one of us on the floor playing with Annabelle? I brought her a new toy. Maybe Morgan could bring it out and Annabelle's beautiful blue eyes will light up." I turn to Gavin to see what he thinks.

"Man, you think of everything," Morgan says.

"I'm back!" Imogen yells from the foyer. "Where's my niece?"

She rounds the corner, still taking off her gloves and coat before tossing them on the back of the couch. Then she snatches Annabelle out of Morgan's hold. Annabelle starts crying.

Morgan laughs. "She doesn't like you."

"She does. I'm her aunt."

"That doesn't mean she has to like you."

Morgan and Imogen continue to bicker, so Ford pulls Annabelle away, holding her so she stops crying. But she grabs at her shoes, crying some more.

"You're going to mess with the pictures, you two, and I want this goddamn Connecticut-style ivory cable knit sweater off before my skin catches fire." He tugs again on the collar.

"It's not a straitjacket," I mumble.

"Might as well be. This isn't me." Ford scratches his stomach, lifting the sweater up. Sure enough, his stomach is completely red.

I gasp. "Ford!" I lift it back up. "You're completely red and angry."

"Isn't he always red and angry?" Imogen says dryly.

"His skin. Look."

Gavin is busy setting up the lights and preparing for the photo shoot. Besides being a freelance journalist, he's also a great photographer, so he agreed to take these pictures himself to keep things low-key and so fewer people traipse through the Jacobs' home.

"You need to go change." I take Annabelle from Ford, holding her to my hip. "Just put on something nice."

"No, it's fine. I can wear it." He scratches again.

"Are you allergic to something?"

"Not that I know of. Let's just take the damn pictures." He looks at Gavin. "Where do you want us?"

"By the tree is good, but—"

"Just snap a few. She's happy right now. We don't have all day," Ford demands, coming off arrogant and better than.

We go over and stand by the tree.

"Oh, what a beautiful family," Morgan coos, but I think she's making fun of us.

"You look like one of those families from Connecticut. The straitlaced, no-fun couples." Imogen laughs.

I turn to Ford mid-snap.

"Try to face the camera, Lena," Gavin says.

Ford turns to me. "What?"

I look at Gavin and back at Ford. "This isn't us. Let's change. We don't have to be perfect. We're not perfect and I don't want us to be perfect." I set Annabelle down and unbutton her dress from the back. "Morgan, can you change her into Ford's jersey he had made for her? She loves wearing that like she knows it's his number. And just those leggings and socks. No shoes." I look at Gavin. "Sorry, we'll be back."

"Lena, it's fine. I'll wear it and so will Annabelle." Ford chases after me as I head for the staircase to go up to my room.

"No. It's not us. I think I was trying to make us who I thought the world should see, but that's not us." I take the hem of his sweater and pull it up and over his body. "Oh, Ford. Why didn't you say anything?"

"A little pain for you to get what you want isn't a big deal."

My shoulders fall and I stare at him long and hard. "Thank you. But go change into something comfortable."

We all reconvene ten minutes later. I change into jeans and a fitted red sweater. This is how we would hang around the house.

"It would be so cute if you were all wearing Ford's jersey," Imogen says.

"Oh yeah, I don't have one," I say.

Ford enters the room in a button-down with the sleeves rolled up and the top two buttons undone. His hair isn't as gelled as before and he's barefoot, wearing a pair of jeans.

"You never bought your fiancée your jersey?" Imogen smacks Ford on the back of the head as he passes her.

"You want one?" He looks at me as if surprised that I would.

While all the wives wear their husbands' numbers at the game, I felt foolish buying one myself at the gift shop. "No. I'm fine."

"I can get you one."

"Can we take the pictures now?" Gavin interrupts.

"Sorry. Yes," I say.

We pose at the bottom of the tree. I purposely keep my ring front and center. Then we take pictures where we're playing with Annabelle, and others of Ford and me staring at one another. Those are the hardest. By the end, I actually felt as though we're a little family.

While Gavin packs up, Ford takes Annabelle into the kitchen with Morgan and Imogen, Bennie demanding Annabelle be the first to taste his new applesauce recipe.

"Thanks so much for doing this," I say.

Gavin organizes all his equipment and the doorman comes up to fetch it and bring it down for him. I chat with Gavin for a bit while all this is happening and then walk him out.

"There are rumors," he says. "I think you should know."

"What do you mean?" My forehead creases.

"Rumors that this is all fake. That Ford is using you. That maybe you're part of it too. There's word that Otis Sandersville might have some interest in Jacobs Enterprises and this is all very convenient."

I haven't heard any rumors—at least nothing has come up from my searches and Google alerts—but I guess when *you're* the story, no one tells you. "They're wrong. We're very happy." I hold up my left hand and smile.

His eyebrows scrunch. "You've been seen without that ring more than you have with it."

"I don't know what to tell you. We're a couple and we're very happy." I feel sweat form on my temples.

He nods and rocks back on his heels. "Then answer me this... why haven't you two been seen together since the party where you were introduced to Otis Sandersville and his wife, Penny?"

Ugh. It's only a matter of time before these rumors

make it from Manhattan's upper crust into the press. "I've been to his games, and besides that, we've just been busy. I am planning a wedding after all." Note to self, make some wedding plans publicly.

He puts his hand on my arm. "If you ever want to talk—coffee, dinner, whatever—I'm here for you."

"That's real big of you, Gavin." Ford enters the room and makes his presence known. He stalks over and kisses my cheek. "Baby, Annabelle wants you."

"I should go. Thank you again, Gavin." I hug him briefly, feeling uncomfortable now. I walk to the edge of the foyer and hide just around the corner so I can still hear them.

"Let me call the elevator for you," Ford says.

"Thank you again for the opportunity to have the exclusive," Gavin says.

"You're welcome. A friend of Lena's is a friend of mine until they sneak around trying to dig up shit that isn't true. I'm head over heels in love with Lena Boyd, and if you want to print that go ahead. Otherwise, I suggest you don't go throwing accusations around. I know you're desperate to be in my fiancée's panties, but sorry, they're all mine."

I gasp and cover my mouth. The elevator arrives, and I wait to hear the doors close and Ford's steps walking back my way before I step out in front of him.

"What did you say?" I ask, although I already know.

"The truth." He sidesteps me and walks back to the kitchen.

Head over heels in love with me? Nice line, Ford.

Chapter 26

"I've kept many secrets in my life, believe me. Yours is
safe with me."

Lena

I'm still thinking about Ford's words to Gavin and him saying he's going to woo me when I arrive at the facility my father lives in. No one knows me here, mostly because I don't come very often. Which is horrible, I know. But every time I come, Dad and I sit in silence while he stares out the window of the community room they wheel him out to. Or I end up talking to other visitors more than Dad. Then again, maybe I'm still bitter about the fact that he didn't much care for my well-being growing up and now I'm responsible to care for his.

I sign in and show my ID to the staff member before heading down the hall. I still remember the way to his room, and I stop just before I reach it, gripping the small plant in my hands.

Then I smack on a smile and round the corner, knocking on his door. "Dad?"

He's lying in bed with his helmet on. His head turns in my direction, and if I didn't know better, I'd think he recognized me. For a fleeting second, I saw his lips tip before they didn't. Then again, right after the accident, I saw a lot of things the doctors said weren't there. They said it was in my head because I hoped so desperately that he'd get better.

I sit on a chair close to the bed. "Merry Christmas." I put the plant on the window ledge that overlooks the garden where other families visit their loved ones during the warmer months.

"Knock, knock. I heard Gregg had a guest." A male nurse with olive skin and dark hair comes in wearing scrubs with little Santas all over them. "Looks like Santa delivered your gift." He takes a cloth and wipes my dad's mouth. "If I'd known, I would've gotten you all dressed up and ready."

Is there judgment in his tone?

"I'm sorry. I moved out of state recently." I feel like an idiot for voicing my lame excuse.

He smiles at me. "I know."

"You know?" My forehead wrinkles.

The nurse checks Dad's vitals and situates my dad just so. Dad doesn't fight him, nor does he acknowledge we're in the room.

"I do read magazines. Congratulations." Then he turns to my dad. "I told Gregg about it and shared some pictures with him." He nods at the nightstand where there's the *People* magazine with our Christmas pictures in it that came out a few days ago.

"Oh." Guilt weighs heavy in my stomach.

"Relax. You look all pale and like you're gonna throw up. And I clean up enough messes a day. I don't need to clean up after healthy people too."

"You probably think I'm a horrible daughter," I blurt.

"I think you have a life, and I think it's hard to see a loved one in this state. Then you come here and you're left feeling unfulfilled because he doesn't interact with you."

"He was an alcoholic." I want to take back the words as soon as they leave my mouth. This man doesn't care about my issues.

The nurse stops fussing with my dad and sits in the chair next to me. He holds out his hand for mine and I place it in his.

"Listen. I'm not judging you. I'm sorry, I get a little protective of my patients. I've only been with your dad for about nine months. But I do understand that things happen in people's lives. Things people can do to others that cause them pain. And just because his brain no longer functions like it did once doesn't mean those things are any less painful for you or that you have to forgive him. In fact, it probably makes it harder because now you know you can't get what you need from him—his acknowledgment of whatever he put you through and his apology for doing so."

"How much do you know?"

"We have case files, Lena. You're his only living relative. Your mom died young and… I don't need all the specifics. I can put two and two together. Most relatives either come daily or not at all. Rarely do I see the in-between." He pats my hand. "But talk to him and have a nice visit. I know you think he doesn't remember, doesn't know who you are, but do any of us really know for certain?"

He stands and pats my dad's leg. "Now be nice, Gregg, so that maybe she'll come back again." He stops just shy of the door. "I'm Bruno, if you need me."

"Thank you, Bruno."

After he leaves, the room is silent and I glance at the magazine. Sliding my chair over closer, I lean in and whisper, "It's fake. The engagement. I'm getting married but only for a short time, then I'll be getting a divorce."

There's no emotion on his face and his eyes continue to stare at the television.

"But it's complicated. Twisted really, because I fell for

him. I fell for a man who breaks hearts and carries on his way. He says I'm different, but why would I be so special to be the one to lock down a man like him? Why me?"

Still nothing.

I sit in the chair, staring at a man I don't really know anymore. Picking up the magazine, I scroll through the pictures.

"We sure sell the happily ever after," I say, running my hand down the page with Ford, Annabelle, and me. Shutting the magazine, not wanting to torment myself any longer, I toss it on the table.

Everything from my childhood swirls around in my head. All the shit Dad put me through, and here I am taking time out of my day to make sure he has a visitor. He didn't care when he left me in that car parked in the back of a factory lot. He didn't care when I wouldn't hear from him for an entire week. When I had to make excuses to the landlord about the rent, had to find a way of feeding myself. Where was he for me then?

"I always thought I had good confidence. Especially given my childhood. Hell, I've fought for every damn thing I've accomplished. I'm an incredible woman and I know that. Deep down, I know. So why am I doubting that I can be enough for him to remain this new version of himself?"

"Oh, Bruno said Gregg had a visitor?" A man walks in dressed in jeans and a Christmas sweater that could win first place in an ugly Christmas sweater contest.

"Hi," I say tentatively.

"You probably don't remember me. I'm Ivan." He stops by my dad. "What's up, Gregg?" He sits in the chair next to me. "Looks like you were in a confessional or something."

"Should I know you?" I ask.

"Back when you were younger, I was your dad's sponsor… for AA."

I rock my head back, not really remembering him.

"I think we only met once. He was protective of you."

"You come and visit him?" I ask, surprised.

"Try to once a month. It's a good reminder for me, which I know sounds bad."

I shake my head. "If it stops one person from drinking and driving, then it's worth it." And I mean that wholeheartedly.

"He used to talk about you at the meetings."

"For those split seconds he was clean?" This is why I never come. All seeing my dad does is remind me how horrible my childhood was and the fact that I couldn't get him to clean up his act.

"How about we take a walk outside?" Ivan stands from his chair.

"I should get going," I say, standing and grabbing my purse.

"I think there are some things you need to know. Humor me for a few minutes."

Since I never took off my jacket, I nod, and he leads me out of my dad's room and out a side door.

The wind whips my face. "I think we could've talked in there. He doesn't know what we're saying."

He's quiet and I regret my comment. "I was the child of an alcoholic mother. And I swore to myself I'd never drink, but obviously you've guessed that I'm a recovering alcoholic, so that didn't work out so well for me. But growing up, I always wondered why she couldn't stop. I assume you've had similar thoughts?"

I shrug and stuff my hands into my pockets.

"You've done amazing things in your life. Your dad was so proud when you graduated high school and got that scholarship to college. He said he had nothing to do with it. That it was all you."

It was all me. Everything was always left up to me. All my success—me.

"He'd brag about you, but after you left for college, I think he got lonely."

"I was lonely my entire childhood," I snip, feeling defensive.

He glances my way. "The road you were on was a hard one. I'm not here to say how great of a father you had. Having a similar path to adulthood as you, I understand your bitterness. You're pissed off. Why weren't you good enough for him to stop?"

I stop walking, repeating the words over in my head. "Why wasn't I?"

"Lena, it took me decades to figure out what I'm about to tell you. And now that you're engaged, I'm hoping to spare you the heartache I caused myself."

"What are you talking about?"

He stops at the now empty fountain that has a sculpture of a koi fish at the top. In the warmer months, that fish would spray water out of its mouth. I wait for him to give me his other piece of advice.

"Your dad failed you."

I wrap my arms around myself. That's not news. "I know."

"But him failing you has no bearing on you. Do you understand what I mean?" Ivan turns toward me, his breath coming out in white puffs. "Failing you was his decision, not yours."

"I know that."

"Do you? If so, then you're a lot smarter than I was. I always felt like I wasn't good enough. Why would anyone waste their time on me? My own mother couldn't clean up her act to give me a half-decent childhood, so why would a stranger who has no obligation do right by me?" His bushy eyebrows rise. "Took me two divorces and a long stint in rehab before a therapist got that through to me. I'm a product of my mother's failure, but I was worthy. Her failure as a mother had nothing to do with me."

I go back over his words in my head.

"Not to mention the fear of being rejected."

I hold up my hand. "I get it. I know what you're saying."

He bends down, lowering his voice. I'm not sure if he's worried the concrete koi fish might hear him or what because there's no one else in this garden. "I'm sorry for eavesdropping outside Gregg's door, but when I heard what you told him, I couldn't let another one of us drown in self-doubt."

My gaze flies to his. He overheard what I told my dad.

I open my mouth, but he shakes his head. "I've kept many secrets in my life, believe me. Yours is safe with me."

I release a breath, hoping he doesn't run to the press. They'd pay a lot of money for this intel, and I barely know this man.

We walk back inside while I sort through everything Ivan said and the feelings that go along with our conversation. I didn't realize I had so many issues from my childhood until someone else I cared about wanted to be a part of my life. Here I've been blaming Ford, accusing him of being the problem, but really, it's on me. I'm the one who messed this whole thing up.

Chapter 27

"Worthy?"

Ford

I'm going to be honest, I've never "wooed" a woman before. I've never bought flowers or chocolates for someone I'm sleeping with. But then Lena doesn't strike me as the kind of person who would like the cliché and I'm sure anything cliché wouldn't change her opinion of me. I have to go outside the box, something to really show her I've changed.

I know we need to be seen in public but I don't want her to think I'm doing this for the press and I sure as shit don't want to spend my night signing autographs.

So, while Morgan once again watches Annabelle, I go into my parents' media room, setting it up for a movie night—and not the Netflix and chill kind. I've picked all the classic romance movies like *Casablanca*, *Breakfast at Tiffany's*, *Sleepless in Seattle*, and *When Harry Met Sally*. I make some popcorn and arrange every candy imaginable since I don't know what she likes. Then I arranged some blankets and pillows on the couch.

I knock on her bedroom door, hoping the element of surprise works in my favor.

"Come in," she says and disappointment floods me as I creak the door open.

In my head, she was going to be lounging on the bed in

lingerie. No such luck. She's sitting cross-legged on the four-poster bed in her usual matching pajama pants and tank top with a sweater over it.

"Hey," she says, looking up to see me. "Everything good?" She glances over her shoulder to the clock. It's later than I would usually bother her, but I didn't want my family interrupting. Since I pocketed Morgan some money, we should be good.

I break the distance, holding on to one of the poster bed rails to inspect what she's doing. She has a magazine spread out in front of her.

"It amazes me the shitty job some **PR** reps do for their clients. They could control some of the crap that ends up in here." She flips the page. "You're lucky to have me." Then she chuckles.

"I am. We are."

She raises her eyes to meet mine. "Thanks."

"Will you come with me somewhere tonight?" I ask, my patience wearing thin and wanting to get this date started.

"I'm in my pajamas. Where did you want to go?"

I love the way she doesn't give me a straight-up no, but rather an "is it worth it" question.

"You don't have to get dressed. We're not leaving the penthouse."

She tilts her head and does the whole chewing her lip thing that drives me crazy. "What is it?"

I nod to the door. "Come and find out."

"Ford," she says with a hint of unsteadiness in her tone. "What are you doing?"

I walk to the side of the bed and hold out my hand. "I already warned you, I'm wooing you."

She stares at my hand for what feels like a lifetime

before sliding her palm into mine and allowing me to help her rise off the bed. "You're really doing this?"

I stop her once she's off the bed and before she can walk away. Her sweater is slightly open and gives me a glimpse of her hardened nipples poking through the thin fabric of her tank top. Pulling my gaze so she doesn't think I only want sex from her, I focus on her eyes. "I warned you I was. Did you not believe me?"

A breath releases from her. "I do now, but I…"

I press my finger to her lips. "No Lena. I don't want to hear any of the bullshit. At least allow me to prove you wrong."

"Okay, but…" she starts.

I give her a stern look, resulting in her concerned expression turning into a smile. She nods.

"Good. We're on the same page now."

I take her hand in mine, leading her out of her room. "Wait, my phone." She turns back, but I grip her hand harder.

"You do not need your phone tonight."

"Okay," she says way more freely than I thought she would.

I walk us out of her bedroom. As quietly as I can, I guide her down the hallway so as not to wake anyone because I don't want to answer any questions or have Imogen thinking she can join us.

Heading downstairs and past my dad's office, I open the door to the theater room. A room my parents converted from a library because they were sick of hearing loud televisions blaring in the middle of the condo.

"We're watching a movie?" she asks, walking in and her hand running along the edge of the gray couch. In front of the couch, I placed a few big LoveSac bean bag chairs and blankets. The tray of candy and popcorn is behind us.

"Movie night." I hold my hand out. "Pick your seat."

"This is fun. What are we watching?" She sits down on the LoveSac for two.

It's the first time I've ever second-guessed where I should sit with a woman, but I'm in this to win it, so I sit next to her. She doesn't look upset so I take it as a good sign.

"I have a few classic romance movies ready to go."

"Oh…" Her tone doesn't have one hint of excitement.

"I thought…"

She shakes her head to stop me. "It's great."

I pick up the remote and turn back to her. "Clearly, it's not."

She smiles and nibbles her bottom lip. "I just…"

"Spit it out, Lena."

She shrugs. "I know you don't want to watch that kind of movie and I'd rather we both enjoy tonight."

"I'll enjoy just being next to you."

She chuckles. "What did you just say, Ford Jacobs? That's some swoon-worthy lingo."

I grin at her. "What can I say, you pull the romantic out of me."

She shakes her head and peeks up at me through her hooded eyelids. Damn, she's beautiful and if I don't win her over, I'm clearly a pathetic loser. "And they keep coming." I watch her for a moment, waiting for her to continue. "I appreciate the sentiment and the gesture, but let's watch *Yellowstone*."

I'm not complaining at all. Hell, lately with Annabelle and games, I've had no time to catch up on the show. "You sure?"

She wiggles her butt into the cushion and grabs the popcorn. "Definitely."

I press a few buttons on the remote to bring up *Yellowstone*, then stop for a moment. "Wait. Is this because you want to see Rip?"

Her head falls back in laughter. "He does make the show more appealing, but don't worry, you're a lot like him."

My forehead creases. "I'm nothing like Rip." The man is alpha times ten. I like to think I'm a catch, but damn, Rip is a man's man.

"Sure, you are." She leans forward, her hand on my chest and her lips millimeters from mine. "The exterior might be hard to break through but once you get inside, you see how soft and mushy you really are. Beth is his soft spot."

I inch forward and kiss her lips briefly. "And you're my soft spot."

She says nothing and I can still see doubt in her features, but there's also hope there now, too. That's a good sign. "All right, let's watch."

She turns away to face the television and snuggles under a blanket. I click the remote to start the episode. She opens the blanket and pulls it over me, positioning the popcorn between us. A man could get used to a life like this.

My stomach is crazy with butterflies when our hands brush in the popcorn and I internally tell myself to calm the fuck down. I'm not thirteen years old. I'm Ford fucking Jacobs, right wing for the Florida Fury. I've got game.

So, I slide my hand under the blanket, landing on the soft fabric of her pajama pants. I don't think it's my imagination that she opens her legs, welcoming my touch. I run my hand up a little higher and through the light of the television, I glance over to her, but her eyes are solely focused on the television.

As though someone up there is on my side, Rip and Beth start going at it on screen. My hand slides farther north on Lena's legs and she pretends to be watching the episode, not paying any attention to me. I'm starved for her touch and I want her again. This wasn't my plan, but it feels impossible to keep myself in check when she's this near. I want her all the time. Which I never thought would happen to me. To want the same woman repeatedly, never getting enough? Of course, she doesn't believe me, I barely believe it myself.

I continue my venture, a soft breath falling from her lips and this time when I look at her, her eyes are poised right in my direction. I'm sure there's an invitation there, so I don't stop until she clamps her legs shut, locking my hand between her thighs.

"We should go for a walk. Have you ever gone for a walk in Central Park?"

"Lena," I say her name with the clear indication I know what she's doing.

"What?"

"My hand is locked between your delicious thighs, and I'd bet my inheritance you want me, do you not want this to happen? You can tell me."

She shakes her head. "No, I want this, it's just…" She flings off the blanket and rolls off the LoveSac. My hand is in just as much disbelief as I am that it didn't keep her interested. "I went to see my dad and I think I'm all messed in the head. But I want this." She waves a finger between us. "I know I'm worthy."

I laugh and her eyes narrow at me. "Worthy?"

Her shoulders sink and she's giving me that same look

she did before this fake engagement. Like I'm the scum on the bottom of her shoe.

"Sorry," I say, standing, knowing that we need to move this somewhere else. Clearly, we're not at the making out while watching TV shows stage just yet. We have a lot of shit to talk about.

"Let's go for that walk." I hold out my hand and turn off *Yellowstone*.

She accepts my hand with a smile and we head out of the theater room.

I guess this is what people do when they're trying to build a relationship.

CHAPTER 28

"I'm a fucking adult, and you're my fiancée."

Lena

The minute we walk out of the Jacobs' condo building, a whoosh of wind whips us right in the face.

"You sure about this?" Ford asks, putting on a Florida Fury hat and his gloves.

The street is mostly absent of people since it's eleven o'clock, but the light snow sprinkling down from the sky makes the city look magical. I wind my arm through Ford's. "I haven't experienced snow yet this year."

"There was snow on the ground when we flew in," he says, leading us across the street to Central Park.

"It's not the same as when it's falling from the sky. Even when I didn't have a home and the snow should have scared me since it meant winter was approaching, I always loved watching it come down. Especially the first snowfall."

He stops right before we walk into the park and looks down at me. "You missed it this year."

I nod. "I know. My first time ever."

An expression of gratitude crosses his face because I wouldn't have missed it if I wasn't pretending to be his fiancée. "Thank you."

"You don't have to thank me, I'm getting something out of the deal. I'm a big girl."

"Next year you won't miss it. I promise."

It's the insinuation that we'd be together next year that lights up my insides. "Are you the weatherman?"

"I know how you feel about money, Lena, but money can get us anywhere we want to go at a moment's notice. The first sign of snowfall in New York and we'll be on a plane back here."

I rest my head on his shoulder. "I'm sorry," I murmur, not always great at apologies. "I never should've underestimated you. I never should've put the brakes on us."

His feet slow to a stop once again. At this rate, we'll never get through the park before it closes. Although I sense Ford won't care to follow the rules anyway. "You don't have to apologize. I understand."

I shake my head and turn to him, staring up at his big blue eyes. All I used to see was arrogance and humor, but now they're soft and loving. "I fell for you and because of that I should've given you a chance to prove me wrong, not just cut it off."

"You were scared." His hands mold to my hips, pulling me to him.

I nod. "I was." Not wanting to look him straight in the eye, I turn and continue walking. "I went to see my dad today."

"Lena," he says my name with sympathy. "I would've gone with you if you told me that's where you were going."

I shake my head. "It was a good visit. Another guy he knew came to see him at the same time I was there and for the first time I understood why I felt the way I did. My dad's failure at being a father was hurting my future. Hurting my future with you. He promised so many times to change, Ford. So many and I was constantly disappointed. But that doesn't mean that every man will disappoint me. And it doesn't mean I'm not worthy of finding a man who loves me completely."

He tugs me back with our adjoined hands, but I shake my head, refusing to let him see the tears in my eyes, not quite ready to show him my vulnerability. But as always, he doesn't take no for an answer and yanks harder until I fall into his chest. His hand comes down and cradles my cheek. "I think I need to explain some things to you. I think you need my side of this story."

"Nope."

He swipes a tear away. "Yes. I haven't explained a lot to you and just expected you to believe me and that was wrong because the man you dealt with in the past isn't someone made to be a boyfriend. The stubborn side of me thought you should just go along with what I said but I understand the walls. Hell, I've put up walls my entire life to not be used because of my last name."

"Don't you ever think I could be using you?"

He laughs. "You're much too sweet to ever use anyone. When I found out I was going to be a dad, I wanted to run. Typical, right?"

I say nothing because the truth is I was surprised when he wanted to be a part of his daughter's life.

"Even before I took the paternity test, I think I knew. It was this gut feeling inside of me and I thought to myself, how on earth will I raise a little human and not screw them up. Even after I knew Britney was carrying my child, I didn't really engage. I didn't go to the ultrasounds, I didn't even really visit her. I threw money at her because that's what Jacobs' do."

"It's a lot of change."

"I'm ashamed to admit, there were nights I thought about giving her a large sum of money to just go away, find someone else to be a father to my child. Out of sight, out of mind." He hangs his head low.

"But?" I ask.

His face lights up. "I realized I had to deal with the consequences of my actions. Once the shock of the situation wore off, I knew I'd never forgive myself if I wasn't a father to my child. The first time I saw Annabelle, I was hooked. You've asked me before what's changed. How I adapted so fast to having Annabelle in my life and honestly, I just wanted the best for her. I was scared out of my mind, but I pushed forward because she's my daughter and deserved the best. It's sad that I needed to see her in order to find that drive inside of me but I'm proud of the way I've stepped up. One day she'll find out the person her dad was before she was born, but hopefully I'll have proved to her that I'm not that guy by then."

I sigh. "Ford, just because you liked to party and sleep with women doesn't make you a bad person."

"Come on Lena, you know as well as I do, I didn't have a lot of respect for those women."

I exhale a breath. "Most only wanted you because of who you are. You used one another."

He shrugs. "Still. I want Annabelle to be proud that I'm her dad. As crazy as it is, she changed me. She's the one who put me on the straight and narrow. I'd rather spend a night in with her than do anything else. Well, that's not entirely true."

I wait for him to finish, unsure where he's going.

"I'd rather us spend the night with Annabelle doing nothing but playing with her."

A smile tilts up my lips because that's a nice night to me too.

I stop us once again and link my hands around his neck, pressing my chest to his. "I think I'm ready now."

"Are you sure?" he asks, winding his arms around my waist and pulling me in the rest of the distance.

My neck cranes to look up to him. "Positive. I want to be with you."

He bends down and when his lips are millimeters from mine, he whispers, "About fucking time, Lena Boyd." And then he places his lips on mine and his tongue slides into my mouth, gliding along mine. I moan into his kiss, having missed it. He steps back way too fast. "Have you seen enough of the snow?"

I laugh because I feel like we're barely in Central Park. "Yep. But where will we go?"

"Looks like we're going for high school vibes. I'm taking you to my childhood bedroom."

I giggle, but he grabs my hand and escorts me out of Central Park back into his parents' condo building all while my stomach stirs with butterflies.

*W*e tiptoe into the penthouse, taking off our shoes and coats quietly. Neither one of us looks at one another, like we're seventeen and about to both lose our virginity. Then Ford links his fingers around mine and slowly walks me to the staircase and up to the top floor.

Ford's bedroom is the farthest down the hall, but I'm aware that I'll have to be quiet tonight because the rest of his family is right down the hall. That's going to be hard since I already want to moan with desire at the mere thought of what we're about to do.

His bedroom door creaks, but he continues in and shuts and locks the door behind us. I make my way over to his bed, sitting down and looking around. As my eyes soak in the room, they land on him standing by the door, watching me. "God, you're beautiful," he says, his breath labored like we've already made out for an hour.

"You have me in your room, you don't need to sweet-talk me."

He strips off his sweater and walks over to me with his T-shirt on but grabs the hem and shrugs that off too when he reaches me. "I'm not sweet-talking you. It's the truth."

"Isn't it my job to strip you?"

He makes me widen my legs and steps between them before he takes my face in his hands, tilting my neck so I look up at him. "I really wish I had you alone."

"We are alone," I say.

He stares blankly and shakes his head. "You know what I mean." He licks the pad of his thumb and runs it along my bottom lip, his eyes solely fixed on mine. "I want to hear you cry out."

I open my mouth slightly, and my tongue comes out, sliding along my bottom lip.

"I love your lips."

The tips of my mouth rises into a smile, but then he falls to his knees, his thumb slipping from my mouth. His hands slide up my torso to my shoulders, peeling away the sweater over my tank top. I know my nipples are poking through the thin fabric of my shirt and the fact that he keeps glancing at my chest confirms it.

"Please Ford, I'm aching to have you," I say, my core pulsing with the need to have his hands all over me, in me, but he's continuing to undress me at a torturous pace.

"I do love when you beg." He winks and again I'm thrown that this man is all mine. What was I thinking pushing him away?

I bring my legs around his waist and link my ankles, locking him in and then I take the hem of my tank top and raise it up off over my chest. "Whoa. Whoa. Whoa. That's my job."

But I do it too fast and instead of being disappointed, he stares at my breasts, his hands gliding up my torso and taking each one in his hands. "You have no idea the dirty thoughts I've had about these tits." His thumbs run over my nipples and I clench below.

"What thoughts?" My breath comes out sounding wanton, which is exactly what I am right now.

"I want to fuck them. I want to come all over them and I want to motorboat them." He inches forward and flicks his tongue along my nipple.

"I think that can be arranged." My fingers push through the hair at the back of his head.

He chuckles into my chest, burying his face between them. Before I realize it, he's inching up off the floor and I'm unlinking my legs. He gets me on my back and crawls on top of me. His mattress is plush and soft and smells just like him.

There's something about being in his childhood room that turns me on even more. He pulls down his sweatpants and just as I am, he's bare of any undergarments. "I really need you right now." He buries his head into my neck and one hand slides down the front of my pajama pants, stroking me. "God, you're soaked."

"I have an IUD," I say because waiting for him to put a condom on right now might just kill me.

He freezes and holds himself up by his forearms, staring down at me. Shit. This would take some serious trust for him to believe me after Britney. Then he sits back on his ankles and tugs down my pajama pants. "I'm clean. Tested after I found out Britney was pregnant and haven't been with anyone since."

My face heats having to be honest with him. "I haven't been with anyone in over a year."

He quirks his eyebrow.

"What can I say? Your dad keeps me busy."

"Fuck Lena, don't mention my dad when you're naked, okay?" Then he lies on top of me and the tip of his dick breaches my opening. "Never again."

I laugh and my head falls to the side. "Okay."

He smiles as he inches inside of me slowly, our eyes locked. This time it feels different than the hotel. This time it's like promises are being made between us.

Once he's completely filled me, my core aches for him to move. He does a small circle with his hips and then draws out of me and back in. All at a painfully slow pace.

"God, Ford," I whisper and he smashes his lips to mine.

"You're so damn wet and soft and fuck, this is killing me," he pants in my ear. I'm only getting more and more turned on.

His thrusts become faster and deeper and I cling to him to make sure he doesn't stop. Not like he would. Our bodies are slick with sweat as we slide together. Whispering of curse words and praises exchange between us. I slide my hand down between us, finding my clit and between me fingering my clit and his pelvis bone drilling in, my orgasm floods me until I can no longer hold on and my back arches off the bed. A strangled cry erupting up my throat, which Ford swallows with a kiss.

He grinds into me once, twice, and the final time he's deeper than he's been and he stills, his body trembling as he comes. His body falls and I hold the weight of him in my arms, never wanting to move from this position.

"You're spending the night here," he softly says into my ear.

"Your parents."

"I'm a fucking adult, and you're my fiancée. What are they going to say?"

He inches up off me and stares down with his crystal blue eyes. Yeah, like I could ever say no.

Chapter 29

"Either you're in or you're out of her life."

Ford

*C*hristmas morning started way too early.

Although Annabelle couldn't open any gifts herself, she's happily playing with her toys. Lena is on the couch, snug under a blanket and drinking her coffee, and I'm admiring her from across the room. I keep thinking of ways to show her I'm not going to have second thoughts, but it's a hard thing to prove.

My mom's cell phone rings and she mindlessly answers it because she's so enthralled with Annabelle. "Yes, Anessa, Merry Christmas to you."

Then there's silence. I'm the only one really paying attention because I'd like to know who's showing up here on Christmas.

"Okay. Let me discuss it with Mr. Jacobs and one of us will be down." My mom's face is pale when she hangs up the phone and motions to my dad to go to another room.

"What is it?" I ask.

She stops in front of me. "You might as well come too."

Lena sits up, but I wave her back down. Surely there isn't anything PR-related that needs handling on Christmas.

We go to my dad's office and my mom shuts the door. I notice her hands shaking as she clenches them.

"What's wrong, Gabi?" my dad asks in his usual gruff way.

"We have a guest downstairs."

"A guest? It's nine o'clock in the morning on Christmas." My dad, along with the rest of the family, is still in his pajamas.

My mom looks at me, and immediately my gut clenches and nausea hits me in the back of the throat. Before she says it, I know. "Britney."

Everything as I know it turns black. How could she come back now?

I storm out of my dad's office and hammer the elevator button until it arrives. When I step in, Lena walks into view, but the doors shut before she can reach me. How dare Britney show up now, on Christmas morning, after leaving me high and dry with our daughter?

When I reach the ground floor, Anessa gives me an apologetic look. Because my life is all over the fucking magazines and newspapers and internet everyone knows who Britney is. The baby mama. My one-night stand. The woman who left her baby.

"Britney," I say through gritted teeth.

She looks okay. Her blonde hair is now brunette, and her makeup is less overdone than before. She's dressed in a big puffy jacket and jeans with boots. I have no idea where she's even from.

"Hi, Ford." She raises her hand in a weak wave.

"What do you want?" I'm seething but trying to keep it together.

"I want to see her," she says.

"No."

The elevator dings and out files my mom, dad, and

Lena. Britney looks over. I'm relieved they didn't bring Annabelle down with them.

"Please. I know what I wrote, what I did, but—"

"Ford." Lena comes alongside of me, her hand on my arm.

I look down at her and see the sympathy in her eyes. She's wrong. I'm not letting this woman see Annabelle right now. We're her family.

"Let's take this upstairs," my dad says.

I raise my hand. "Absolutely not."

"Well, we're not going to stand in the lobby and air all our family business." My dad's tone brooks no argument.

I stare at Britney, anger for the way she's treated her daughter consuming me. "I'm going to get dressed and I'll meet you outside the building in fifteen minutes."

"Okay," she says.

I storm back to the elevators.

"Thank you, Anessa," my mom says and we all get in.

After the doors shut, I yell, "How could she come back?"

"It's only been a few months. Maybe she had a change of heart?" Lena tugs on my arm, her way of cooling me down. For a moment, it works.

Annabelle's mother has returned, and that terrifies me as much as it eases me. I don't want her to grow up without a mother, but now that I've had her to myself, I don't want to share her. Even so, I would never keep her from Britney if I thought Britney had her shit together. But I can't allow her mother to come in and out of Annabelle's life as she pleases. How will that make Annabelle feel as she grows up?

We arrive at the penthouse and I'm surprised that my parents have said nothing.

"Annabelle can stay here. I'm going out by myself.

Britney needs to answer some questions before she sees her." I walk upstairs to my childhood room.

Lena slides in right behind me, sitting on the bed. "I think you need to remember Annabelle does need a mother in her life. I know you're angry but—"

I take off my pajama pants and Lena lowers her head, covering her eyes. "You've seen my dick already."

"I know, but we're not like—"

"We're engaged. Technically my dick is still yours."

She keeps covering her eyes. "Don't be so vulgar."

"You liked it when I was vulgar," I remind her, and her cheeks flush.

"Well, now we're just friends."

"I'd rather be a real couple who were still fucking."

"Let's just stay on task."

I pull on a pair of jeans and take off my shirt. She's back to looking at me and I don't miss the way her eyes flare when she looks at my chest. Hell, at least I know she's still physically attracted to me.

"You can do more than just look."

Her shoulders fall and she whines, "Ford, you have more important things to deal with right now than getting your dick inside me."

"Keep talking dirty to me," I egg her on, because it's easier than dealing with what is going on downstairs. I have to address this situation that could change my daughter's outlook on life. I can't screw this up. I have to make sure I look out for her and do what's best for her.

"She's Annabelle's mother."

"Doesn't deserve to be," I say, throwing on a long-sleeve tee and reaching for a sweatshirt.

"Regardless," her voice softens, "she is. She's her one and only mother."

And I know she has a point. Nothing will change that fact.

"You're more of a mother to Annabelle than she is." I sit on the bed next to Lena, desperate to pull her into my lap.

"Maybe, but in the end, she only has one true biological mother. And regardless of who you marry and who comes into her daily life, Annabelle's going to want a relationship with her. At the very least she'll want to know." She places her hand on my shoulder.

"What do you expect me to do? Open my door after she just left her? And didn't even give her to me, but to a friend while I had to play a hockey game?"

"Maybe it was all too much for her. Maybe she couldn't handle the stress one more minute. I know it's crazy, but you handled the transition so smoothly. Most new parents don't adapt to change like you did."

"I had no choice. She's my daughter. My responsibility."

Her eyes illuminate with a soft gaze. "You truly are remarkable."

"Yet we're not a couple," I say dryly.

"Let's table that conversation for right now. Go to Britney and straighten this out. If you want me to bring Annabelle down to meet you, let me know. I'm happy to." She stands and I follow suit.

My hand cradles her head and my thumb brushes her cheekbone. "You're the amazing one. You should be wishing she'd go away. The three of us could be a family."

She shakes her head. "We can make a bigger circle for our family if need be."

"Are you admitting that there's a chance of us being a family?"

"I never said I didn't want it. I simply voiced my concern."

I step closer. "Then give me a shot. Give me a shot to convince you."

"You shouldn't need to do that. I should believe you."

She continues to blame herself while I know I'm the cause of her doubt. Aiden's right. She saw way too much shit about me.

She adds, "I'm going to see my dad again today."

"Oh?" I've yet to remove my hand from her face and I don't want to.

"I didn't say that because I expect you to come. I just wanted you to know. In case the Britney thing runs late."

"I want to go with you," I say.

She shakes her head. "No, he doesn't even remember me."

"I'm going."

"Go take care of your business first."

I groan and kiss her on the forehead. "Thanks for talking sense into me."

She laughs. "A few months ago, you would have kicked me out and said how wrong I was."

"What can I say? I didn't realize how much I loved a bossy, uptight woman back then."

She shakes her head and steps away, my hand dropping between us. I watch her leave the room before I grab my wallet and head out.

***

Britney's at the corner by the entrance to Central Park, her arms wrapped around herself. She doesn't have any luggage or bags with her. It's hard to believe it was only a few months ago that I agreed to the fake engagement and walked Annabelle through here to see the vibrant colors of fall. Now the trees are bare and there's a soft dusting of snow on the ground.

I jog across the street to join Britney.

"I'm sorry for showing up like that. I just had to see her. It's Christmas," she says by way of explanation.

"You could've called me." I nod to start walking through the park, and I have no idea if it's to get her away from Annabelle or just because I need to walk.

We end up by the pond and sit on the bench.

"How is she?" Britney asks.

"She's good."

"Your fiancée? When I heard it was Lena, I was surprised, to say the least. Does Annabelle think she's…" Her voice becomes choked up.

Britney met Lena a few times to handle the PR when it first hit the press that I was going to be a father.

"She's six months old, she doesn't think anything. But she does like Lena."

"That's good. I mean—"

"What do you want?" I ask, needing to get to the point.

She shifts to face me more. "I want to see her. I think I made a mistake. I'm her mother."

"You are her mother, but what's changed from when you walked out on her?"

"I saw the pictures. All three of you in the magazine."

I stand, annoyed that my suspicions were correct. This is a jealousy thing. Gavin's pictures of Lena, Annabelle, and me came out yesterday.

I take a few steps away then circle back. "Is that why you're here? Jealousy? If you can't have her, no one should?" My voice is like venom, and I hate hearing it, but I have to protect Annabelle right now.

"I'm not jealous. Not of the family. But seeing the

picture of your fiancée giving Annabelle a gift and her eyes are all lit up like she's giving her the fucking moon… it stung. I won't deny it." She takes out her gloves and puts them on before holding her hands together in her lap.

"She's not a toy you can pick up and play with when you feel like it. Either you're in or you're out of her life."

She nods. "I'm in."

I sit on the bench, remembering what Lena said. Britney is Annabelle's mother whether I like it or not. No one can replace her in Annabelle's life. "Are you one hundred percent sure?"

She stares at the pond that's yet to freeze over because it's too early in the season. "Yes."

"Then I think we should have papers drawn up. A custody agreement."

"With lawyers?"

"Yeah." I run a hand through my hair. "Where are you living right now?"

"Pittsburgh. Back with my parents. I don't have the money to live in Florida."

"You had a place, remember? I was paying for it."

She nods a couple times. "I know, but when people figured out I was the mother of your baby, I didn't like the attention. Some people were really mean."

I shrug. "People can be assholes."

We're both silent for a beat.

"Can I see her?" she asks.

No is on the tip of my tongue, but it's not going to make a difference to Annabelle right now.

"Yes, but after that, I want you to really think about this, Britney. Do you want to be in her life? If you do, then let's figure something out, but if you can't commit to being a constant presence, then please think about her needs and her well-being. I won't allow her to be hurt."

She nods eagerly.

I pull out my phone and message Lena that we're coming up to the penthouse.

"Let's go." I stand and nod in the direction of the building.

"Do you think she'll even remember me?" she asks, and I can tell she's nervous now.

I want to answer honestly and say probably not, but I shrug. "I don't know. I guess we'll find out."

Each step closer to the building, I want to put my hand across her chest to stop her from moving forward, to spare my daughter the pain of a mother who might abandon her. How do I allow Britney into Annabelle's life if she's only going to destroy her? Britney left her once. Who's to say she won't do it again? It's then I realize that I now understand what Lena's been concerned about with me this whole time.

CHAPTER 30

Lena

The elevator dings and we all stare at one another, Imogen looking as if she might blow her gasket. Annabelle is oblivious, sitting in Mrs. Jacobs' lap while Morgan shows her how to play with one of the toys she got for Christmas.

The deep inhale behind me a second later tells me they've arrived. I'd be lying if I said I didn't want to stand up and demand Britney leave, but I meant what I said to Ford. She's Annabelle's mother and nothing will change that. Sure, someone can step into the role of mother for her and heal the wound Britney might leave, but she's still the woman who gave Annabelle life.

"Annabelle," Britney whispers, coming across the room.

"Gutsy," Imogen says a little too loudly, but if Britney heard her, she doesn't show it.

Britney stops in front of Mrs. Jacobs. I've never known Ford's mom to be mean, but she has a murderous expression right now. Britney picks up Annabelle off Mrs. Jacobs' lap and holds Annabelle, singing a song I don't know, twirling her around the room.

At first Annabelle is looking around, unsure, and her gaze stops on her dad.

Imogen huffs next to me. "Sure, she doesn't cry with her."

I watch Ford intently. His jaw is tense, his teeth clenched, but he's not stopping Britney.

"She's gotten so big," Britney says, more to herself than anyone else, I think.

"That's what happens when you vanish," Imogen says, bitterness in her tone.

Mrs. Jacobs stands. "I'll get more coffee."

Mr. Jacobs follows her. I'm surprised that a man who wants to be so involved in everything has no say about what is transpiring right now.

I pat Imogen's leg. "I think I'm going to go get dressed."

She grabs my hand, stopping me, and leans in. "You need to protect your spot in this family."

I shake my head. "I'm not fearful of my spot." The words ring true to me. I don't have one ounce of fear that Ford would want Britney. And I do believe she should have a role in Annabelle's life as long as it can be consistent.

Imogen looks at me as though I'm crazy. "Why?"

I look across the room at Ford and he's staring back at me, clearly unsure what he should be doing. Like watching his daughter with Britney is a car accident he can't strip his eyes away from. A small part of me somehow knows that I need to go to him and tell him this will all work out. Give him the reassurance he's lacking. He's not used to facing things outside of his control.

I smile at Imogen and go to leave the room, squeezing Ford's shoulder on my way past.

He follows me out of the room then stops me with his hand on my wrist, tugging me back to him.

"You're leaving?" he asks in a hushed voice.

"I think it's better if I'm not around. I'm going to head out. Should be beautiful on Christmas morning."

He frowns. "But I want you here."

I place my hand on his chest. "You don't need me here, Ford. Let Britney spend some time with her daughter. See what she's really here for. Having me here will only complicate matters."

He stares at me for a beat, not saying anything. Then he slides my hair behind my ear, leans in and whispers, "Thank you."

I shake my head. "I didn't do anything."

"You make me a better person."

"Ford, you are a good person." I place my hand over his heart. "Trust yourself."

We stare at one another for a moment, but Britney screeches, stripping our attention away.

"She spit up on her," I hear Imogen say then laughs. "I guess we should've told you she just ate."

Ford places a chaste kiss on my lips then returns to the room to help and I decide this is my opportunity to sneak out.

CHAPTER 31

"I don't want space."

Ford

I sit on the couch and watch Britney play with Annabelle, but all I can think about is Lena. I hate that she felt she needed to leave. Britney's appearance must be hard for her too and instead of assuring her things are okay between the two of us and it doesn't matter that Britney is here, I'm making sure this woman doesn't kidnap our daughter.

"Her smile is like yours," Britney says, looking at me. "What do you think she got from me?"

My entire family has left the room by now, none of them wanting to deal with this. Hell, back in the day, I would've hightailed it too.

I shrug. "I don't know."

"Come on. She has your eyes." She raises Annabelle in the air.

I've noticed that since it's been just the two of us, Britney seems to be much more her old self and less the heartbroken mother.

"You're so lucky, your daddy gets a lot of women because of those eyes," she coos at Annabelle. Britney smiles at me, setting Annabelle in her lap. "So you're engaged? I never thought I'd see the day."

I nod.

"What, can't you talk to me about her?"

I shrug. "Don't want to is more like it."

She huffs. "If we're going to co-parent, you have to be civil to me."

I glance at my watch. "I am. I had a pressing appointment I missed in order to allow you to visit with Annabelle. That's pretty damn civil, if you ask me."

She strips her gaze from me. "Do you think this is easy?"

"Did you think it was easy for me when I had to play an entire hockey game knowing my child's mother had left her and I was now solely responsible?"

She shakes her head. "I wasn't in a good space. I missed my old life."

I remain silent, collecting my thoughts. Lena's words ring in my ear once again, reminding me that regardless of the fact that I loathe what Britney did to our daughter, she is still her mother. "And now?"

"I want to be a mother to her." I hear the but in her tone, so I wait for her to finish. "But will you let me?"

"It's not up to me."

She sets Annabelle in her bouncy chair, securing her in. Then Britney crawls toward me. "Are you happy, Ford? I heard that the marriage thing might be a sham?"

I watch her come toward me, wondering what the fuck she thinks she's doing. "They don't know what they're talking about. I'm very happy."

My gaze falls to Annabelle. She's enthralled with the spinning bunny on the bar across from her. She keeps hitting it to make it twirl and she watches it before doing it again.

"We could be a family. Raise her together." Britney sits back on her ankles in front of me, sliding her hands up my thighs. "I hate the idea of moving her from house to house. Not being able to spend holidays with her."

I wiggle out of her hold, but she's got me caged in. Her one hand slowly inches up my thigh.

I put a hand over hers to stop her. "There is no us." My voice is ice cold.

She raises up on her feet. "We were good together. Remember the night we were together?"

Sadly, I was half in the bag. More than half, if I'm being honest.

She sits in my lap and wraps her arms around my neck.

"Get off me," I bite out.

"You haven't stopped me yet. There must be a reason for that?" Her voice is low and breathy.

"The reason is that I don't want my daughter to think I'm aggressive with women." I take her arms and unwind them from around my neck, but she puts them right back and tightens her grip. "I'm not interested. That option isn't on the table."

I stand to get her off, but she hangs on me like a monkey. "She's not your type."

"And let me guess, you are?" I try to get her hands from around my neck, but seriously what does she do, vise grip exercises? I lose my footing and stumble, ending up on top of her on the couch.

"I can give you the kind of thrills she can't." She locks one leg around mine, then another. I feel as though I'm stuck in an octopus with no hope of escaping.

"You have no idea what you're talking about. Let go of me now."

Then the elevator doors ding. I push off the couch using every bit of my strength to free myself right as Lena turns the corner to take in the scene.

Of course, it couldn't be Imogen or Morgan. It had to be Lena. Fuck my life.

Lena splashes on a fake-as-shit smile. "Looks like you two are getting along great. I'll leave you alone." Then she heads up the stairs—assuming I was just what? Fucking around with Britney in front of Annabelle? Is that how low she actually thinks of me?

"You need to leave," I say, picking up Annabelle from the bouncy chair.

"No," Britney whines. "You can't be serious? You're going to run after her? Since when do you do that?" Her voice is full of anger.

I pause with my hands under Annabelle. That's why Britney ran, left Annabelle with me. She'd tried seducing me a few nights before she left. Except she was much pushier, had lingerie on and the whole bit. Wanted to strip me down and give me a lap dance. All of which I denied and left.

"You wanted me to chase you," I say more to myself than her. How could I be so stupid? This didn't have anything to do with her being overwhelmed about being a new mother—or at least not entirely.

"Well, I am the mother of your child." She sits up on the couch, straightening her shirt.

"What the hell were you thinking?"

She stands, her face contorted in anger now. "I thought it would be too much for you to take care of her on your own. That you'd beg me to come back, change your mind and give us a shot. But now." She points upstairs. "She stepped into the role that's mine."

I shake my head, trying to make sense of this whole thing. "Role? We had a one-night stand." Annabelle puts her head on my shoulder, and I run my hand down her back.

"Exactly! Do you have any idea how much work I put into you that night? How long it took me to get you to notice me?"

I barely remember the night we had sex. I always used a condom, but... "Please tell me you didn't..."

She smiles and looks away.

"What the hell!"

Annabelle startles in my arms. She doesn't need to be here for this conversation.

"Morgan!" I yell, hoping she hears me.

She peeks down the round staircase because she's probably been eavesdropping this whole time.

"Can you take Annabelle upstairs?"

She rushes down, still in her pajamas, and takes Annabelle out of my arms.

"Wait! She's my daughter too," Britney says.

"You left her. You want to see her, get a lawyer."

Morgan smiles and leaves, her footsteps faster when she gets to the stairs.

Once I know she's out of earshot, I step closer to Britney. "Are you suggesting you got pregnant on purpose?"

"You can't blame me, Ford. It takes two." She raises her hands, but her cocky demeanor tells me her goal that night was to get pregnant and I was the fool who fell for it. Because I like to party and have fun, I was an easy mark.

My head falls forward and I shake it. Britney's right, she's not entirely to blame. I was right there with her even if I was drunk. I lift my gaze to hers. "We will never be anything more than co-parents to Annabelle because I love the woman upstairs. Do you understand that? If you want to be a part of Annabelle's life, the door is open, but the role of my wife is taken."

"Until you get bored, and from the looks of her, that's gonna be pretty fast."

"Out!" I yell, pointing at the elevator, my anger bursting out of me. "Get the fuck out of here."

"Come on, Ford." Britney saunters up to me. This girl won't quit. "Give me a chance. I like to play and have fun. We could bring other women in if you want." Her hands raise to my chest, and I grip her wrists.

"I only want one woman and it's not you." I stare coldly at her and I see the point when she finally gets it—there is not and never will be an us.

She steps away from me and collects her things. "I'm going to sue you for custody. I'm her mother and everyone knows the moms win."

"Go ahead and try. I'm sure your track record will speak well for you."

I follow her to the elevator and press the down button for her.

"I'm serious, Ford, I'll keep her in Pittsburgh. Away from you."

"Again, try it." A calmness falls over me. "But before you do that, think of what's best for your daughter and whether that's you. I want you to be a part of Annabelle's life, but from this point forward, we'll talk through lawyers. You want to see her again, get a lawyer, Britney."

The elevator arrives and she steps in. "You just made the worst mistake of your life. You think you've changed?" She guffaws. "Men like you never do."

The doors slide closed and my head drops forward. I'm thankful that's finally over. A part of me wants to disappear with Annabelle so Britney can never get her hands on her.

I jog up the stairs and knock on the guest room door.

"Come in," Lena says.

When I open the door, I find her packing. "Where are you going?"

"I'm going to go back to Florida."

"What about the party on New Year's Eve?"

"I'll come back that day. If anyone asks, you can just say I'm not feeling well. Have the week to do as you wish."

I stand idly by the door. "You don't believe what you saw, do you?"

She glances over with a soft smile. I can tell she doesn't know what to believe. "I think you need to get some things straight in your life."

I break the distance between us and place my hands over hers, stopping her from packing. "I only want you. You and Annabelle."

"But whether you like it or not, Britney's in the mix too. And I just can't…"

"Can't what?" I ask, sitting on the couch, taking out every item she puts in the suitcase.

Eventually she huffs and glares at me. "I can't be here, stuck in the middle, swaying how you feel one way or another. Finding you in compromising positions."

"That wasn't me. She wouldn't let me go. She just admitted she coerced me into getting her pregnant." I raise my hands. "And yeah, I know I played my part."

She situates herself between my legs. My eyes close as Lena runs her fingers through my hair. Impulsively, my hands land on her hips to keep her steady.

"I know you've changed, Ford. And I have no doubt you'd make a wonderful husband and father. Don't ever think you wouldn't." She places a kiss on my forehead.

I tug her into me. "Why are you doing this?"

"I'm not doing anything. You just need to figure out things with Britney. I'm giving you the space you need to do that."

"I don't want space," I tell her, speaking into her stomach.

She lays her head on mine. "I'm sorry for screwing this

entire thing up before. It's all on me." She steps back. "But while I'm gone really think about what you want for you *and* Annabelle. We'll figure out the stuff between us after you know that."

I can't even make sense of what is happening in this moment.

She repacks her suitcase, zips it, and heads toward the door. "The arrangement remains. I'll be at the party and any other engagement we need to attend. In the meantime, figure out this thing with Britney for Annabelle's sake."

My heart cracks as she opens the door and walks out on me.

CHAPTER 32

"It's nice to have you back."

Lena

Flying commercial sucks after flying private, but I'm at Ford's place now, alone. He hasn't tried to call me or text me, which I'm thankful for. I barely had it in me to walk away from him in New York. Seeing him on top of Britney broke me. I know it shouldn't have. I know it wasn't how it appeared. I believe all of that, but he does need to figure out how she fits into his life and I think that's best done without me around.

The week has gone by slowly. I've spent most of it recollecting my childhood. I never realized how messed up I am from it. I met Paisley for coffee, and she's referred me to a colleague I'll start seeing next week after the party.

The Jacobs are sending their private plane to take us back to New York City. Aiden, Saige, Maksim, Paisley, Tweetie, and Tedi are all invited to the huge New Year's Eve party that the Jacobs are having.

I've just finished packing my bag and am ready to head to the airport when my phone rings. I see Gavin's name on it, and I roll my eyes. "Hey, Gavin, can I call you back? I was just about to leave the house for the airport."

"Lena, I just want to warn you that a story is running that your engagement is fake. It's also talking about how you inserted yourself between Ford and his baby mama and stole him away. I got word of it when a colleague of mine who works for some low-rent online gossip mag called to see if I had a comment. He knew I'd done a couple interviews with you guys."

"How?" I shake my head, knowing those who dig hard enough can find anything. And sometimes they run with a story even if they don't have all the proof they need. And if I'm honest, Britney's name flashes through my head too.

"I just wanted to give you a heads-up."

"It's not fake," I say.

He chuckles. "It was though, wasn't it?"

I say nothing.

"It was all so sudden, then Eli Jacobs was looking around for companies to buy him out. It's a journalistic dream to uncover all this. You hid it well, but I know it was fake until I came for the holiday pictures."

"What are you talking about?"

"When Ford approached me in the foyer of the penthouse… I saw it in him. The jealousy in his eyes. It shouldn't be a surprise that once he was around you more, he'd fall for you. You're an amazing woman, Lena. Any man would be lucky to have you."

I sit on the couch to collect my thoughts. "Thank you."

"That's my one stand-up male moment, because I would've fought him for you if I thought I stood half a chance."

"Gavin—"

"No, I'm just telling you this so you can do damage control. I want this to work for you."

"Thanks." And I mean that. Although I never felt that way for Gavin, I'm thankful he's giving me a heads-up so I can spin this story.

"Go do what you do best." He hangs up.

I hold my phone for a second before I search all the

internet sites that usually report hockey news. None of the stories are there yet, which means the rumors aren't being fueled by hockey fans. They're being spread by people interested in the other side—Jacobs Enterprises.

So I head over to the gossip sites that usually report when businesses are failing, stock tips, and who's sleeping with who. Sure enough, there it is. Eli Jacobs forces son to marry to pretend he's an upstanding family man. The article tears apart the entire family, but primarily Ford, referring to him as a playboy and spoiled silver-spooned jackass. It says he'll never grow up and it's hard to swallow that he's a father.

The more I read, the madder I get. I dial Mr. Jacobs on my way out the door and talk to him from the back seat of the car taking me to the airport.

"We have a problem." I send him the link to the story, not wanting to involve Ford unless I have to. I hate myself for treating him the same way that article spoke about him because he has changed. I was just too scared to admit it.

I wait for Mr. Jacobs to read the article and hear him groan a few times. "Who is this and how do they know so much?"

"I don't know. I think it's speculation honestly. There's no one who knows for certain who would talk."

"We have the party tonight. You'll have to sell it to Otis Sandersville."

I glance out the window at the palm trees whipping past. "I'll be in the city by early afternoon. We can figure out a game plan."

He's silent for a while. "Okay, we'll talk then. Are you filling in Ford?"

"You can since I'll be on the plane."

"Right," he says, then he's quiet again. "Lena, he's been miserable…"

"With all due respect, Mr. Jacobs, let's just put out this fire."

"I'm just saying that I've never seen him so upset." He huffs. "That's all."

"I'll get on this article and see if I can figure out who their source was. There's a good chance we might never know. Talk to you soon." I ignore his comments about Ford. I cannot deal with that right now. I need to focus on my job.

I end up at the airport around the same time as everyone else, and this time it feels natural for me to navigate flying in a private jet. Oh, how things have changed.

"You sure have become accustomed to flying private," Tweetie says. "Ouch."

I turn to see him buckled over and staring at Tedi, who must've just smacked him.

"I didn't say anything offensive. I just meant she knows the ins and outs. Hell, she should be happy because she's special."

"Special?" I ask.

Tedi waves him off. "Don't pay any attention to Tweetie. He's just overzealous because he got asked to come with you all."

Tweetie scoffs. "Ford lost the bet. That's huge considering how competitive he is."

I stop what I'm doing and catch Maksim glaring at Tweetie.

"This is why you don't get invited," Aiden says.

"What are you talking about, Tweetie?" I hold up my hand to the other two guys so they don't speak.

"I made a bet with Ford that he'd be celibate for two months. But he told me that he lost because he slept with you."

I glance at Aiden and Maksim, who are pretending they're not paying attention.

"And what did he lose for this bet?"

"Bragging rights. Which we realized a long time ago is enough for Ford. He doesn't need to gain anything material. Hell, he can buy anything he wants. But he just gave in when it came to you. That's huge in Ford's book." Tweetie smiles. I have to say, it does make my stomach flutter that Ford was willing to lose because he couldn't stop himself from sleeping with me. "The man has it bad."

"We should go. We're going to miss our plane." I turn and they all follow.

I hear Tweetie sticking up for himself as to why he said anything and how it's a good thing, not a bad thing. I can't say I disagree.

---

*W*e land, and while the others go to the hotel, I take a cab to the Jacobs' residence. The stories have spread from the original website to more mainstream outlets and we have no choice but to send out a press release at this point.

The elevator doors ding and Ford's standing in the foyer waiting for me. His back is leaned against the wall, one hand stuffed in the pocket of his jeans and the other holding his phone, his thumb scrolling.

His eyes take me in and it sucks the last breath out of me. A smile forms on his lips. "Hey."

"Hi. Where's Annabelle?" God, I've missed her so much.

"She's sleeping. Should be up soon though."

I nod. "Your dad?"

"Expecting you." He pushes off the wall and holds out his arm for me to go first.

I lead the way to Mr. Jacobs' office. He's at his desk, teetering a pen back and forth on his desk and staring at his view of Central Park.

"Mr. Jacobs," I say, stepping in and sitting across from him.

"I have my plan ready." He leans back in his chair. "At the party tonight, Ford will give a speech. One that you'll write." He looks at me from under his eyebrows.

"I can write my own speech," Ford says.

"I know you can, but we have to do damage control. It has to be perfect. It needs to detail the rush of events, the fact that he fell hard and fast, and he's heard the rumors but…" He waves to me. "You understand, right?"

I raise my hand as though to ask a question, and he nods. "I think we need to put out a press release and go with no comment at this point. Ford and I will play up our engagement. Maybe get caught in a kiss on the balcony on purpose. We can be convincing without a speech. A speech looks like a cover-up and there's too much room for error."

I hate disagreeing with Mr. Jacobs, but there's only one way to turn this around and spin it back our way and that's with our actions. We can't give any credence to the rumors by defending ourselves against them.

"People are enamored by grand gestures. If Ford stops the party and gives a speech about how much he loves you, that will endear them to you both. As long as you cry and meet him halfway in the room, sealing it with a kiss. Convince them you two are the real deal."

I nod because this is my job. The one part I've never really cared for while working for the Jacobses is that Mr. Jacobs didn't always trust my decisions. That's what you get with a powerful man who isn't used to his ideas being questioned though.

"Okay, I'll get to work on it." I stand.

"Lena?" Mr. Jacobs catches me right before I leave, and I turn back around. "It's nice to have you back."

"Thank you," I say and nod, not meeting Ford's gaze as I sneak out of the room to go write the speech.

Before I get too far, I hear Mr. Jacobs say, "Ford, you stay here and shut the door."

I blow out a breath. I had hoped to catch him for a moment. To do what, I don't know. I just miss being around him. I feel as though we've fallen so far down, I don't know how to claw my way back up to him. So much has happened in such a short time, it feels daunting to think we could ever put this all behind us. That I could ever put my past where it belongs—in the rearview mirror.

CHAPTER 33

Ford

I sit at the desk across from my father, leaning back and resting my ankle on my knee. I really wanted to talk to Lena, but at the same time, I don't know what to say. When she stepped off the elevator, I wanted to rush to her, take her head in my hands, and kiss the living crap out of her.

"You've been moping this entire week." He leans back in his chair.

"I've been handling Annabelle. And I've done plenty."

"You love Lena," he says, no question in his tone.

I say nothing.

"It's okay, she loves you too."

A rush of air leaves me. "I think maybe there's just too much shit between us."

Britney called me two days ago to say she's not ready to be a mother. I think once she realized there really would be no *us*, she must've thought about what that would mean for her life and raising our daughter without me by her side. My heart broke for Annabelle, but I'll be the best mom and dad she needs.

"That's ridiculous. I'm giving up my entire company for your mother." Dad stares at the park again. "Life is too short." He turns to me. "Do you know why I allowed you to continue playing hockey through college?"

I shake my head. "Why?"

"I wanted you to have that because you had to come on board, learn the ropes so you could take the reins at Jacobs Enterprises. I never thought you'd fight me on taking your rightful place, nor did I ever think you'd go pro." I open my mouth to speak, but he holds up his hand. "Let's face it, Ford, it takes dedication to play any sport in a professional capacity. People don't give a shit what family you come from, and it wasn't as though you came out of the womb with a puck and stick. You weren't a natural."

"Well, this is a great pep talk. Thanks, Dad."

He blows out a breath. "Do I have to tell you that I don't want you to marry that girl in order for you to go fight for her?"

I scowl. "What does that mean?"

"You've worked yourself to the bone for your hockey career. That's why I never understood why you constantly did shit off the ice that would threaten your spot on the team. Of course, the selfish side of me wants you to come on board here and take over, but I knew a long time ago that you inherited your mother's stubborn side. You weren't going to bow down to me. And I admire and respect that because I couldn't do the same to my dad."

"You're being awfully complimentary today."

"Call it nostalgia. I want you, Imogen, and Morgan to be happy. We have all this, and for what? To feel trapped every day? I shouldn't have pressured you as much as I did. And honestly, I should've never put you and Lena in the position I did. Forcing you two to pretend you're in love?" He shakes his head. "I'm ashamed of myself, because you both look miserable."

"It's fine."

"No, it's not."

I slide to the edge of my chair. "I'll manage with Annabelle. We'll be fine."

"Sometimes life doesn't give you a redo."

I look at my hands. "I know." Standing, I head to the door. "See you tonight, Dad."

I open the door and shut it behind me. Coming through the family room, I already hear Lena in the kitchen with Annabelle. I lean my shoulder along the kitchen doorjamb, watching her with my daughter.

"I swear she's grown. Is she sitting up on her own yet?" Lena asks Morgan.

"It's only been a week," my sister says with a smile.

Lena has Annabelle in her arms, dancing them around. "Oh, how I missed you, little girl." She nuzzles Annabelle's neck and continues moving around the kitchen as though it's their own dance floor.

Morgan looks at me for a moment, questions as to why I'm not coming in filling her eyes.

But I walk up to my room and shut the door. Lena's already made it clear what she wants from me—nothing. Don't count your boy out yet though. I have a plan.

J'm getting ready in my room, and my mind won't stop whirling about what I have planned tonight. I probably should've filled my dad in earlier, but I didn't want to give him time to talk me out of it.

Unable to wait any longer before I see her, I head across the hall and knock on Lena's door.

"Come in." She's opening the box I sent for her earlier. "Ford, you don't have to do this anymore."

I shut her door and lock it. "Tell me."

"What?" She turns around, forehead creased in confusion.

"Tell me you don't love me."

She huffs. She's dressed in a robe, naked under it I bet, but I force myself not to focus on that.

"Why are you doing this?" She picks up the box of lingerie. "And please take this back."

I wrap my hand around her waist and tug her toward me. The box falls to the floor and the panties and bra spill out onto the floor, along with my note. God, she feels so good in my arms.

"Tell me I'm wrong. Tell me, and I'll walk away and we can see each other when we need to for the sake of this plan. Make me think I'm crazy for knowing there's something here between us."

She shakes her head. "Ford… I don't…"

I smash my lips to hers, unable to hold myself back. She's all I've been thinking about for the past week, and I call bullshit on the fact that she doesn't feel for me the way I feel for her.

I lick the seam of her lips and she opens for me on a breathy moan. I take full advantage. Her fingers grip my shoulders and I slide my hand down between her legs, pushing the robe out of the way.

"I'm going to give you that blush tonight, and all night, every time I look at you, I'm gonna remember the way you came on my hand."

I slide my finger through her folds and she arches her back. Holding her up, I step us toward the wall, using it to leverage her so I can untie her robe and reveal her beautiful naked body. She releases a long exhale when I push a finger inside her.

"Tell me you can live without this," I say, pushing

another finger in. "That you don't want me just as much as I want you."

"I do," she cries out, grinding along my palm.

"We're supposed to be together. You're mine. All fucking mine." I bury my head in her neck, nipping and sucking and licking, tracing my way up to her mouth before I take her lips again.

"Yours," she pants. "Always yours."

"Finally," I say and thrust a third finger in, grinding my palm along her clit.

She rides my hand, my fingers coated in her wetness. She smells of lavender and vanilla.

"I fucking love you, Lena," I admit, overcome with emotion and needing her to know.

She moans, her head falling to the wall. She's there, right at the brink, trying to drag out her orgasm. I increase my pace and her hands move to my wrist, clamping down.

"Go, I'll catch you."

She releases my hand and stills, crying out and falling forward until her head hits my shoulder. Her pussy spasms around my fingers as I slow my movements and slide them out of her, bringing them to my mouth, loving her fucking taste.

"Ford," she sighs, pulling back and staring at me, her cheeks the perfect shade of pink.

"You're beautiful."

"But what does this mean?"

I kiss her forehead and step back. "Be ready in twenty."

I walk out, knowing that she does love me. She can't deny it anymore. Now I just have to get her to see that we can handle anything that comes our way.

CHAPTER 34

Lena

’m still wet as we’re sliding out of the limo at the event. The more I think about Ford coming into my room and the way I rode his hand, the more turned on and confused I am.

"You have the speech, right?" I whisper to Ford as we approach the doors.

He smiles at me and pats his jacket. With his hand on the small of my back, he ushers us into the warmth of the venue. We check our coats and head into the party.

I’ve wanted to talk to him about what happened earlier in my room, but he keeps dodging the topic. I’m taking it as a bad sign for our future.

Aiden comes up to us as soon as we enter. "Did you hear about the trades?"

"No. I’ve been kinda busy." Ford puts his arm around my waist and tugs me next to him, his thumb slowly moving along my hip bone. A girl could go delirious from that move. "Who did we take?"

"Cory Freeman. A rookie." Aiden looks at Maksim, who’s just joined us.

Ford stiffens next to me. "And?"

"Warner Langley," Aiden says and steps back.

"What? Why would they take that prick?" Ford’s mad,

but then he glances at me and I see something switch in his brain. "That asshole isn't ruining my night. Just don't tell Imogen."

"Why would Imogen care?" Aiden asks.

"We'll talk about it another time. We have to handle something more pressing right now." Ford leads me over to the bar.

"Why don't you like Warner Langley?" I ask.

"He's just a jerk. That's all." He orders us two drinks. A whiskey for him and an Aperol spritz for me. "Let's just enjoy our night."

"Okay."

I try to bring up the topic of us again, but then we're told to sit down for dinner. Since we're at the table with the rest of the hockey players, there's no time to talk about us.

As we're finishing our meals, I lean forward to ask if maybe we can go out into the hallway to be alone, but Ford beats me to it, kissing me on the cheek.

"I'll be right back," he says.

I watch him head over to his dad. They talk for a moment, then his dad ushers him outside. He doesn't look angry, but Mr. Jacobs is an expert at masking his face in front of others. He should take up high stakes poker.

For the next hour, I talk to everyone at the party. I can't help but feel as though there are whispers going on behind my back. People speculating that our relationship is fake. And here I am making the rounds without him.

I glance at my phone and see that it's almost midnight. Thank goodness this New Year's Eve party is almost over, but Ford has yet to give his speech. Maybe he's having second thoughts?

The music slows to a lull before stopping, and all eyes fall to the stage where Ford now has the microphone in his hand. "Excuse me, everyone."

Nervousness fires up in my belly because I know what's coming. I know every word written on that paper and I need to be prepared to sell this on my end.

Ford's gaze finds mine with that cocky smirk that I shouldn't love, but I do. "Sorry for interrupting your night, but it's almost midnight and I've been dodging my girl all night while waiting for the clock to run out."

I tense, not understanding what he's saying. This isn't part of the speech I gave him.

He pulls the piece of paper from his pocket and I relax a bit. "I was supposed to come up here and give this speech. A speech that Lena wrote to convince you all that we're in love and ready to get married. To make sure you don't believe the articles going around questioning our engagement, when in fact, they're true."

I gasp then glance at Otis and Penny Sandersville before closing my eyes. They were looking at one another, their mouths hanging open.

"The truth is, when I proposed to Lena Boyd, I kind of loathed her."

Tweetie laughs and Tedi elbows him in the gut.

"I did it because I was irresponsible and got a woman I barely knew pregnant. That woman left me with our daughter, and my dad needed us to look like a wholesome family, like we had it all together, so he could sell the company. I wanted him to sell so he wouldn't harp on me to stop playing hockey and take over the family business. But almost instantly, as soon as our sham had started, this weird feeling came over me whenever Lena was around.

"I didn't know it then, but I now know it as love." He rips up the paper. "I'm not going to read this prepared speech about how much we love each other and how happy we are because the truth is that we've found ourselves in this hole that neither one of us knows how to get out of."

I breathe deeply, unshed tears burning my eyes.

"Lena Boyd, I fucking love you. I love the way you challenge me and don't take my shit. I love the way you love my daughter and treat her as your own. I love the way you helped me without me ever having to ask. And I love the fact that you put one hundred percent of yourself in anything worth doing. There's a lot more I love about you, but those are just between us." He winks, and the crowd laughs.

"I know we lost our way during this fake engagement, but I'm here. All I know is that I love you and that has to be enough. Enough for us to get through a lot of these problems we're facing. The insecurities we might have."

He steps down from the stage.

"One year ago, I kissed you at midnight on New Year's Eve, and this year I want to be the man you kiss again. But this time, I want you to kiss me because you love me and because I'm the man you want in your life."

He reaches me and drops the microphone to his side.

"Ford," I say, barely able to speak.

He cradles my face in his hand as he always does.

"Ten… nine…" the band leader starts the countdown.

Our eyes remain locked.

"Eight… five… three…"

Ford waits patiently, but he knows. He's always known.

"One. Happy—"

I rise up on my tiptoes and smash my lips to Ford's. He picks me up, my feet floating off the floor.

Everyone screams, "Happy New Year!" There are a few claps, but I hope everyone else is kissing the one they love.

We draw back and I rest my forehead on his.

"I love you," I say.

"I know." He kisses me again.

Who said you can't have it all? I might've gone through hell to get here, but maybe I wouldn't have appreciated it like I do now.

"That's an awfully big smile," he says.

"Well, I just locked down Ford Jacobs. I'm a lucky girl."

He laughs. "I'm the lucky one."

"True." I smile. "You are lucky."

"You could fight me on it just a little."

"Nope." I inch forward. "Take me to the hotel."

"How did you know?" he asks, lowering my feet to the floor.

"It's my job to know what you're going to do before you do it." I turn to walk out, waving goodbye to our friends.

"Not anymore, and you're insinuating that I can't surprise you."

I turn around to walk backward. "I hate to break it to you, but I don't think you can."

"Are you challenging me?" He raises an eyebrow.

I stop short of the doors. "Hey, you have the rest of our lives to surprise me."

Then he drops to one knee, pulling a box out of his pocket. He slides off the ring I was wearing and pockets it. "Will you marry me, Lena? For real this time?"

Inside the box is a modest but elegant ring. Something way more me.

"Damn it, Ford. You were supposed to wait to surprise me." Tears sting my eyes.

Murmurs start behind him when a few bystanders notice what's going on.

"Answer, Lena," he says.

"Yes. Yes." I chuckle as he slides the ring on my finger.

I'm about to kiss him, but he ushers me out, signaling for the limo. "If we don't get out now, we never will."

He gets me into the limo, then his lips are on mine right away.

I finally have it all, and what do you know? I've never felt as secure as I do right now.

EPILOGUE

"She's literally my world."

Ford

nnabelle turns one today. I can't believe it. I also can't believe Lena invited Warner fucking Langley to the party. But she said the entire team needed to be included. She didn't like my argument that we're not in kindergarten and don't have to invite the entire team.

Since the trade, I've dodged Langley in the locker room and only talk to him when I have to on the ice. So far, we've been able to steer clear of one another. So explain to me why he accepted the invitation and is sitting out on the patio by my pool?

"Just relax. Whatever your beef was, you have to let it go." Lena pats me on the ass, getting more dip to put out. She wouldn't let me cater the party.

The paperwork has all been handled terminating Britney's parental rights. The day my lawyer received the paperwork back from Britney, signed, was a hard one. I'm sad for Annabelle that her biological mother couldn't step up and be what she needed. But I feel strongly that this is better than having a parent who pops in and out of her life whenever she feels like it.

Still, I hate that a part of me is always waiting for her to knock on the door and change her mind again. Will I feel this way our entire lives? Even if she no longer has any legal right to Annabelle, there's nothing stopping her from showing up and causing problems.

"You have no idea what he did," I say.

Just thinking about it makes me homicidal. I've yet to tell Lena, mostly because I'm loving our life right now. We fuck nonstop and we do all this shit like go to the zoo and other crap kids like. Annabelle is walking, so lately I've been baby-proofing. Plus, it's not really my story to tell. It's Imogen's, and although Lena will be my wife in a few short weeks, I need to clear it with my sister first.

"Because you won't tell me."

"I'll tell you tonight, and then you'll be pissed you invited him."

"Fine. Anyway, the new guy Cory seems nice," she says.

"He's cool. I think Aiden's a little worried. The kid is fast." I take her in my arms. "When are all these people leaving?" I nuzzle my head into her neck. "I want you alone."

Right now, we're in this dream sleep schedule with Annabelle. She sleeps, like, twelve hours a night plus two naps. The alone time we've gotten as a result has been great for our sex life.

"Soon. It's a one-year-old's party. She'll fall asleep and then you can give me a massage." She wiggles out of my hold and takes the dip outside where most of the food is.

I follow Lena because yeah, I'm whipped and proud of it.

Annabelle cries and toddles up to me, plastering herself to my leg. I reach down and get her, holding her in my arms.

"Tweetie scared her," Tedi says and shrugs.

"Beautiful family you got here," Warner says from next to me.

I tense, my jaw clenched. "Thanks." I refrain from saying anything else.

Lena comes over and Annabelle reaches for her. It was a sad day when that started, but my teammates who already have kids promise that my time will come again. Lena takes Annabelle and grabs a few Goldfish crackers. Annabelle devours them. How we're ever going to get her to cake time without her crashing is anyone's guess. Her head falls on Lena's shoulder and Lena rocks her while talking to someone else.

I sit down with my friends but can't stop admiring the scene in front of me. My entire family is here, and my dad actually has a tan because he and my mom just got back from a Mediterranean cruise. Otis still wanted to buy controlling interest in the company after I came clean on New Year's Eve. Said he appreciated that I did what was right and put my heart on the line. I have my dad to thank for that. When I cornered Dad at his table that night and we went outside to talk, he didn't put up a fight about me telling the truth during my speech. That's the closest I've ever felt to my father—when he put my happiness above what was best for the company. We've gotten along much better ever since.

I watch as Lena blows some bubbles for Annabelle to chase. I want to experience it all over again with Lena, except I want to see her belly swollen, hold her hand during the birth. See Annabelle as a big sister.

"You've got it bad," Tweetie says next to me, clasping me on the shoulder.

"What?"

"You can't stop staring at her and you've had her in your bed for almost a year."

"And I hope I never stop staring. I can't imagine I ever would. She's literally my world."

He just chuckles and ventures off somewhere.

Eventually I'm dragged up to get the cake, and we engage Annabelle, who isn't having any of it. She doesn't want to be in the high chair, which results in Lena giving me an "I told you so" look because I tend to feed Annabelle while we're sitting on the floor. I sit at the coffee table and Annabelle walks around and grazes off the plate. It works for us.

Lena started her own PR firm down here. She only has a few clients so far, but I know it will be successful. After all, I'm her biggest client, how could it not be? Even if I don't give her problems to deal with like I used to.

The cake gets smashed, the presents are opened, and my daughter is out cold by the time darkness falls. Everyone slowly wanders out, saying good night. Most overstay a one-year-old's birthday in the first place. I'm not sure if the party is really for Annabelle or us honestly.

"Where's Imogen?" Morgan asks, collecting her purse and my mom's.

We all look around. She's nowhere to be found.

Mom passes Annabelle to Lena so she can get ready to leave, kissing her granddaughter on her forehead.

Imogen comes down the stairs and stops when she notices all of us staring at her. She looks just fucked with her hair messy and her clothing askew.

Anger strikes me like the crack of a whip. Tell me she didn't… "Where were you?"

"I fell asleep in the guest room," she says.

But another set of footsteps barrel down after her. "Gen, we gotta talk."

My entire body goes rigid when Warner Langley comes down still buttoning his shorts.

"I fucking warned you what would happen." I cock my fist back and punch him in the face.

He stumbles against the wall before sinking down to his ass.

"Ford!" my dad yells from behind me.

I guess the demon hasn't been exorcised out of me just yet. Good thing I know a good PR person.

THE END

Cockamamie Unicorn Ramblings

Ford, oh Ford. He's the type of character we love to write. The banter between him and Lena came onto the page so easily. We both love an arrogant guy who says and does whatever he wants. They're always the most fun to see fall. ;)

We had a lot of ideas for this book and one big one for the end didn't pan out how we hoped. We loved the idea for the scene, but who knows… maybe it'll work for a different book down the road. Sometimes the stories go in a different direction once we start writing.

We haven't written a single dad since Confessions from a Naughty Nanny and we missed it so much. There's something about having kids in the picture that makes these stories especially swoony. We can't wait to tackle this trope again. *cough-Jed's book*

Without our team you wouldn't have any of our books! Seriously, they take on a lot of the work off our hands so that we can write!

Danielle Sanchez and the entire Wildfire Marketing Solutions team.

Cassie from Joy Editing for line edits.

Ellie from My Brother's Editor for line edits.

My Brother's Editor for proofreading.

Hang Le for the cover and branding for the entire series. Those colors!

Wander Aguiar for our muse, Ford.

Bloggers who consistently carve out time to read, review and/or promote our work.

Piper Rayne Unicorns who love our characters like as much as we do! Thank you!

Readers who took the time to read our story when there's so many choices out there.

Yes, Warner Langley, Ford's archenemy is up next, but first you'll get to travel down to the tropics with the hockey hotties to celebrate Ford and Lena's wedding in, Tropical Hat Trick (Hockey Hotties #3.5). If you read Cory and Ande's story in The Color Theory anthology, just know that we're expanding the story to include all POV's for the next three Florida Fury players!

xo,
Piper & Rayne

About Piper & Rayne

Piper Rayne is a USA Today Bestselling Author duo who write "heartwarming humor with a side of sizzle" about families, whether that be blood or found. They both have e-readers full of one-clickable books, they're married to husbands who drive them to drink, and they're both chauffeurs to their kids. Most of all, they love hot heroes and quirky heroines who make them laugh, and they hope you do, too!

Also by Piper Rayne

Hockey Hotties

My Lucky #13

The Trouble with #9

Faking it with #41

Sneaking around with #34

Second Shot with #76

Offside with #55

Kingsmen Football Stars

You had your chance, Lee Burrows

You can't kiss the Nanny, Brady Banks

Over my Brother's Dead Body, Chase Andrews

The Baileys

Lessons from a One-Night Stand

Advice from a Jilted Bride

Birth of a Baby Daddy

Operation Bailey Wedding (Novella)

Falling for My Brother's Best Friend

Demise of a Self-Centered Playboy

Confessions of a Naughty Nanny

Operation Bailey Babies (Novella)

Secrets of the World's Worst Matchmaker

Winning My Best Friend's Girl

Rules for Dating your Ex

Operation Bailey Birthday (Novella)

The Greenes

My Beautiful Neighbor

My Almost Ex

My Vegas Groom

The Greene Family Summer Bash

My Sister's Flirty Friend

My Unexpected Surprise

My Famous Frenemy

The Greene Family Vacation

My Scorned Best Friend

My Fake Fiancé

My Brother's Forbidden Friend

The Modern Love World

Charmed by the Bartender

Hooked by the Boxer

Mad about the Banker

The Single Dad's Club

Real Deal

Dirty Talker

Sexy Beast

Hollywood Hearts

Mister Mom

Animal Attraction

Domestic Bliss

Bedroom Games

Cold as Ice

On Thin Ice

Break the Ice

Box Set

Charity Case

Manic Monday

Afternoon Delight

Happy Hour

Blue Collar Brothers

Flirting with Fire

Crushing on the Cop

Engaged to the EMT

White Collar Brothers

Sexy Filthy Boss

Dirty Flirty Enemy

Wild Steamy Hook-up

The Rooftop Crew

My Bestie's Ex

A Royal Mistake

The Rival Roomies

Our Star-Crossed Kiss

The Do-Over

A Co-Workers Crush